AGAGUK

AGAGUK

by YVES THÉRIAULT

Translated by Miriam Chapin

McGRAW-HILL RYERSON TORONTO

FOREWORD

The action of this novel takes place among the Eskimos, as they were about twenty years ago. It is undeniable that their life today has been modified by the invasion of progress in the Arctic. The author intends to make this the subject of another story.

AGAGUK   PART ONE   CONTENTS

AGAGUK   PART TWO   CONTENTS

THIS TRANSLATION WAS MADE POSSIBLE
BY A GRANT FROM THE CANADA COUNCIL

PART ONE

CHAPTER 1/INIKSAK
The Promised Land

When he had reached maturity and proved his manhood, Agaguk took a rifle, a leather water bottle and a haunch of dried meat; with them he set out across the land of the endless tundra, flat and monotonous like the winter sky, without horizon and without trees.

He felt for the right places with a practised foot, avoiding the burrows of the small animals. When he found a solid hillock with no breaks in its sides, he walked around to measure it; then he drove in a couple of sticks and made his shelter of caribou skins. He would build his igloo later when the snow came. He spent a week there, studying the tracks of animals, looking at the sky, observing the winds and the way the clouds moved over the land.

He dug into the tundra with his knife, making a hole the width of three hands and elbow-deep. Water came in to cover the bottom: such a well would be enough for survival. During the week Agaguk took six foxes in the traps he set, two badgers, and when a caribou came near the hillock he brought it down with a single shot.

Hurriedly he smoked part of the meat for the return trip. Then he scattered the rest around so that the foxes and the wolves would learn to come to feed near this mound while he was away. His return to the village took two days walking due north. When he arrived, he did not go to the hut where Ramook lived. The fact that this man was his father did not matter any more. Since the old man had taken a Montagnais woman—the hated breed—to replace his dead wife, Agaguk considered that all ties were broken. He could feel he was free. He was eighteen years old, a good hunter already. He knew how to dress skins; all that was useful knowledge.

There was Iriook to think of. She too was free, for her father and mother were both dead now. She lived alone in a hut around which Ayallik and the others came to prowl. A month before, Agaguk had rushed just in time toward the screaming girl, to snatch her from Ghorok's arms.

"She's mine," Agaguk had declared. "Leave her alone."

As soon as Ghorok had gone out of the hut, she had raised her eyes to Agaguk's face, with a tender look, more submissive than he would have believed possible.

"I did not know I belonged to you," she said.

"You do," he answered.

She smiled mysteriously. "I'm glad."

From that day on, Agaguk worked hard to carry out his plan. He would find a small hill, far away on the tundra, and he would build a hut. In snow time, an igloo, a very big igloo, solid enough to stand against all winds. They would live there, he and the girl, far from Ramook, from Ghorok, from Ayallik, from all the others. They would not remember those men; they would make a new beginning.

So Agaguk had gathered together all that was necessary, the provisions, the caribou skins for a low temporary hut. He had cut two long poles. Then, with his weapons oiled and his knife sharpened, he had started out with his two dogs as companions toward the south-east, toward the country where people said the half-breeds lived, the country the white men called Ungava.

The Eskimos knew something of the geography of these lands, by their memories of hunting trips long ago, by the old men's tales, by the smells carried on the winds, by the colour of the sky and the migrations of the animals. Toward the evening sun lay a great water, but it was said that it pushed within the land. White men called it Hudson Bay. It was said that other Eskimos like those of Agaguk's village lived on the other side. Toward the morning sun, after four days of crossing the tundra, was a desolate barren land, a stony country with terrible winters, empty of all visible life. There also was a great water, but very far away and ravaged by storms. A man must never venture upon it in a kayak. In the country of the North Star, toward the north, according to what the white men said, there was again water, then immense islands under eternal snow, where the Eskimos lived in igloos all the time. To the south, after the mossy tundra, lay the tree country, the country of hills, of queer beasts, of white men and their towns, and of Indians too, Montagnais, Abenakis, Ojibways, half-breeds. But the distance was so great toward the rising or the setting sun, toward the North Star or the tree country that no one thought much about them. Here was the tundra, here was the pleasant and familiar country: men could be content here, Agaguk like the rest.

Halfway between his village and the territory called Ungava, Agaguk found the place he had dreamed of, the little hill he measured and marked out, a kind of firm island that was hardly a swelling in the spongy brown moss, this living layer hiding the thousand-year-old permafrost. It was to this hillock that he would bring Iriook to live out their destiny.

So he returned to the village to find the girl. "We shall leave in three days," he said. "What will you bring?"

"Not much. One bundle, no more. And my dogs."

"That's all?"

"I have nothing but you," she said.

Agaguk got ready two packs, his and the girl's. They shared in common the poles for a bigger hut and all the caribou and seal skins Agaguk possessed. There were the rawhide thongs, and the needles made of seal's teeth, the iron pots, the tools. There was also a metal stove to burn oil or fat, a purchase of Agaguk's at the white men's store, near the Great Water. It was a precious possession which Iriook examined all over, never tiring of admiring it. "It will be pleasant in the igloo with that stove," she said and she touched it gently, almost timidly.

In the girl's pack there was also fat to last a month, pemmican, white man's matches and tea. A missionary, a man in a long robe, with a thin face and heavy eyebrows, had taught her to drink tea. It was comforting, he said, and he was indeed right. That was the only teaching that Iriook remembered of all that the man had said. For a box of tea that Oonak let her have, she paid two fox skins: it was expensive, but Agaguk too liked tea.

One morning the man and the girl took to the trail. Packs on back, Agaguk's two dogs and Iriook's three held to their wrists by strong leashes, they left without goodbyes, without looking back, turning toward the deserted tundra.

CHAPTER 2/A'NGNAK
The Female

Because it was summer, the first day's march was slow and troublesome. The packs were heavy, the dogs nervous on their leashes. It was farther than Agaguk had foreseen. He had to stop often to identify landmarks on the tundra; the faint track of mukluks in the moss, or a hardly perceptible dip on the horizon, here and there some tiny nipple of earth. As any Eskimo does, Agaguk had scored on his memory the road he must follow to find his chosen hill.

When the sun had gone down, he thought it was time to halt. Together they ate, and went straight to sleep. Once during the march he had felt a pleasant stirring; his blood ran faster, his flesh thrilled. Behind him followed this girl, Iriook, the object of his dreaming, of his desire for many months. And she was there, docile, all his. Nevertheless, he had felt in a confused fashion that the journey set a goal which he ought not to overtake prematurely. Over there, at their destination, in their own country and on their own acres of ground, only there would he acknowledge the right to have her.

That first night under the stars, they slept chastely side by side. It was the same the second night. On the third day, when they reached the place Agaguk had chosen, he relieved the girl of her burden and threw his own load on the ground. Without waiting, he pulled Iriook down, slipped off the caribou pants she wore, then his own, and possessed her silently. She moaned but once and was quiescent. Soon they were mating savagely on the damp and resilient surface of the tundra.

When he was spent, when all of him was emptied, he rolled over beside the girl and they both slept, half naked under the leaden sky. A hawk flying very high passed overhead, coming from the forests of the south and travelling to the lands farther north, where it might still find weasels in their brown summer fur. The bird did not see that the pemmican Iriook had carried had fallen from her pack and lay on the moss. . . .

They had arrived well before the end of the day, but when they woke up the sun had gone down. Agaguk put his new wife to work in a hurry. They drove in the shortest poles and made a temporary shelter for that night. The tent was cramped; they had to secure the dried meat and the fat between them while they slept, to keep it away from animals. In the morning they built the bigger hut, roomy, sufficient until winter when it would be time for the igloo. They worked in silence, pitching in to the job with all their might.

Iriook was short and stocky, with a sound, smooth face from which her impassive, shiny eyes looked out expressionless. When she smiled she was pretty, for her teeth were not yet worn by chewing skins. But she seldom smiled that day, there was so much to do; she had no time for any niceties.

Agaguk was taller than she, and rather heavy. He seemed older than his eighteen years. A gaze accustomed to bear the terrible reflection of the sun on the snow shone from a face already ravaged by wind and cold. He could see as far as a hawk and even farther. He pointed his finger at a weasel moving a hundred yards away, a beast big as his fist, brown as the tundra: it was witchcraft.

Stripped, Agaguk was handsome because his skin was smooth and dark, and his muscles rippled underneath like bands of steel ready to relax. Iriook had a thick body and very short thighs. Her breasts were small, but round and full, with almost black nipples and no halos. She was gentle, with never any roughness. She was strong too, like Agaguk, capable of lifting heavy weights.

They spent what was left of the day in building the hut. When the evening came, there would be nothing to do by lamplight but prepare the bed of trampled moss, bury halfway in the ground the stone upon which Iriook would set the stove and cook the meal. Agaguk had made a hole for the smoke and ventilation in the top of the hut. In the low opening by which they would enter, squatting down, they would hang a skin and anchor it firmly with heavy stones, so they would be shut in for the night, and wolves and foxes could not get in. Nothing, no one could penetrate that hut without awakening the occupants. That was the essential thing.

"You like it?" asked Agaguk.

Practically, he added, "You'll be able to cook the meals comfortably, chew the skins, sew—"

"Yes," she answered. With tenderness, yet so slight that one had to divine the feeling. Why search for words when gestures are enough?

After a little while she said, "I would not have asked for it any other way—this hut."

When she had gone to sleep, Agaguk slipped out and sat at the edge of the hillock to look at the stars. Under that light the tundra was lovely, quiet, immense. On the western horizon he could see the golden band of the midnight sun, the eternal light.

A shadow passed close by. Agaguk crept quickly into the hut, and grabbed his loaded rifle. Outside again, he ran swiftly over the spongy moss. He picked up the wolf's trail a kilometer on, coming so near that the beast did not even sense his approaching death. Agaguk fired. The shot crackled in the night. The wolf leaped high, faltered, fell head first.

When Agaguk came back to the hut, he hung the carcass high on the poles. So the dead beast would be out of reach of the other wolves or foxes that would come, drawn by the smell of fresh blood. His having sown the remains of the caribou around the hill was paying off already. The wolf was sniffing the moss when Agaguk fired at it. This would be a first skin to trade with the white men. Also, Iriook would twist thread from the entrails, and as for the flesh, it would make new bait for the other meat-eaters and the gnawing animals.

Iriook was awake when he came back and slid in beside her. "It was you who fired a shot, Agaguk?"

"Yes."

"Why?"

"I killed a wolf."

She sighed contentedly. Agaguk felt completely happy. He was a man. He had a wife of his own, a hut, two guns and ammunition, the freedom of the tundra, a life to live.

A plane purred far overhead, but Agaguk did not hear it. He was asleep. Like the hawk during the day, the plane was not at all concerned with that hut, a tiny excrescence on the tundra, like a mole hill.

CHAPTER 3/ANGON
The Male

The time went by, one day, two, still more, a week. Already there were several skins stretched on the drying racks. They were summer skins, worth little in trade, but to capture these animals taught Agaguk the many secrets of his surroundings. The tundra held mysteries, as many as the forest or the mountain country. Burrows in the moss, trails hardly visible, hourly habits of the beasts. Insects that it was good to know about also lived in these grounds. Birds sometimes flew across the sky and alighted for a moment, most of them desirable food for happy days. Over the surface of the ground moved the weasels, the mink making their way south, the sinuous martens with their precious fur, or the muskrats. There were the taller animals too, caribou, wolves, foxes, easy to see; sometimes came a bear, wandering alone over the great plain. The humble ones were a multitude, field mice, gray mice, moss rats, all the invisible nibblers that came out at night, sneaking under the sides of the hut, gnawing at the provisions, munching the pemmican, treating themselves to the fat, even spoiling the rawhide pantaloons and mukluks, eating the fur lining of the parkas where the sweat and salt of the body makes them succulent.

Sometimes came a chunky brown rabbit, nimble as a gust of wind. For every one of these beasts, Agaguk ordained a destiny, became a god, suddenly from his own needs and those of Iriook. Traps for the rodents, snares for the rabbits and the martens, foot traps for the minks that would not damage the precious fur; a bullet for the caribou, the wolves and foxes, a bullet fired straight, without pity, guided by the Eskimo's unfailing eye.

Agaguk became vain with all the knowledge he acquired. Before Iriook he shamelessly boasted he would get rich out of it. He never stopped talking about what he had accomplished before. But if he boasted of his own prowess, sometimes Iriook's eyes showed a glint of mischief. When he called himself by that proud name, *Inuk*, Man, she answered back at once, "Half-breed!"

That was the worst of insults, but she said it laughing, in a moment of fun. Then she snuggled up to Agaguk, slipped her hands under his parka, tickled and pinched his bare skin. When he yelled for mercy, she rolled over on her back in her turn and he possessed her savagely. So it was in the morning at waking and at night after eating. They never tired, daily seeking the satiation which they never seemed to attain. They were alone with this animal joy, alone on the great tundra. Their solitude was precious to them; they marvelled at the eternal renewal of their delight, of their potency.

In his free hours Agaguk set new traps or went to visit the ones he had already in place. The circuit made, he sat down, legs folded under him, rifle on haunches, and waited for a wolf or a fox to pass by. Sometimes it would be a caribou that came bounding from afar. He would bring it down with a single shot, and he and his wife would quickly smoke the chunks of meat. So the stores of preserved meat accumulated.

The men of the North, the men of the eternal snows make their provisions of seal meat, but where Agaguk lived it was not yet the Arctic, and it was not the forest either. It was beyond the tree line, beyond the Laurentian shield, on the infinite tundra, land of changelessness. They often had to depend on other meat, that of caribou and bear, even of the beasts of prey if there was need.

One morning Agaguk said, "There are people farther north. They call them the People of the Top of the World. Two of them came to the village one winter."

"I wasn't there," said Iriook. "I was out hunting with my father. He was still alive then. But I heard about them."

"They were people like us," Agaguk said.

"I know."

"They live in igloos the year round."

"Don't they mind?"

"I know I wouldn't. . . ."

He was sincere. Agaguk would have liked to live in an igloo

the year round. He did not like the huts. But he was born on the tundra and he would die there. So be it.

A few days after that, one evening the wind rose; it shook the hut all night and was still raging in the morning. A great fluid powerful mass swept the tundra; it came from the south, bringing strange unfamiliar smells.

"What's that smell on the wind?" asked Iriook.

"You've seen a tree?"

"No."

He pointed south. "Down there are many of them. I went up in the priest's Big Bird, once when he went to get medicines in the other lands."

"Those to the south?"

"Yes. The Father called it Quebec. Lake—wait, I can't remember the name. . . ."

He tried again, but the sounds were too bizarre for him, too soft, too much like a whisper. He gave up.

"We were away three days."

"And what did you see down there?" questioned Iriook.

"White men, half-breeds, Montagnais. They live in wooden houses with chimneys, like the houses at the post at the Great Bay. Like the trader's house."

Iriook's eyes were dreamy.

"Is a tree pretty?"

Agaguk shrugged his shoulders. "When there are too many trees you can't see the animals. They call that the forest. I would be a poor hunter in a place like that, I'd get lost."

"Are there many trees in a forest?"

"We flew over them for four hours—nothing but trees."

"There are many of them," Iriook concluded calmly.

She was already sitting on the moss bed. On her knees she held the wolf's intestines, well dried in long greenish strings. While she listened to Agaguk talk, she chewed tirelessly on the entrails, softening them, stretching them, twisting them into fine needlefuls of *babiche* for the hems and seams of their winter garments.

High up in the hut, near the smoke hole, the fox and the caribou skins were hanging. Later, before the cold weather, Iriook would chew all of the caribou skins to soften them. Sewing the fox skins to them for trimming or for lining, she would make two heavy parkas and pantaloons tied in at the ankle. This would be their winter wardrobe, and a luxury to boot, since last winter's clothes were still in good shape. But she had promised to be a good wife and she kept her word.

The wind grew stronger. For a while, Agaguk had tried to divert his thoughts from it by talking. But ever since it screamed louder over the tundra, he had fallen silent. His face was sullen, his eyes shone with a queer light. The gusts shook the hut, moving the poles; the skins rattled on the supports. Suddenly Agaguk rolled on the ground and fastened his hands on a dryer made of seal bones. With one squeeze he broke it in a hundred pieces, and yelled in an extraordinary shriek of rage such as Iriook had never heard from any man.

Frozen in fright, she stared at her husband.

"What's the trouble?" she asked.

He was gasping, his eyes were bulging, he had foam at the corners of his mouth.

"The wind!" he cried. "It is stronger than I am. Nothing must be stronger than I am."

He repeated it, his body trembling.

"You hear me? Nothing!"

Then he stretched out, flat on his belly, his head between his arms, beside Iriook. For a moment she looked at him, her lacquer eyes betraying nothing of her thoughts. When Agaguk's breathing became regular, she went back to chewing carefully. That day he did not go to his traps. He slept until their evening meal. And because the wind still whistled when night fell, he remained seated before the fire somberly watching Iriook sleep.

In the morning the sun was shining over the tundra and the wind was only a warm gentle breeze. Nevertheless, hardly a meter below the moss lay the permafrost, the eternal ice going down one or two hundred meters deep, keeping the nights cool, preventing the growth of the trees, even keeping the taller bushes from finding nourishment. Only the moss, the lichens, sometimes a pallid clump of grass and mangy bush-growth could live; and for the summer only, the insects and the small animals that could emigrate to a warmer climate in a hurry when the cold came, or dig in for a hibernation very close to death while they waited for the return of spring.

The only things that moved over the tundra in winter were the big animals, the wolves, Tiriganiak the white fox, sometimes a hungry caribou, a solitary male that had not followed the herd toward the tree country where even in winter they might find bark and tender young twigs to chew. Half crazy, then, were the beasts hemmed in by the cold, fleeing toward the barren lands and certain death, whether it would come by the bitter weather, or from the pitiless bullet of an Eskimo rifle.

Agaguk went out in the sun, sniffed the breeze. Iriook, awakened, came beside him. The tundra was refreshed, the warm wind had made the flowers open, blue and yellow here and there, with a few timid scattered red ones. They were a decoration on the drab plain.

"I smell water," Agaguk said, hesitating at first. He seemed hesitant. He sniffed again, thought a while, drew a long breath. "It is water."

This time he was certain. He pointed where the warm wind was coming from. "There is a river."

13

A river, the place where the mink go to drink, the place to set traps when the fall comes and the furs are prime, where sometimes muskrats live in the water. Other life would exist on the banks of the river, otters maybe, fishers surely, and birds, big fat birds well nourished on mud larvae and little fish.

"I'm going there," he said.

There was a heavy sound, sort of a distant rumbling, seeming to come out of the bowels of the earth.

"The wind coming again?" asked Iriook.

But Agaguk shook his head smiling. "No."

"What is it?"

"It's what happens when there is a warm wind. My father before me spoke of it, others before him—they sing of it in the igloos in winter. You never heard it? When the warm wind blows, that is the time for such things."

"*Nuna aodlaklok?*" cried Iriook.

"That's right. The earth moves. It is always so during the warm wind."

Under the thawing crust, the permafrost endures this new warm wave. Then the eternal ice cracks and splits. The mass wavers, growls, and the earth moves. The phenomenon is common enough. Most Eskimos pay no attention to it. What does it matter, so long as the huts stand firm?

A weasel ran past them, probably fleeing its flooded burrow.

"*Nuna aodlaklok?*" moaned Iriook. "And if the earth moves again, shall we die?"

"No."

Agaguk was still sniffing the wind. "There is a river over there, I'm sure of it now. And I'm going there."

"Why?"

"To find water. And if there is any, we'll go live there."

"Will you be long?"

"*Nauna.*"

"You don't know? One day—two days?"

"Two days. If the smell of water comes on the wind, the river can't be far away. I don't know the country yet."

"Two days—and if the earth moves again?"

"It's moved once. If there is no other warm wind, it will not move. But the warm wind won't come back."

"Why? How do you know?"

"Because it has gone away toward the ice at the Top of the World. It will die there."

"I wasn't afraid of anything but that," she said.

"You see, it's gone away."

"Yes."

"Today the wind is from the west. It carries the smell of the river, it's a good wind."

"It's a good wind."

"You won't be afraid to stay alone, if I go?"

"I've got my rifle and some bullets. I won't be afraid."

Agaguk got ready his pack, pemmican, fat to make a fire with, bullets for his rifle, a caribou skin to sleep on.

He set out without looking back once. Standing in front of the hut, Iriook watched him walking rapidly over the tundra for an hour. Then he was out of sight.

He found the river at the end of the second day. It was really a torrent, a brook rather than a river. In several places he could reach the farther bank in one jump. Nevertheless the approaches to the stream were everywhere marked with animals' tracks. Agaguk found bird droppings there and even saw a wild goose watching him patiently from a tangle of water plants on the opposite bank. Slowly, carefully he raised his gun to his shoulder. When he fired the goose beat its wings once, then floated out of the weeds, killed instantly, its neck clearly cut by the bullet. Agaguk ate it right away.

There was a little grass in the brook, in the quiet places, and some reeds. A few bushes succeeded in growing on the edge, protected from the permafrost by the sun-warmed water that soaked into the ground. It wasn't much, but he could make a fire in dry weather and the brushwood would serve as a blind. Agaguk took a whole day to explore the course of the river and its surroundings. Farther on, he found fast water, even rapids, which would freeze later than the pools when autumn came. That would be the place where the fur-bearing beasts would come to drink. He marked the spot in his memory, fixing its position by the faint undulations in the tundra, and when night fell, he recognized the stars that would guide him when he came again.

When he got back to the hut, he found Iriook crying. "What's the matter with you?" he asked.

"You've been gone so long. I thought you were dead."

She kept on crying. "Shut up," Agaguk said rudely. "You see, I'm back."

But she could not stop. He touched her arm hesitatingly, and she wept even more. "I want you to stop," he yelled suddenly.

Iriook shook her head and kept on crying, her face buried in her hands. Then, because her tears overwhelmed Agaguk, because he felt powerless to make her stop, he was seized with an hysterical rage. He beat her, with his feet and fists, furiously, until she fell fainting. He took a long time to calm down. Then he came to lie beside her, and when she opened her eyes, and stirred moaning, he possessed her brutally.

CHAPTER 5/MIKIGIAK
The Trap

Agaguk and Iriook carried the dismantled hut on their backs, along with their provisions, their weapons, the tools, traps and hides, all the way to the edge of the river Agaguk had found. There they built their home again. The task did not take long—three long supports stuck in the ground, tied in a bundle at the top, to make a triangular structure. In two places they put horizontal crosspieces to hold the poles together, and over the frame they hung the caribou skins that had been scraped clean of their fur. The top of the cone was the air hole; on one of the flaps was a low opening closed by a freely hanging skin. Rawhide laces held the hides to the poles.

Inside, near the entrance, they put the flat stone where they would set the stove, and made a bed of moss along the sidewall. The tools, these objects which were their only belongings, hung on the horizontal bars. High up in the cone the pemmican was slung, held by thongs and out of the reach of the small animals, and in a sack were the bricks of fat and caribou tallow. The two guns stood by the door.

They were finishing their new installation when they heard someone in the distance. "*Inuk*," said Iriook, looking over the plain. Pointing, she repeated, "Look, a man is coming."

Agaguk recognized Ghorok from the village. Lots of stories were told about that man. The witch doctors no longer kept their former hold on the tribes; still Ghorok retained a witch doctor's prestige, the domination of a cruel and determined man over his companions. He owned a collection of more or less obvious tricks, learned from a cousin of his who had been a feared sorcerer in one of the shore tribes. Certainly that was not enough to make him as feared in his village as he would have liked to be. But it was enough for the chief Ramook to

17

recognize his usefulness and make him his right-hand man. How much complicity in their manoeuvres, how much co-operation they gave each other! It was a sort of united front, which made Ghorok more powerful than his magic alone would have done. In spite of everything he impressed the more superstitious, and even those who did not believe in his magic were in the habit of calling Ghorok the sorcerer. Was he not brought to the igloos to cure the most absurd ailments? Did not some old women confide their hopes, their ambitions, even their destinies to Ghorok, who would then set himself to make for one a little bag of strange mixtures for another an amulet with a hundred outlandish powers?

Sorcerer in one way, accomplice and disciple of Ramook in another, he was feared and even hated in the tribe. But who would have dared affront him? And now, what brought him to Agaguk's camp?

Ghorok grunted a brief greeting, then squatted down and ate silently what was offered him as a sign of hospitality. He had a greedy look in his eye. Agaguk did not like his presence and felt ill at ease. Ghorok said he had gone hunting, and had walked farther than he meant to. So he had noticed Agaguk's hut and made his way to it. Before leaving, he leaned forward, his face close to his host's. "There is a new man in the village," he said. "A white trader. With a Montagnais to help him."

Agaguk shrugged his shoulders. "So?" he said.

"It's nearer to go there than to walk to the Great Bay."

"Yes."

"If you go there, the trader will be pleased. He hasn't as many skins as he would like."

"What's he got to trade?"

"Bullets—" Ghorok patted his belt. "Lots of bullets—salt, sugar, tea."

"That all?"

"He's got knives, and he still has three rifles."

"And if I go to him?"

"He will be pleased, that's sure."

Ghorok examined the hanging skins. "He takes everything," he said. "He'll even take the summer furs, fox, muskrat, weasel. Ivory knives for salt."

"Why are you so anxious I should go?"

"No reason. I'm just speaking about it." His glance was furtive, his manner deceitful.

Iriook made a gesture with her hand. The light of the stove cast a monstrous shadow of it on the wall of the hut. "The white man's helper is a Montagnais?" she said. But she did not use the name of the tribe. Instead she used a contemptuous, insulting word, *Irkrelret*, "the lousy ones."

Ghorok spread his hand on his thigh. He shrugged his shoulders. "He's only a man." He smiled, showing his yellow teeth. "Since he trades, and the white man trades too, there is nothing to say about them."

"*Anartok*," Iriook spat out. It was a dirty word, the worst possible insult.

The two men were silent. Ghorok roused himself to take leave. He rubbed his hands, he licked his lips to show that he had eaten well and was completely restored. "What I told you of this matter is just to make conversation," he concluded.

When he had gone Agaguk went to sit down by the fire. Iriook had not moved. "He wants you to go?" she asked. "Why?" She spoke evenly, without expression.

"I don't know."

"*Krablunak ayortok!*"

Agaguk grimaced. "How can you say the white man is no good?"

Iriook seemed angry. "If he was any good," she declared, "would he go to trade in a village of ten huts? Count them on your fingers. And he has travelled all this distance for so little? It's because he's not wanted anywhere else, that's sure. If the Company learns he is there, it will send the police."

She had never said so much before.

"My rifle is old," said Agaguk. "I could do with a new one." He looked up over his head, reckoning the skins set to dry, the others in a bundle. "Here, the hunting will be good," he went on. "If I had more steel traps, white man's traps—"

He pointed with his finger. "That caribou skin—"

"I wanted to make you a parka of it."

"And the wolf skins. I have three ivory knives. Other skins. Maybe it would be enough for a rifle."

Iriook was silent. She had said all she could say. Now the man must decide.

"I'll go tomorrow," Agaguk said. "The trip will be worth the trouble."

"And if Ghorok should come back while I'm alone?"

"You have your gun."

"Yes, I have my gun."

CHAPTER 6/ANGAYUK'AK
The Trader

Ayallik, Tugugak and Ignek met Agaguk when he entered the village. "There's a trader here," said Ayallik.

It seemed they did not know about the visit Ghorok had made to Agaguk's hut. Ayallik pointed to the bundle of skins. "Is that all you brought?"

"Yes."

"It's not much."

"It's enough," Agaguk retorted drily.

Tugugak growled something Agaguk did not understand, and Ignek shook his head. "Times have changed," he said.

Ayallik smiled. His toothless mouth with the blackened gums looked like some evil cave. "There's whisky," he said. "You want some? The white man trades in that—"

Agaguk looked at him in surprise. The liquor traffic was forbidden in the territories. Was this then the mystery? The people welcomed this man gladly because he bartered alcohol for furs. "Ghorok didn't tell me that," muttered Agaguk.

"He went to your hut?"

"Yes."

"What for?"

"I don't know. Maybe to tell me the white man was here—"

"Was Iriook there?" asked Ignek.

"Yes."

"Ghorok knows her. He's a devil. He didn't want to say anything in front of her. And you see, you came anyhow."

"I don't want whisky. I want a rifle, some salt, some tea, some bullets. Perhaps a steel knife—"

Tugugak touched the bundle of skins with his toes and made a face. *Ayornarman*, he said with a sigh.

"Why do you say it's no use?"

"*Krablunak ayortok*," cried Tugugak.

21

"That's what Iriook said," said Agaguk. "The white man is no good. She guessed it."

"You see," Ayallik said. "You see. I was right. Ghorok was very careful not to say anything before her." Ayallik had been drinking, as was easy to see by his gestures.

"What's the white man's name?" asked Agaguk.

"Brown." Ayallik pronounced it "braoune," dragging out the final syllable.

"I'll go see him," said Agaguk.

"It's that hut over there," said Ignek. "The last one, where you used to live. But since it's empty, the white man lives there."

Agaguk went on, his bundle of skins in his hand. When he entered the hut the white man was alone. He looked up and smiled at Agaguk. He was a tall, thin, almost emaciated man, with a sunken face and strange eyes in deep sockets. He had long yellow teeth like a wolf's.

"I have some furs," said Agaguk. The man understood Eskimo and spoke it.

"What do you want in trade?"

"A gun, three boxes of ammunition, some salt, some tea. If possible, a steel knife."

The man looked at the bundle on the ground, smiled again. "Let's see the skins." He spoke Eskimo not at all badly. But it was plain he had learned it with the *Kidlinermeun*, the farthest tribes, way in the North, on the edge of the habitable lands.

Agaguk slowly undid the bundle. He spread out the little skins first, those of the weasels with the poor summer pelts. Then the wolfskins, much better; two of them were big ones with good fur. There were six wolfskins, ten fox. And then there was the big caribou hide, which Iriook had cleaned and scraped so carefully. Brown hardly looked at them. He rolled up the bundle and threw it behind him in the hut. "You don't want liquor?" he asked.

"No," said Agaguk, stubbornly. He counted on his fingers. "One rifle, three boxes of ammunition, some salt—"

"I know, I know," Brown interrupted him. He reached behind him, picked up a bag of salt and put it on the floor between Agaguk and himself.

"There you are."

Agaguk waited a moment, then patiently repeated, "I want a rifle—"

The white man broke in with a gesture. He pointed to the bag of salt and grinned wickedly.

"*Nao*," said Agaguk. "You don't understand. Where is the gun, where are the shells?"

The man laughed, sneering at him. "No gun, no shells, no tea, no knife. Nothing but the salt," he said.

"And my skins?"

"You don't want liquor?"

"I want a gun, tea—"

Brown lifted his hand and slapped his thigh. "Oh shut up!"

"Then give me my furs. I won't trade with you."

"Take the salt. It's all you'll get."

"No. Give me back my furs. I'll go to the Company post on Great Bay. I'll tell the police what you're doing here."

Brown stood up. Agaguk, suddenly uneasy, rose too. The white man had a revolver in his hand.

"Get out!"

"I want my furs."

The white man fired, not at Agaguk, but in the air, toward the smoke hole. Agaguk spat on the floor, deliberately, toward Brown. Then he left, his back stiff. Outside he waited a moment to see if the white man would come after him. But Brown did not come out, and since no one from the huts came to his aid after the shot, he went to Ramook's, his father's. He looked worried, scowling. At Ramook's he found no one pleased to see him again; there was no word of greeting, after all these months of absence. He glanced at the Indian woman who lived with the old man in his usual contemptuous manner.

"You got oil for the lamps?" he asked Ramook.

The old chief pointed to a tin of kerosene by the door.

"Tonight," Agaguk said, "I'll be needing it."

CHAPTER 7/TOKONIK
Death

Stretched out on the moss behind the largest hut, the one where his father lived, Agaguk did nothing the rest of the day. When Tugugak or one of the others came to ask him questions about the new country where he lived, the hunting there, the water, the caribou, he hardly answered. They understood quickly that he did not want to talk. They left him to his thoughts. But at nightfall, Tugugak said to Ayallik, "Agaguk is very angry. I've never seen him like this."

They all guessed it was on account of the white man, but they did not talk about it. What happened between Agaguk and the white man did not concern them. To many of the men in the village, it was a good thing to have the white man selling whisky. To take Agaguk's side would be to dry up the source of their pleasure. To take the white man's side would be to set Agaguk against them; he could invoke the traditions, the solidarity of the tribe. They knew he was vindictive, dangerous in his silence and his savage determination. He lay stretched out there, without speaking a word. He was in trouble with the white man. All right. To meddle in this matter would bring nothing but quarrels. Better leave him alone. For the moment, wisdom prescribed silence, imposed pretended indifference. But within themselves, they could not help thinking. Not to get one's due for a bundle of furs is an affair between Eskimo and trader.

Warned by the men, the women squatting before the huts and chewing skins also avoided talking over the affair. If Agaguk was there next morning, if he had forgotten the incident, there would still be time to inquire about Iriook, who had been a daughter of the tribe.

The evening came. It was not real evening, for it there was no longer the midnight sun, it meant the equinox was drawing near. Soon would come the cold, the snow, the winter night, this constant dusk, without let-up. Every hour monotonously the same as the other before it was enough to drive the most reasonable white man crazy. For the Eskimo, it was an accepted part of his life. There is the half-day of the summer nights, especially on the western horizon where lies the long golden ribbon that never vanishes entirely and that bathes the tundra in a phantasmagoric half-light. In this the tundra of Labrador and northern Quebec is different from the far North. The six months of Arctic night with the eternal ice, the six months of shining day which follow are not the tundra's. The midnight sun creates only a half-day, the winter night is only a half-darkness. In this latitude the transitory state remains. It is not the Arctic, but neither has it the varied fairness of happier climes.

There are flowers on this tundra, once the snow melts, red or yellow, sometimes white. They blossom at the end of June. For a week, sometimes two, they cover the moss, and then the tundra is wonderful. But this is the only moment of color. By July the hot sun turns the moss yellow and fades the flowers. It is the sign that winter is near, that soon will come the frosty nights of August. From early October and sometimes before September ends the snow flies in the dry wind. Soon it will be time for the igloos. It is still only a foreboding; there are warm hours in the middle of the day, and the snow that comes in gusts is not the real snow of winter. It is only a white powder, fine and light as an angel's breath. The wind makes it dance over the plains blackened by the freeze, throws it into the air where it whirls a while before it falls to earth, to begin again its dance in long elegant swirls. The true snow will come later, solid, heavy, hard. In a few hours it will cover all the tundra with a layer a meter thick. A little later the first blizzard will blow, adding another meter and more to the first. By January there are five meters of snow on the tundra, a hard mass as dense as cement, on which nevertheless life must continue to be lived. So it goes from October to the end of April.

Often the Eskimo must leave his igloo, when the blizzard buries it, and build another. Some tribes let their igloos be covered under the successive layers, merely digging out the entrance tunnels after each storm. Agaguk chose this alternative. He had never rebuilt an igloo. He liked better to place it with care on a site wisely chosen, the rear against the worst driving winds; or at the top of some little rise of ground which would assure him enough height to make up for the first meter of snow and perhaps the second after a long winter; with its misery, its dangers, its monotony, in June the treacherous weather makes the bogs dangerous. When that time comes, the heat in the igloos becomes unbearable, the blocks of ice slump. Then the need to build the hut is evident as soon as the black tundra shows through the snow.

Then the time has come for the Eskimo to think of the summer hunting, the essential hunting that will provide the smoked meat for winter, the reserves of fat, the piles of bones and finally the ivory to make tools.

They call themselves *Inuk*, man, *Inuit*, men. There are no other men than they, the Eskimos, the *Inuit*. They have names of contempt for all other races, for the whites, for the Montagnais, for all those who come from the south, Abenakis, Apaches, Half-breeds, Shoshones, Snakes, all the Indians of the forest regions across Canada, all those who are not Children of the Sky, masters of the Top of the World. Only the Eskimo is an *Inuk*, a man, "Look at that man coming," will mean an Eskimo, no other.

In Ramook's village it already looked like wintertime. They were smoking caribou meat in several huts, and the most able hunters came in with full hands, bringing more meat to smoke next day. That was one reason why no one had paid much attention to Agaguk's trouble. Before the inexorable seasons the Eskimo has but one thought in his head, to provide for the cruel winter, to profit from the great summer hunts. Agaguk could then dwell all day on the white man's behaviour, could work himself up to a cold, dull, implacable rage, without attracting attention. Night came, without moon or star or midnight sun, or so little that there was no light. Agaguk, still alone, stayed motionless, lying on the moss.

The Montagnais woman came out to offer him a handful of pemmican boiled in water. He spat in her face, as he always did since his father had brought this woman into the igloo. A Reservation woman from the south, she had a bad smell, she was queer-looking, with her thick face, her animal eyes, her cotton dresses like a white woman's. Ramook had tried to teach her how to chew the skins and sew them, but she had laughed in his face.

Ramook came in his turn, stood near his son for a moment, hesitated and sought for words. But not knowing what to say, he went back. In the village silence fell little by little. The men were eating at this hour. Soon stuffed, they would go to sleep, snug against their wives. Strangely Tugugak was singing in his hut, at the top of his lungs. The white man's liquor was not milk. The night grew darker and the silence deepened, broken now and then by a dog's short bark or a woman's spasmodic groan or the wailing of a child. Tugugak sang no more. The silence was complete.

Agaguk got up, went near Ramook's hut and surveyed the agglomeration of the village. Nothing moved at the white man's hut. It also was in darkness. Where did his Montagnais sleep? Agaguk did not question, he waited. The power of man against beast is exactly this immobility, this waiting, the patience of a thousand years. When he was sure everybody was asleep, he slid his arm under the caribou skin flap at the entrance to Ramook's hut, felt around, and found the kerosene tin. He pulled it out without a sound and went with supple padded steps toward the white man's hut, gliding through the night like another shadow. Like a ferret he slipped into the trader's dwelling.

Brown was sleeping on his back with his mouth open. He was snoring. His arm lay along his body, a pistol in his hand.

Agaguk's eyes, growing used to the darkness, could make out the outlines of this stretched-out form. Seeing the weapon, he smiled mysteriously, quizzically. A moment he stood there, calculating. Then he seized his bundle of furs and threw it outside.

With soft movements he unscrewed the cap of the kerosene tin. He was ready. He fished out of his pocket a big match, a white man's match. His movements became a sort of rhythmic ritual like an ancient religious dance. In a wide precise arc he raised his arm; the kerosene spurted from the tin and drenched the man. At the same instant the match flamed, touched the liquid, and Brown, screaming terribly, became a living torch.

Agaguk was out in one swift dive, grabbing up his bundle as he fled, and in an instant was far away looking at the hell which he had started. The screams of the white man were soon quieted. Then the Montagnais ran from somewhere and beat in vain on the sides of the hut. In the time it took the village to wake and come to Brown's rescue, the dwelling was already a pyre, casting for miles around its light of death.

Agaguk, pack on back, took off from the village with long strides, toward the river where Iriook was waiting. As a cold wind was whistling over the tundra and the wolves would be hungry, Agaguk quickly forgot the deed he had just done. Nothing was on his mind but the rustling emptiness of the tundra, the effort of his muscles, the howling of the wolves which the wind carried to his ears.

In the village, there remained by now nothing of the hut that had once been his. And of Brown, only a shapeless charred mass, stinking of roast pig.

CHAPTER 8/INU'SIK
Life

Iriook was not expecting Agaguk so soon. When she saw him arrive, still carrying his furs, with nothing in exchange for them, she did not say anything for a moment. Finally she asked, "You're back empty-handed?"

"Yes."

"What happened?"

He shrugged his shoulders and stacked his gun beside the entrance of the hut.

"What happened?" Iriook insisted.

"Nothing."

That evening the man stayed outside a long time, watching the horizon. Many times he had looked back in his flight from the village, uneasy in fear of pursuit. The tundra remained blank. But this evening, he still waited. The midnight sun made a golden band on the horizon. Against that light silhouettes showed up clearly. Agaguk watched, but nothing came. Now he was sure that nothing would come. The tribe would not seek any other vengeance. The victim was a white man, the guilty man one of their own. Even though Agaguk had in a sense rejected the tribe to go to live far away, the solidarity would triumph. But a doubt lingered in his mind, even so. How could he be assured in his beliefs when it is so hard to foresee another's reactions, even living together? He must take any possible setbacks into account.

Nothing among the *Inuit* was the way it used to be; the purity of intention, the blind attachment to tradition, these were no longer as powerful. The evil spread by the white man grew, this development of the individual more and more setting his will against environment. With Agaguk, it showed itself in the flight toward solitude, liberation. With the others, what form might not this new emancipation take? Could

Agaguk count on their holding to the traditional rules if he, in his turn, had cared for them so little that he had taken upon himself to leave with Iriook? Would Ayallik, deprived of the white man's whisky, dream of revenge? He was a danger; so were Tugugak and the others. But that night nothing appeared on the horizon, no one came.

When long hours had passed, when all risk of immediate pursuit was over, Agaguk went into the hut and stretched out by Iriook. With a firm hand he pulled off her pantaloons and threw them far off. Iriook half woke, moaned happily and opened wide her strong heavy thighs. When their breathing was back to normal, and the long cry of the woman was swallowed up in the silence of the tundra, Agaguk relaxed, fully restored.

In the morning when he woke, Iriook was not at his side. He found her vomiting painfully on the river bank. "What's the matter?" he asked anxiously.

But in his confusion he already knew the answer to his question.

"This has gone on for some months already," said Iriook. She counted on her fingers. "He will be born in the snow time," she said.

All that day Agaguk worked away without saying a word. He tended the traps along the stream and caught a few fish. With his knife he cut some straight branches from the bushes and made a sort of dam to form a little bay. Here the muskrats would come to be captured. With one motion Agaguk could block the exit. It was an old method, learned from the Montagnais, men whom he considered little better than animals but who knew how to hunt furs. Once the rats were prisoners behind his dam, it would be easy to club them on their sensitive muzzles. And there would be furs enough for a big trade.

But while he did all this, Agaguk's thoughts were elsewhere. Iriook's news brought a great light into his soul, a happiness he did not know how to express. Like a marvellous hope and a kind of tenderness, he felt a need to solace and love, of which he did not know the meaning. That evening, while they were eating, he smiled at Iriook. She had rarely seen him smile. "It will be a boy," he said.

He did not look at her when he spoke. Bending over, he bit

with his strong teeth into a fish he had caught some minutes before and which was still wriggling. He tore off the raw flesh and spit out the tiny bones. "It will be a boy," he repeated.

He was not asking a question, he was making a statement. He was sure fate would have it so. Iriook ate little. Since the morning she felt ill. In the middle of her breast lay a heavy, unmoving load.

"I wish it for you," she said.

Agaguk nodded and went on eating. It must be a boy. A girl would be a burden, a useless mouth to nourish on this tundra where every hour of living is a fight against nature. Her eyes dreamy, Iriook repeated smiling, "It will be a boy. I wish it— for you." This time Agaguk looked her in the face. "The good spirits are not our enemies," he said.

He spoke softly, murmuring the words, and put out his hand to touch Iriook. When they had finished their supper, Agaguk took the dishes and went himself to rinse them at the river, an extraordinary thing for him to do. "Leave them," said Iriook, "I must keep on with my life."

But he did not answer. "Leave them, leave them," protested Iriook.

He kept on rinsing the dishes. "I must work," said Iriook impatiently.

Agaguk was living in a dream. "Tomorrow," he said, "tomorrow."

He spoke little, made no grave declaration; only he had this look of seeing wonders, of being intoxicated without wearying. Later they went to bed on the moss but Agaguk did not touch his wife. He lay stretched on his back near her, his eyes wide open.

After a while Iriook murmured, "Nothing is forbidden, nothing. My mother told me so long ago."

Agaguk turned toward her with an astonished gaze. She smiled in the darkness, indulgent and patient. "In the last days, when the child will soon be born, then it is better to wait. But this evening, especially this evening, nothing is forbidden."

Then savagely, in a great surge of his whole body, he was upon her.

"But never as before," he said, his mouth close to his wife's ear, "never as before." He attained a new passion, gestures which did not resemble anything they had done before. He had generated life in this woman; he acquired suddenly a force, the greatest of all, a power which seemed to him almost magical.

Their coitus was brutal, almost mad. Iriook cried out in pleasure, and Agaguk's wail could have been heard far over the tundra. What they discovered surpassed the closed world of their understanding, that of the tribe, the barren soil, the daily drudgery. They were united not only by the flesh, but through the soul, the heart, the mind. And above all by a sort of roaring power within, which threw them one upon the other, magnificent animals. It was a deliverance from the past years and an entry into wonderful and gentle realms.

All the next day Agaguk dreamed of this boy that he was soon to possess. When he set a trap and hid it under the moss, he thought of the day when he would teach the child this art. Not at once all the complex sciences; first the child must learn to live. He would teach him to walk, to dip up water. He would show him how to swim in the river, to tell the cold from the hot weather, the bad wind from the generous mild breezes. The child would be near him, within reach of his hand. Iriook would sew him a parka of the finest skins, according to his size, small and beautiful. And Agaguk would take the child hunting, in the moss where he could find the badgers' burrows, on the sharp banks of the river, on the wet ground where he could pick up the tracks of the animals come to quench their thirst at the watercourse. Each track, each footprint would mean to him an image of the beast and its habits.

So, look at this wolf track. You see how he treads? One foot before the other, nervously advancing, eternally careful, every sense alert . . . the fox, more confident in his muscles, so fast in the leap, drinks with his paws apart, see? Like this . . . this star-shaped print is the mink's, that three-toed paw is the wolverine's . . . here the weasel, there a muskrat . . . do you understand? You must learn to recognize them, to know, to have judgment on such things. Every track is an image, never forget that.

This beast here, see, this wolf, has not set his feet on the ground as another wolf would have done. Why? He was afraid.

Something was moving on the other side of the river. He was watching every moment, but he drank just the same. For he had as much thirst as he had fear. For him there was no choice. A river with its water means survival. So he will survive. A muskrat whose track comes to here, then turns back, suddenly more compact, the prints close together, disappears under that grass over there, do you know what that means? He disturbed a mink and is being followed, so he flees . . . come, come with me to that clump of grass, look, here is the mink's track. It meets that of the muskrat. Good, come and look, there! Blood and fur. A muskrat is dead, devoured by the mink. For them also, one or the other, the price of survival. The muskrat is sacrificed that the mink may live. For one dead, ten are born. The muskrat's litters are frequent and numerous, while the female mink gives birth to only two or three little ones. So then it is fair that more muskrats die the prey of mink than mink as the prey of muskrats. The Spirits have so decreed.

But there were not only the animals; there were also the weapons. This is a rifle. Look how it is made. This is the barrel where the steel bullet comes out. Here is the inside of it, here is the stock. Look how the weapon is loaded, how you must shoulder it, how to fire it. See that caribou running there . . . I press here, the bullet flies out, it strikes the animal. I did not aim at the animal itself, but a little in front of it. When the bullet reaches the place where the animal is at the moment when I press the trigger, can you understand that he will no longer be there? So I aim a little in front, like this—a very little, but it is enough, and the caribou falls, my son.

He would tell everything to this first witness he would have. Every day he would show him the mysteries of their own survival, in accordance with that of the tundra's animals. How to tend a trap, how to kill the beast, how sometimes to spare it because at certain seasons there is nothing to use it for, and the day will come when it is precious. The dressing of the furs, the preservation of the meat by smoking or drying, the knowledge of which animals give plenty of fat with which to render the precious oil.

And so that these tasks may be done at the proper times, all the other skills, all are just as essential—how to recognize the smell of an animal in the wind, how to know the tricks of the beast whose track one follows, how to guess the habitual path of the mink going down to drink—to foresee the acts of each one and possibly outwit him. Beasts with fur for trade, beasts with fur for clothing, from which to make parkas and the walls of the hut, beasts whose hides will make more or less supple leather, beasts with short hair whose hides serve for beds or seats, beasts with good food flesh, beasts with fat that will give oil for the cold season. . . .

The caribou furnishes food and clothing, the fox furnishes clothing and fur for trade. But only the surplus is to be traded. The same goes for the wolf, but for them there is also the government bounty. As for the mink, the muskrat, the weasel, the badger, the fisher and the wolverine, they are bearers of excellent and precious furs. The carcass feeds the dogs, and so each one to his needs and satisfactions.

Every day, dreamed Agaguk, every day something new to teach the child, so that his knowledge will be complete. But still more, more than all that, no child in all the tribes would receive such an education as he would give him. Agaguk swore it by the Good and the Bad Spirits. They would talk of him in all the igloos and at the Top of the World. This would be Agaguk's child, the handsomest and the most cherished in all the universe.

CHAPTER 9/TOKONGAYUT
The Dead Man

In the village, after Brown's death, the Montagnais who had been his helper had cursed at everyone who came near. They had not paid any attention. A Montagnais doesn't amount to anything. Why bother with him? Nevertheless Tugugak, his expression somber and his look cruel, talked of going to punish Agaguk, whom he suspected of the crime and who had thus deprived them of their source of brandy. Some of the others dissuaded him and their reasoning was sound. Sooner or later the R.C.M.P. would have come and imprisoned Brown, this white man who sold the illegal goods. The man who had caused his disappearance had only anticipated the men of the law. How could one know by how much time?

They would not attempt any revenge against Agaguk who was after all the son of Chief Ramook, and so deserving a certain respect. As for reporting Brown's death to the white men, well—they held long palavers. Around their chief, Ramook, were grouped Ayallik, Tugugak, Hayuluk, Ghorok and a few others. The Montagnais had left for the free south, a pack of furs on his back. "Who gave them to him?" demanded Ayallik. It must have been a gift. It was easy to see that there was nothing left in Brown's hut, once the fire went out, except the charred remains of the white man, which they made haste to bury. "Someone gave them to him to keep him quiet."

Ramook, for it was he, said nothing. Like the others, he shrugged his shoulders. Ayallik was right. It was to keep the man quiet that he had given him the furs. But that kindly gesture, that logical offering, did not ensure the man's discretion.

On the other hand, the R.C.M.P. might not trouble themselves about the affair, unless there was a formal complaint. Who was this white man? Where had he come from? And since he was engaged in an illegal traffic, would they really try to punish his murderer? This Eskimo reasoning was surely not that of the R.C.M.P., but it served to calm the anxiety of Ramook and the people of his tribe. They deduced, in their own particular logic, that if the white man was a bad man no one would seek to punish anyone for his death. The authorities would probably judge that it was better to let things go, to pigeonhole the affair and not talk about it. All this palaver was in vain.

They chose to do nothing, to say nothing. If the constables came, they would pretend ignorance. They would know nothing of what had happened and still less of why. The tribal solidarity on which Agaguk had counted held firm. Life went back to normal, and after a few days no one spoke any more about the trader and his horrible death. However, Ramook's doubts persisted. He had paid the Montagnais generously for his silence, but as the days went by he was sorry he hadn't killed him. That would have been a surer way to buy his discretion. Surer anyhow than relying on a simple bundle of furs. Ramook knew the price of a delation, and some days he was not at all confident that the Montagnais would not have recourse to one. But as he was naturally rash, little inclined to worry, he longed to regain his peace of mind. He called the men together and proclaimed a celebration.

It was an escape as good as any, for him as well as for the tribe. Certainly, after the drinking, the chance orgies with the docile women, no one bothered any more about the recent melodrama. Especially as Tugugak had found the hiding-place of the white man's brandy dug in the moss and skillfully camouflaged near the hut he had when he was alive. Tugugak thought of trading it himself, but he had no leisure for that after Ramook decided on the feast. Tugugak gave up the gallon cans of liquor in exchange for some fine furs, one for each of the acknowledged men of the tribe who would be present at the festival. He gained riches at one stroke, with no bargaining.

They drank. They fornicated for three days and four nights. Few husbands searched out their wives, for that would have been neither much fun nor sporting; alcohol rendered its normal service, and they cared little for legitimate intercourse.

It was the kind of feast Ramook had wanted. Hunting being better in new territory, why sheathe the weapons?

When the cans were empty, they slept off their drunkenness, in a dreamless sleep from which they awakened to their ordinary life. Fifteen days after Brown's death, no trace of his stay in the tribe remained. Ayallik buried the empty tins in the tundra, far from the village and deep in the moss. They cleaned up the site of Brown's hut, burying the cinders, raking the moss over it, so carefully that after a day of sun and morning dew, it did not show any more.

CHAPTER 10/OKIOK
Winter

The weeks passed and became months. Near the river, far from the village, Agaguk and Iriook followed their destiny. Now the woman's parka bulged in front. Her belly swelled. Within, the new life grew each day. And every night Iriook, in panic, implored the Spirits to make this weight in her a boy.

On the tundra, the wind grew sharp. In the morning it was cold and the frost covered the dark moss with whiteness. Sometimes the odor of snow came in the clear blue sky. Then Agaguk stood before the hut and scanned the north. One evening he said, "Tomorrow the snow will come."

And the next morning indeed the snow did come, first a gust of wind, a terrible driving wind. The snow came from the north, riding the wind. It was a white fluid wall, which darkened the world. Then everything was enveloped by the icy, dense flakes, hitting the skin like chick peas. Contrary to the usual course, everything was covered, buried in a few hours. When the wind let up and the pale sun returned, three days had gone by. The tundra had become again the snow plain, the polar vastness. Seven months of misery began, for the distracted and famished animals as well as for the men who would have to survive in this deceitful environment.

With this first new snow, Agaguk built his igloo. Then he transferred all they owned to it and took down the hut. "When will be your time?" he asked that evening. He had touched this belly that was like a balloon and that compelled the woman to walk awkwardly in the igloo.

"Surely three more months," said Iriook. "Surely three, maybe four. Why do you ask?"

"I was waiting for the snow," he said. "To barter the skins I have here—we need salt, bullets—"

"I need some things too."

"A rifle for you," said Agaguk. "Yours is old."

"I don't need that."

"Yes, you might."

He was making calculations. "We lack a lot of things."

Iriook agreed. "When will you go?"

"Early tomorrow, with the dogs."

"And when will you be back?"

"It takes four days to go to the Company's village on the Big Water. Four to return. I shall stay there one whole day."

She said nothing, but the look she turned on Agaguk was eloquent. What would he do over there? What would happen to him?

"You've been to the Company's village before," she said. "What's it like there? I've never been there, me." She felt brave enough to go with him, even if the child within her was becoming a burden.

Agaguk raised his shoulders. "There's nothing there. The trading post, the igloos, that's all. I'll be there only one day, maybe less. . . ."

Iriook did not feel reassured. "There's nothing else?" she insisted.

"What do you expect?" Agaguk answered harshly.

At daybreak the next morning he harnessed the dogs and came near Iriook, not knowing what to say. But he stood beside her and felt the woman's hand rest on his arm. That had to suffice. "I'll be waiting," she said. "Come home quickly."

A crack of the long whip, the man's shout, brought the dogs to their feet, whining. The animals leaped in the traces at the second stroke of the whip, broke the runners free and the outfit took off. The sled carried what was needed to feed the dogs, and the fat, the ammunition, the bundle of furs, the caribou skins in which Agaguk would roll himself for the night, the igloo lamp and the pemmican.

Agaguk had slipped the long snow knife in his belt, the tool with which to build a night's igloo, and another knife, shorter, to finish off and cut up any game he might bring down along the way. How could he know what would be the luck of the road?

Standing, one foot on each sled runner, he let himself be pulled along by the dogs. The load was not heavy, for on his return he would have to bring whatever he got in exchange. The surface was hard and compact, the sled glided along without difficulty, and the dogs ran willingly. Here on the tundra, the snow is not treacherous. The ground is even, without cracks. The snow piles up without faults, unlike that on the islands to the north, where in the polar ice abysses open up ready to swallow man and dog team together. The dogs have a nose for these dangers. The head dog can recognize the sure footing. He distrusts the hand's breadth crust of snow, barely covering a crevasse twenty meters deep. He goes around the danger and avoids it. But this makes necessary a zigzag course, sometimes a very slow one.

On the tundra there is none of that, but instead a rapid run in a straight line. It went so smoothly that Agaguk could hope to cover in three days a distance that formerly took him four to walk. But then he had a savage wind to fight, the snow was not frozen and crisp as it was now, just right for speed.

He let the dogs travel without a halt until evening. At first he had driven them hard, but after a while he decided that he would cover more ground before night if he let them take their own gait, and they would not be exhausted. The evening gray was showing in the east when he stopped.

The dogs were still frisky, though covered with ice. Agaguk undid his bundle and threw a frozen fish to each one, which they devoured instantly. They kept circling around him, hoping for another morsel, but he was not moved. He knew that a dog on the trail ought to eat only a little at a time and that he runs much better with an empty belly. Rationing thus had its usefulness, aside from lightening the load to draw, in making sure that the sled dogs would be eager. Disappointed in their hopes, they wandered aimlessly for a moment. The head dog and a jealous bitch fought a brief battle. Soon one of the dogs dug a hole in the snow, using his muzzle and his paws. He slid in to sleep, having created his own igloo to his own measure and for his own needs. The others did the same, one by one. In a few minutes they were all out of sight in their improvised burrows. Their warmth made the snow at the opening crumble, blocking the entrance and hiding it. A gust of wind spread a fine snow over all, and soon no trace of the dogs remained. They could sleep in peace, warm and in comfort.

In his turn Agaguk built an igloo, putting it together in a hurry and making it just big enough for himself. Tomorrow the wind would begin to pull it apart. He carried all the sled load inside, out of danger from wind, dogs and wolves, then he placed the stone lamp on the floor; it was a more primitive utensil than the metal stove that Iriook was so proud of. That stove, which the white man had thought up for Eskimo use, and sold at the company store, was a sort of wick affair in which they burned the ordinary heavy impure oil distilled from animal fats or from the seal and whale blubber they hunted at sea.

In the cramped space of the igloo, the stone lamp, which also used the oil by means of a woven wick, was just as good as a stove and took up much less room. While the flame gave him warmth and light, Agaguk melted some snow in a pot and put the pemmican to boil. As soon as it was ready, he devoured it, then he let the liquid boil until it was reduced to tasteless bouillon. Having eaten and drunk, he took out his pipe and tobacco. He smoked peacefully, unmoving, letting himself soak in the damp, soft heat of the igloo, a heat that made him dull and sleepy. Then he laid one of the caribou skins on the ground, folded it in two and lay down, rolling himself in the other skin.

When he woke up in the morning, he was ready to resume his journey, every muscle relaxed, his energy renewed. It was another fine day, almost without wind, and the dogs could again run at their usual pace. As before, Agaguk traveled standing on the sled runners, except for a few moments at a time when he felt numbed. Then he ran alongside the outfit or behind it at the same rate as the animals. It took him three and a half days to reach the post.

It was a collection of a dozen grayish houses, with a few igloos on the edge. A radio antenna stuck up thirty meters in the air, a thin steel obelisk. At the entrance to the village, an enormous reservoir of heavy oil supplied heat to the houses, and near the Company warehouse a smaller building from which came crackling noises, sheltered a diesel electric generator. That was all.

The monotony of these few buildings succeeded the desolation of the plain; they were no less desolate—in fact they made the desert seem more vast, they extended its boundaries. Here, in a blizzard, a man could go out merely to pass from one house to another, and without realizing it blunder off in the wrong direction, to be lost in the white turmoil and perish before he could be found. It happened often, and more than one white man living in the Arctic would not dare stick his nose outside during a blizzard unless for some desperate emergency. When the wind rose, driving a wall of snow before it, when this swirling, blinding, deadly mass came down on the post, there was nothing to do but to sit at home and wait for good weather to return. Only so could one survive.

When Agaguk came into the village, his eyebrows and cheeks covered with frost, his team was worn out. For a moment his heart stopped. He was passing the R.C.M.P. post, a bigger and better kept house than the others. A constable hailed him. "Where are you from?"

Agaguk halted his dogs. His stomach in a tight knot, he pointed back in the direction of his village, which was also the direction of his hut. It was a vague gesture. "I come from there."

"How far?"

Agaguk counted on his fingers. "Three days' travel, maybe four . . . ." He waved his arm to sky and sun. "According to the weather," he added.

The policeman came over to him. Agaguk could not move. Since the man had spoken to him, he had thought of but one thing—the flame lighted in the night, the expiation on the pyre which he had destined for the trader Brown.

"What do you come here for?" asked the constable. Agaguk took a long deep breath and found his voice. "To trade my furs."

The policeman looked over the outfit, and even touched the bundle of skins. Satisfied, he motioned briefly. "All right," he said.

Agaguk whipped up his dogs. But he put so much force into his gesture, his whole attitude was so strange, that the policeman watched him curiously as he went along toward the trading post. Then, bored all at once, he shrugged his shoulders and turned back into the R.C.M.P. office.

CHAPTER 11/AMERK
The Furs

In front of the Company's establishment, Agaguk tied his lead dog to the post planted there for the purpose. Then he took the heavy bundle of furs on his back and went into the store. There was no one there but the clerk, a tall, thin Scotsman, with reddish hair and a mournful, unhealthy face. He said nothing, gave no welcome when the Eskimo entered. His expression remained cool and watchful. He had glanced at the bundle, but that look betrayed no interest. He waited while Agaguk undid the straps and spread the skins on the floor. "I've come to trade my furs," said Agaguk.

The man nodded slowly. "The price of furs is very low," he said.

Agaguk shrugged. He had been hearing that for so many years. And others before him had been able to learn it by heart, so many times was it said and repeated. "Very low," the man said again in a lugubrious tone.

Agaguk lifted the first lot of furs, fifteen mink, almost all first-call. The man McTavish spread them out on the counter and examined them one by one. His look was brief, that of an expert. He knew how to discover the smallest rubbed spot, the bruise that spoiled the workable part of the skin. If it was summer fur or the velvety fur of winter, if it came from a healthy mink or a sick one, if the dressing had been done with care or not, McTavish would find out in the wink of an eye. He threw the inspected skins farther along the counter, the good to one side, the rejected ones to the other. But every time, no matter what Eskimo was concerned, the good skins were rare.

Agaguk watched the performance as it went on. He had a twist at the corner of his mouth, an odd look in his eye. He picked up one of the rejected skins. "What's the matter with this?"

McTavish smiled. He was used to protests. They did not affect him any more; he had exercised this ungrateful trade for twenty years. He pointed to a tiny scratch on the inside of the skin, where it was no more the back and not yet the belly. The scratch did not go through the leather. "Reject," he said.

Agaguk turned red. "It's nothing," he cried, "It doesn't hurt the fur—that's not enough!"

The Scotsman looked coldly at the Eskimo before him. Twenty years of this game, twenty years of this kind of talk, twenty centuries—he grabbed all the skins on the counter, rolled them up and held them out to Agaguk.

"Take your furs away. I don't argue."

The Eskimo looked at him open-mouthed. "Go ahead, you understood, I don't argue."

Agaguk stood a long moment staring at those blue-green eyes, eyes which did not smile and perhaps had never known how to smile. Then he shrugged. "As you like," he said.

He put the skins back on the counter, in front of McTavish. With a sigh the factor unwrapped the bundle and put the skins in the same order as before. After that it went fast. He inspected what remained in silence, the summer mink, the wolf skins, two caribou hides which Agaguk could spare, twenty of fox, as many of badger, a few muskrats. Then the Scotsman added up the total.

It was small. Even less than Agaguk had hoped, allowing for the customary bargaining. But he must have foreseen it. The Company never paid the hoped for price, however low a man set it. It rarely happened that one could get a man-to-man trade, in liberty and frankness. The Company had a monopoly —no competitor. Traders like Brown, illegal opposition, never lasted long. Where could be found the manufactured goods, if not in the Company stores? The factor fixed the price, one must accept his figures. He himself owed his promotion to the success of his bargaining. At the head office, he was judged and weighed in the balance according to the margin he could establish between the market value of the furs and the value he allowed the Eskimos. Besides, by the high mark-up put on the normal prices of the merchandise for sale, mark-up which reduced still further the value of what was brought for barter, the Company had the opportunity to write incredible profits in its books. Against a hydra of this kind, an infinitely powerful monster, what could Agaguk do? Agaguk or anybody else?

"What do you want?" asked McTavish.

Of course, no money. Trade was carried on for the most necessary objects, for everything and nothing in the store. Certain Eskimos hardly succeeded in covering their necessities. They gave up their furs for knick-knacks, things which were of no use to them and often valueless. Like children without any sense at all, they were seized by sudden desires which they could not control. When bad times came, they had nothing, they were defenceless. Like all the other factors who came before him, McTavish willingly let them waste the fruit of their painful hunting expeditions.

Agaguk, thinking for himself, had always bought carefully. Perhaps he was different from the other Eskimos, in some remote fibre of his being. Often he had longed for the mechanical toys, the childish trash. He would have liked many of the things in the store, but he had always chosen indispensable things, for which he had come especially to exchange his furs. He listed what he wanted. "A rifle," he said, counting on his fingers. "Some ammunition, twenty boxes. Cotton cloth for my wife, kerosene for the lamp."

The Scotsman put a rifle on the counter. It was a weapon of very ordinary quality, efficient enough but sold in town at a very low price. Beside it he laid the twenty boxes of ammunition, and a tin of kerosene. "Tobacco for my pipe," Agaguk went on. The tobacco came to join the rest. "Salt," continued Agaguk. "A whole sack." He pointed to a fifty-pound sack.

"Half," said McTavish. "No more."

Agaguk bent his head, his face bewildered. The Scotsman knew how much he normally used. He did not intend to let him have more than half a sack. Besides, the bill was paid. "Some cotton cloth," went on Agaguk, resigned. An iron kettle like that one. A shovel, see, like the one hanging there."

"That's all," said McTavish. "Nothing more after the salt."

"What?"

"I said that's all. After the salt, no more."

"Hardly half," cried Agaguk. "I want a lot more things."

"Next time," McTavish cut him short. "Next time."

McTavish had not learned the game yesterday. He was used

to it. Agaguk, not knowing how to count, could not guess that even at the arbitrary price allowed for the furs, the Scotsman had considerably lowered their trading value. He felt no remorse. The Eskimo was not going away with empty hands. He had a gun, bullets, things with which to hunt and to feed himself. He had salt with which to dress the skins and preserve them, oil for his stove and tobacco to smoke. He could do without the rest. A shovel? What on earth for? Cloth for his wife? What good would that do? Nothing useful, that was sure. And the kettle? Nonsense. . . .

According to his way of thinking, everything was going well and the Eskimo was not harmed. McTavish felt no twinge of conscience. After all, Agaguk was not obliged to accept the conditions of the bargain. He could leave, take back the furs, refuse the price he had set. That Agaguk had no other place to sell did not bother the Scotsman at all. It was none of his business nor any fault of his. What could he do about it? He had laid down certain conditions which the Eskimo had definitely accepted. He felt at peace with himself.

The Eskimo gathered up his purchases and carried them out to the sled. He took an hour to pack the load, to feed the dogs, to choke down the rage in his heart which urged him to do something desperate, to take a terrible revenge. He thought again of Brown, whose fate he had sealed. There was no possibility of disposing of the Scotsman in the same way. But was it bearable that the white men must always have the last word? Always, without the Eskimo ever being able to defend himself? But to whom could he complain? The white men, were they not all-powerful, and their interests in these countries all too well protected? He felt his mind confused, he could hardly knot the thongs to hold the load on the sled. The dream of vengeance would not leave his mind, but along with it there rose within him a contrary sentiment, a neutralizing thought that little by little calmed his fury. Vengeance? But how? To go into the store, to strike, to kill? It would be futile, ridiculous even, for they would take him prisoner before he had gone thirty steps in flight. To tell McTavish what he thought of him? He might as well talk to a rock. Agaguk raged at the memory of the man's icy look, the complete indifference he showed openly. What good would talking with him do? It would mean bad days to come. To oppose McTavish could bring no good. The Scotsman would get even for any insult at the next bargaining session. He would remember the Eskimo, keep his face in mind, wait his hour for revenge patiently. Others had tried their luck, Agaguk remembered well. What had happened was still talked about in the igloos. Okarnak had been the latest victim. Now he had to travel three weeks every year to trade his furs at a post farther away than the one that employed McTavish. For Okarnak that was the only way to obtain, if not justice, at least conditions equal to those which McTavish imposed on him before he started to take his revenge.

Nevertheless, outside, in front of the post, Agaguk knew that he could not go home to his igloo like this. Too many contradictory feelings were boiling in his breast. The need to escape somehow grew and grew, demanding immediate satisfaction. He did not identify his desires, he simply took account of their existence and recognized their strength. But in this isolated and inhospitable village, what way of escape could there be?

Under his parka Agaguk touched the beautiful shining mink pelt hidden there, the one that he still kept as his last reserve, which he had not considered offering McTavish to complete his transaction with him. He thought for a moment of going back to McTavish, of offering him this skin, truly a magnificent one, in return for the things he lacked, the kettle, the shovel, the cotton cloth he wanted to bring as a gift for Iriook. He thought of obtaining justice, this time, of insisting, of showing his independence as McTavish had done. But he changed his mind.

The mink skin would bring much more than those objects, which now he no longer wanted so very much, and which Iriook could certainly do without. More than the cloth, the shovel, the pot—something indefinable, this need to escape was suddenly made attainable by the presence of this forgotten bit of fur. He wanted to make some extraordinary gesture, to do something far outside his usual way of life, something that would mark the instant precisely, and for a long time.

Little by little he envisaged this escape, made it clear. Quickly he understood what he had to do. Between that unpleasant moment with McTavish, and his arrival at the igloo where Iriook would be waiting, something must happen, there must be a hiatus. He could not resume his journey, he could not return immediately to his wife. He whipped up his dogs; he felt a sudden lift in his spirits, an enthusiasm he did not try to control; he had made his decision, he knew what he would do. He drove the team straight to an igloo on the outskirts of the village, an igloo larger than the others, topped by a short mast where a tattered flag waved in the wind. It was a place well-known to the Eskimos who passed the word to each other that there a man could satisfy his wants.

Did this igloo enjoy some special protection? Did the authorities shut their eyes to what went on there? Neither Agaguk nor the other Eskimos coming to trade could have said. They knew of its existence, they knew what they would find there.

Once within, Agaguk was brief. He displayed the mink pelt, the choicest of furs. The man who had received him, a half-breed Eskimo and Ojibway, was a trader well known all through the Arctic, who carried on his traffic under the nose of the R.C.M.P. He examined the skin contemptuously.

"You kidding me?"

Here Agaguk felt more sure of himself. He snatched the skin out of the man's hands. "I'll go somewhere else," he said.

This time the threat made sense. He could go somewhere else. A white man in the same village, he said to himself, could fill his needs. The trader shook his head, grimaced. "The price of fur is down," he said.

"It's worth what it's worth."

"One bottle, that's all."

He reached into a cupboard behind him and took out a small bottle of liquor without a label, a syrupy white alcohol, distilled from some filthy mixture, brought there illegally. Agaguk began to stuff the mink skin under his parka. "No," he said.

They were sitting on the ground, their legs folded, and they argued in the flickering light of a little kerosene lamp. A frightful smell of rancid sweat, rotten grease and bad alcohol pervaded the igloo.

"Four bottles or nothing," said Agaguk. The man sighed. The palaver was going according to the rules. He would do well enough out of it, he knew. He took another bottle from the case.

The trader stared at the fur, the beautiful supple mink skin. He knew its worth. The Company would never see the colour of it. Surreptitiously, as the liquor came in, someone would undertake to dispose of it. The beautiful skin would end up with some dishonest buyer in town. There was always somebody to buy unstamped skins. Later it would find its way to Europe. At the going price of mink, the risk was worth while.

"Four bottles," Agaguk repeated firmly.

The man swore vulgarly in the white man's language, but he ended by taking two more bottles from the case and holding them out to Agaguk in exchange for the fur.

Agaguk left at once, bearing the precious flasks hidden under his parka. Outside, he jumped on the sled runners and whipped up the dogs. But he did not go very far over the snow plain. The hour to make camp had not yet come when he stopped his dogs and built an igloo.

He did not delay in carrying out his plan to escape. Feeding the dogs took only a moment, and then came the unloading of the sled, piling things safely in the igloo. Warm, sheltered, the dogs already buried under the snow, he lighted the stone lamp and instead of eating he quickly drank the first bottle. Though his body was not accustomed to alcohol, he nevertheless possessed such great physical strength that he hardly felt the effects of one dose. He drank the next one more slowly.

After a few minutes, he polished it off. His movements were slow and he talked thickly to himself. He could hardly keep awake, but he still fought off his drowsiness. He could not have said what he was thinking. At first he had felt an airy lightness. He was visiting a marvellous country, a fairyland; his drunkenness was euphoria. After that stage, rage possessed him. Immense, domineering, it took hold of him, but before he could yield to his anger, he went to sleep. The alcohol in his veins had conquered all resistance.

In the morning he was sober, but he had a hangover and his head ached. He boiled a little pemmican and after he had eaten that he went out to feed his dogs which were yapping miserably. When he returned, he began to drink again, emptying the two remaining bottles. This time, drunkenness came more slowly. Since he had eaten, his body put up more resistance to the alcohol. He began to sing, a strange outcry without tune or meaning, a sort of animal howling. He beat time, striking his thigh with the palm of his hand. Outside the dogs began to howl in turn. The racket lasted a long time, but it died down, little by little. It was still light when Agaguk went to sleep, slouched against the sack of salt.

He woke at dawn the next day, with a thick mouth and a heavy head. Instinctively he measured out every movement, for each one hurt him. With infinite trouble he got to his feet and went out to feed his dogs. Most of the trip was still ahead of him. The wind was blowing hard and the sky was gray, snow was flying over the tundra. "Blizzard," he said to himself.

But he was not frightened and in spite of the physical ills that weighed on him, his mind and his thoughts were oddly clear. The episode with McTavish no longer made him ashamed; he didn't even care about it. It was over. The hiatus was filled in, he could now go back to Iriook.

He loaded the sled, kicked down the igloo and harnessed the dogs, whipping them joyfully and cursing them, laughing to hear his own voice echo over the ridges of the icy plain. The wind presaged a storm, what matter! The cold had revived him, the blood ran swiftly in his veins, the headache was fast disappearing. Agaguk hurried on. The dogs, eager after the long rest which they were not used to, did their best, and pulled without weakening. But Agaguk knew well that they would not win their race against the blizzard.

Toward five o'clock in the afternoon, when the team had run at full speed all day, the wind freshened, the snow came, hard and stinging. Agaguk did not hesitate. The blizzard's birth is swift. It doesn't strike gradually, but spreads over the plain and covers the whole country before one is aware of it.

Again the igloo. He had provisions and oil, he could wait until good weather returned. The force of the blizzard surprised him, though he had seen many another. A constant roar filled the heavens, the mass of snow driven by the wind beat down on the igloo and shook it. Even the dogs howled their uneasiness, and Agaguk heard their voices mingling with the gigantic sound of the wind raging in the high regions of the sky.

CHAPTER 12/ANORE
The Blizzard

The blizzard lasted two days. It had not completely cleared at the end of that time, but there were left of it only occasional gusts of wind and wreaths of snow over the plain, mere squalls that had lost most of their force. Agaguk stuck his head outdoors and reckoned that he could risk continuing his journey. A thick layer of snow, fine as powder, covered the tundra. The dogs floundered, slipped and fell. This was no easy passage like the one coming. Agaguk cried invectives to his team, sometimes implored the dogs, encouraged them, cracked the whip in the dry air, constantly adding his voice to the irregular barking of the beasts. They took three days to cover the distance, three full days of arduous labour, a struggle for survival.

At Agaguk's igloo, tongues hanging out and all energy drained from their bodies, the dogs sank down exhausted. Iriook was waiting. She showed no uneasiness, no signs of worry; she remembered the lesson she had learned. She greeted him as he had come to expect, tenderly and with an indescribable light in her eyes, but she was careful not to say a word, though Agaguk's wanderings over the snow plain were far from leaving her indifferent. It was not easy to remain impassive, without revealing anything of the hard days she had just lived through, while the blizzard raged and she was desperately worried over what might be happening to Agaguk in this tempest. She said only one thing, coldly and with a pretended indifference. "You've been gone many days."

"It was a long way to the village," Agaguk answered without faltering. "The blizzard made me stop a while."

He lied without knowing how to lie, as Iriook knew perfectly well. But what use would it be to blame him? Since he was there before her, back whole and sound, back at least, that was the essential thing. "You've brought the things you wanted?" she asked at last.

He made a vague gesture, went out and began to carry the bundles he had on the sled into the igloo. He spread his riches on the ice bench. "Your rifle," he said, holding out the new gun.

She took the weapon and held it in her hands a long time, examining it.

"I will teach you to shoot," said Agaguk.

Without a word, but with a funny smile, she opened one of the boxes of shells, took out one and loaded the gun. "Come," she said.

With great difficulty, considering her size, she crawled out through the tunnel, and Agaguk followed. Outside, she pointed to a bush growing on the bank of the river. "You see," she said, "that forked branch, the one on the left? Look."

She lifted the rifle to her shoulder, barely aimed, pressed the trigger. The bullet whistled and the branch flew up, cut in two. Agaguk murmured admiringly, a sort of hoarse grunt deep in his throat. "I have nothing to teach you," he said. "Nothing at all."

He smiled at Iriook and she felt suddenly overwhelmed. Why ask more of her man than this one word which revealed a whole world of thoughts. Agaguk took the rifle from her hands and leaned it against the wall of the igloo. "Help me," he said. "There are more things to carry inside."

In a few minutes the sled was empty. Together they had finished the job and all that Agaguk had brought home was in the igloo. "I wanted to bring you some cotton cloth."

"Some cotton cloth? What for?"

"You've seen the white women? They wear cotton dresses sometimes, when the sun is warm—"

"At the village," said Iriook, "I saw one woman dressed like that. . . ."

He was silent for a moment; then he decided to tell part of the truth, at least what had happened, if not the hurt to his pride which was the worst of all for him. "He did not want to give me the cloth—"

"Who?"

"The man at the Company store."

"You talked about it?"

Agaguk puckered his lips. "According to what he said, I already had all that was coming to me. I wanted an iron pot too, for you. And a shovel for me. The man would not give them to me."

The secret was heavy. So heavy that Agaguk came very near to telling of the rage that had struck so deep and the drunkenness that had followed.

"It's always so, you know that, Agaguk."

It was true but he was not used to it. He might stay silent. What would be the good of telling also what had happened after he left the Company store? Iriook would not understand.

They stayed outside, after they dragged the sled behind the igloo and fastened it there. The wind rose suddenly over the plain, picked up Iriook's cap and carried it away. Agaguk looked at the lowering sky, sniffed the wind and walked out farther to gaze better at the sky.

"What is it?" asked Iriook.

"Another blizzard. It's a bad winter, there's little peace."

They went in through the tunnel, instinctively hastening even though the tempest was still far away, as if they needed quickly the reassuring warmth of the igloo, the peace that reigned there.

"Will it last a long time?" asked Iriook.

"I don't know, four days, maybe more." He saw that she was uneasy.

"What's the matter? Are you afraid?"

"One storm after another. If the whole winter is like that, what shall we do when the baby comes?"

But Agaguk smiled. "To be born at the time of the great cold wind will make him brave and strong. It's a good sign."

The waiting began.

The weather was much the same during the weeks that followed, with few calm days and great storms that came down
from the north.

"I can't help it," Agaguk said one day. "I can't help it."

Indeed there was nothing to do about it. Outside the wind
raged and the snow driven by the tempest fell in great solid
sheets. Agaguk, squatting at the tunnel entrance, had been
looking out over the plain for a good five minutes, what he could
see of it. In the rare periods of calm, the immensity around
them appeared suddenly, infinite and uniform. Then the wind
redoubled. Enormous and powerful, it swept everything before
it, heaving up the snow, throwing it here and there, piling it
against the igloo in a drift that would end by covering over
everything.

Agaguk computed carefully how long this would take. For
Iriook's time was up and soon he would have to think of her
alone. When he came in, he examined the air hole at the top of
the igloo, in the keystone of the vault of hardened snow. The
driven snow had not yet reached that far, but if the blizzard
kept on it would before long. He sat down and took on his lap
the seal-bone knife with which he cut the blocks of snow to
build the igloo. This flat tool served also in case of need to free
an access tunnel blocked by the wind or an air hole buried by
the gusts, as there would be in a few hours. Quickly he shaped
some snow blocks, and at three meters from the igloo in the
direction from which the wind was driving, he built a wall a
meter high, a solid wind-break, two blocks thick, and tapered.

Iriook's condition gave Agaguk's work a feverish energy.
Ordinarily he would probably have let the snow accumulate,
but now he found himself confronted by special circumstances.
He might have to get out in a hurry, the access tunnel must

be open, the ventilation as good as possible. The wind-break might not save the igloo entirely, but it would give Agaguk a few days' leeway. It was a rough device, the only one he could think of. As soon as the job was finished, he went back in. Iriook was sewing by the light of the stove. "Will snow cover the igloo?" she asked.

"I've built a wind-break."

"I heard you tapping the snow blocks."

"Perhaps the wind will drop."

"And if it doesn't?"

"I can't help it," Agaguk said again. He had done the only thing there was to do. For the rest, he must leave it to fate. For an hour he listened, unmoving.

"Will the storm end soon?" asked Iriook.

Agaguk lifted a shoulder and looked away. "It's one of the last," he said. "The wind will shift finally. It must."

The woman did not believe him. "You said that a week ago," she said, "and here's another one. You've been saying that for two months."

"There is nothing I can do," muttered Agaguk.

"We haven't any more pemmican."

"I know."

"And the frozen fish, just look." The hole in the igloo wall where they kept the fish was almost empty. "You haven't killed anything for a month."

"There's nothing to kill. The plain is deserted."

"And the wolves?"

Sometimes when the wind was low, they could hear the famished pack howling.

Agaguk lifted his hand sharply. "There is nothing on the plain," he said stubbornly.

"The wolves—"

"There's nothing." He hated to admit that he had not been able to track the wolves, to get near them. A trap set for a whole month, looked at whenever possible, had been no more successful than his patient ambush in the brush along the river bank. He had also dug away the snow down to the ice on the river, and he dropped a line through a hole in the thick covering, but no fish had taken it. If spring was slow in coming, in a couple of weeks, three at most, they would face famine.

"That caribou meat that we smoked and that you threw to the foxes and the wolves," remarked Iriook gently, "that would have saved us."

Agaguk had shot a male the middle of October. He had looked over their store of pemmican, and decided they had enough. He had skinned the caribou, salted and rolled up the hide. He had kept some of the choice bits of the meat and thrown the rest to the beasts of the tundra. "That would have saved us," Iriook repeated.

Rage swept over Agaguk. Did she have to keep saying it? Must he listen to reproaches now? How was he to know, way back in October, how tough the winter would be? "Shut up," he yelled at the woman.

Iriook bowed her head. She did not want to argue any more. Besides, she admitted that it was not Agaguk's fault, only a lack of foresight. She herself might at that time have asked that the meat be dried and smoked rather than given for fodder to the wild animals which, if they had come on the plain, had not let themselves be caught in traps. Then too, she was carrying the child, another reason to keep quiet. The baby moved in her and she felt ill, with a queer sensation she had not felt before, not exactly a pain, but the root of a pain. It was very far away, very deep in her belly.

Agaguk stood up. With his snow knife he cleared the air hole, which was filling up fast. He worked with angry gestures, with brutal strength.

Seated on the ice bench where the skins had been laid, fur side up, Iriook kept her eyes turned on some image within, some nameless joy. She smiled mysteriously, evoking remote joys known to her alone. A little boy wandering about the igloo? A child playing on the tundra in July? In the silence there was only the sound of Agaguk cutting and trimming the ice.

Then the pain shot through the woman's belly, like a dart. She bent her head and groaned. Agaguk stood still and looked at her. "What's the matter?"

She moved her head slowly from right to left. The pain had stopped as quickly as it had come.

Agaguk insisted. "What's the matter?"

The woman stretched herself out on the skins. Her belly under the parka looked like some monstrous growth. Her eyes closed, she rested. The man put the knife in his belt and went toward her. He would have liked to sit beside her, to make some tender gesture, but he had never learned to do anything like that, and to feel the immediate need of it made him ill at ease. He found some words, not those he would have wished to say, but others, simple ones, meaning nothing. His tone was almost caressing.

"Like some tea?"

Tea was a rare luxury. They kept it for the return from the hunt after a hard day on the tundra, or for a chill, or for times like this, should they ever come. "Would you like some?"

Iriook raised her eyes. Her look was docile, loyal, like that of a wounded animal that trusted its master. Her forehead glistened. "No," she said, "I don't want anything."

A sword of pain went through her body. She grimaced and could not keep from groaning. Agaguk could not move, could not even breathe.

"I think the time has come," Iriook said. "You will know what to do?"

"Yes."

He leaned over her and undressed her. With movements which he managed to make gentle, he slid the parka over the woman's head, unlaced her mukluks and pulled off her skin breeches. Now she was bare, lying on the caribou skin.

It was hot in the igloo, too hot. Even naked, she was sweating. Her body shone in the smoky light of the oil stove, a body become grotesque with its heavy breasts, its enormous belly, its distended pubis spreading the hair wide over the diaphanous skin. In the ballooning belly there was a sudden spasm which wrinkled the tense surface and made Iriook move. Then a large bloody patch appeared on the caribou skin. From the gaping vagina ran a flood of water mixed with blood. The horrified man watched this new phenomenon with clenched fists.

"Now," murmured Iriook, "don't be worried. Old Poktok taught me. It's nothing to worry about. It means my time has come and nothing now can stop the birth."

She spoke in a hoarse, abrupt, uneasy voice, her eyes still closed, her head thrown back on the skins. "Nothing now," she repeated, "nothing can stop it."

And as a sharp pain again passed through her, Agaguk saw her writhe, grimacing, on the couch.

CHAPTER 14/ERNGNIK
The Son

It was first a dull pain in her innermost being, almost imperceptible in origin. Iriook had stiffened in the interval, but the pain passed almost at once, and she took a long breath. Her fingers, clenched tight on the caribou hide, hardly let go before the pain took hold of her more fiercely. Then she groaned weakly, unable to stifle these long moans which were calling Agaguk. After that everything was quiet and silence held the igloo. From without came only the dull roaring of the wind, smothered by the thick walls of the ice dwelling.

And so for a long time the alternation of peace and hell went on for Iriook. Agaguk stood by powerless during the struggle. Embarrassed by his brute strength, humiliated by the uselessness of his muscles, he watched with increasing terror this labour in which man has no place. His wide eyes saw the life move under the tight skin of Iriook's belly. Leaning against the igloo wall, he felt fright overwhelming him as another cry rose to a scream to die away in an animal moan like nothing he had ever heard on the tundra or elsewhere. Then the relaxation took over, each time shorter and shorter, with hardly a moment to gasp for breath. Unable to bear it, suddenly he said in a hoarse voice, "I want to take away your pain."

He did not want her to suffer any more. He wanted all at once to extirpate the pain, to drag it from her body like an evil root to be burned at once. What he wanted henceforth was to save Iriook. Strangely the child to come no longer mattered. "You can't take it away from me," groaned the woman. "You can't. You can do nothing at all, Agaguk."

Then slowly, from the depths of his subconscious, Agaguk felt his rage rising, not in a sharp rush of blood to his head, but in a slow implacable anger, which mounted from his entrails to take over his whole being. A new force existed in him, an extraordinary power which would decide the event. His hands braced against the ice wall, the muscles of his legs taut, his knees bent, he panted, his rage in rhythm with the moans of Iriook, with the fury of her cries. For now she cried without rest. It was no longer a moan, but a long continuous shriek, coming from very far within her, a horrible sound which rose to a mad crescendo.

Sometimes she opened wide her thighs, raising her knees, and her whole body seemed to arch itself. Then she pushed desperately to cast out of herself this living mass which now took too much room within her. At that instant the vagina opened like a mouth, a sort of dark orifice, a monstrosity carved in the lower belly. The woman's cries filled the hut and reverberated in terrifying echoes along the walls and up to the ice dome. Still against the wall, Agaguk had become more beast than man. A hoarse growl came constantly from his throat. His eyes were bloodshot. He shook his head from left to right continually, like an animal ready to leap.

Suddenly Iriook thrust out her thighs and her legs. She writhed and the spasm moved her belly. Pain possessed her entirely. At the moment the child's head appeared.

It was a frightful sight to Agaguk, a hairless skin, bare and shining, a sort of ball that blocked the vagina. Iriook uttered another scream, still louder, and the head made its way more easily. Then Agaguk jumped. Until then he had mastered his rage, but he could no longer. He must fight this great evil in his wife. He must destroy it, drive it away forever. It was a devil, an evil spirit, a malevolent beast to conquer. He rushed at Iriook, threw her on the damp ice, kicked her and hit her with his fist, seeking so to kill the pain, to make it flee the body of his wife. And all the time he yelled like a madman, and his cries mingled with Iriook's as he bit her arm, struck her full in the face. The blood ran from her swollen lips.

Then suddenly the woman had a convulsion of her whole body; she uttered a last scream which was lost in a long stifled sob. Her imploring voice rang in the igloo. "He's out," she howled. "Don't you see? He isn't in me any longer. He's out!"

As calm as the instant before he had been like a wild animal, Agaguk pulled himself together, and saw the child lying between Iriook's thighs. He leaned down, picked up the inert body, and with a swift bite severed the cord. The blood spurted. He took the string which for a long time he had been keeping in his pocket for this very instant, and quickly tied off the sticky, supple cord, close to the baby's stomach.

"He must be made to breathe," said Iriook, her voice sounding far away and sleepy. Agaguk looked at her. Her face was unrecognizable. Blood was running from the wounds he had inflicted on her. Her lip was cut as if by a knife, one of her cheeks was swollen. "He must breathe, hurry!" she begged weakly.

Agaguk took the baby by the feet, and held it at arm's length. With his fat, awkward finger, he cleaned the mucus from inside its mouth. Then he hit the new-born child hard at the base of his spine. The baby twisted in Agaguk's grasp, curled up in a great effort, and then they heard the piercing cry of a healthy, well-born infant, a baby to be proud of. "It's a boy," Agaguk said, in a voice which emotion strangely altered.

With a smile of infinite tenderness, he held the infant in the crook of his arm. Iriook, her eyes closed, was smiling too. "I knew it," she said. "I knew it would be a boy—for a long time, I knew it. . . ."

Agaguk came to squat beside his wife, still lying on the floor. He put the baby on a skin; lifted the woman and laid her on the ice bench, against the warm furs. Then in his turn he stretched out on the couch, putting the baby in the warmth between the two bodies. "Go to sleep," he said to Iriook, "Go to sleep."

The child was quiet. He was breathing well. "Sleep," Agaguk repeated. And he also slept, close against the woman and the child, now all his worldly goods and all his riches.

CHAPTER 15/K'AUMAYOK
The Light

In the morning Agaguk woke first. He had slept a long time, perhaps fifteen hours—he could not have said. The newborn child was still, his eyes shut, wedged between him and Iriook. Agaguk took him in both hands and hefted him. He noticed that the body was thick and hard, the back wide, the legs well made. He would be a fine child, strong and healthy, who would grow up capable and handsome.

Iriook woke and groaned in turning on the couch. Without moving, her head on her arm, she watched the child in Agaguk's arms. Her eyes rested on the head first, still egg-shaped from the pressure of its coming, then on the shoulders, the chest, the prominent lower belly, the bent legs, the tiny dimpled feet. Without a word, she held out her arms. Agaguk laid the child in them.

Iriook brought her breast to the baby's mouth. With her fingers she pressed the nipple between his lips. He began to suck greedily.

"Already?" said Agaguk, who was looking on and marvelling.

"No," Iriook said. "Tomorrow the milk will come, not before. But he has to learn."

The baby sucked at the dry breast, then started to cry at getting nothing out of it. Iriook gave a soft laugh from way down in her throat. "You see?" she said. "He's like you."

Agaguk, intimidated, was squatting in front of the stove and said nothing. After a little he said, "You want some tea?"

"Yes. We'll need water too."

The baby was filthy as if he had rolled in bloody dirt. Iriook spread her legs apart. Agaguk saw the soiled caribou skin, and against the woman's vulva the mass of the afterbirth expelled during her sleep of exhaustion.

"I'll go get some snow," he said, "and melt it. Then I'll heat some water over the fire." But he hesitated to leave. Standing he looked at her. Then he said, "Last night, I hit you."

She put a finger to her face, touched her split lip, her bruised eye, her swollen jaw. "I know."

Agaguk shuffled his feet, and hunted for words. He dared not look her in the face.

"You couldn't do anything about it," she said gently.

"No, I couldn't do anything."

"It's over," she murmured. "The child is born. He's strong. Everything will be all right."

The baby had begun to suck again at the breast which was swollen but still gave no milk. Iriook got up and came to hold him near the stove to warm him. Agaguk took a deep breath, almost a sigh. "I'll go get some snow," he said. "We've got work to do."

He crawled hastily through the tunnel, toward the storm. Outside he saw that the wind break had worked well. The igloo was in no danger of being uncovered. And as the wind had gone down, it looked as if the blizzard was ending.

Left alone within the dwelling, Iriook began to sing to the baby in a soft murmur, a song of ancient time, a lullaby handed down from generation to generation for thousands of years. The baby stopped crying and was tranquil. For a long time Iriook sat on the edge of the ice couch and swayed to the rhythm of the song. She was smiling, her gaze far away, her arms holding her naked little son tight, asleep against her breast.

When Agaguk came back, he brought snow to melt in the iron pot. Soon the water was boiling and they both got to work.

That evening, Iriook cried out in pleasure, mingled with a new pain.

"The milk!" she said.

With her hands cupped she squeezed the fleshy masses of her breasts to knead the congestion in them. She lay down on the couch, took the baby in the crook of her arm and held his mouth against the now generous breast. He sucked with funny noises that made Agaguk laugh. "What shall we name him?" asked Iriook.

"I've picked out a name," answered Agaguk. "He shall be called Tayaout. It's a brave name."

Iriook smiled. "I like the name," she said. "Indeed it is a brave name."

"They sing about him," said Agaguk.

Tayaout, the great hunter, who lived on Lake Aenakdiouak long ago, at the time when the first white men came. Even the police spoke of him with respect, boasting of his ability, his strength, the riches of his fur catch each year, the excellence of his hunting. Tayaout, symbolic name, name of hope and ambition.

"Tayaout," Agaguk repeated gently, rolling the word on his tongue, savouring it gravely, piously.

Iriook contemplated the baby drawing life from her rich breast. "You're named Tayaout," she said, "did you know it?"

CHAPTER 16/NARIAKTITAUTIK
The Hunting Dog

At the village nobody talked any more about Brown's death. Months had gone by. The winter had come and with the winter the devouring cold, the daily misery. They had taken down the huts, erected the igloos, and the rhythm of life had little by little adapted itself to the new and terrifying season. All was immobility—to sleep, to wake, to sit in the igloo without moving, to wait—to eat at times, and go to sleep again.

Sometimes if the wind slackened, the men went out on the plain, looked for trails, set their traps, visited others they had set before. The fur was good but the harvest scanty. Out of ten or twenty traps, they got only two or three takes. There were even whole weeks when nothing came to trip the mechanisms. Then there was only the amorphous, vegetative life. When the wind blew and the storm swept the country, when the temperature sank so low that he risked death a hundred yards from his igloo, the Eskimo slept. Men and women and children were heaped on the ice couch, half-conscious in the foul air of the primitive dwelling, in a kind of animal hibernation.

Then one day the dogs barked, new sounds were heard on the plain. A dog train was in sight. Ayallik gave the alarm. He was returning to the village after visiting his traps. In all the igloos they had heard the team coming, but it was Ayallik who told them who it was before the intruder arrived.

"A policeman," he said.

A head popped out of every tunnel. At Ayallik's announcement, the head withdrew, like an animal diving into its burrow. By the time the policeman was near, Ayallik had already warned every Eskimo.

"Do you suppose he is coming about Brown's death?" asked Ramook. Ayallik made a face.

"What else?" he said.

"He might be on his way to the Islands, farther up."

"He would have started from Coppermine then," said Ayallik.

"You think so?"

"Yes. And he would have traveled in the big bird."

"Maybe."

"On a sled, with dogs," went on Ayallik, "he is surely coming here, not farther on."

Ramook's shoulders were drooping, but his eyes remained alive and wary.

"I depend on the others," he said in a falsely whimpering tone. He pointed to Ayallik, "On you, especially. On Ghorok."

Ayallik grinned. He liked to see Ramook implore his aid. The man had always been his enemy. Perhaps that fact would change nothing in the tribal solidarity which might persist in the days to come, and it was quite possible that Ayallik would suit his behaviour to that of the tribe, but at the moment he took delight in seeing Ramook tremble with humility.

The policeman arrived in the middle of the village and found no one to greet him. This was, for this man who had been trained in Eskimo customs, the sure indication that they were concealing something. He stood in the centre of the circle formed by the igloos for a long moment, knowing that he was being spied upon but pretending to notice nothing. He was tall, almost twice as tall as the Eskimos, blond, with eyes as blue as the sky in spring time. He pulled off his long furred gloves and put them on the bundles of provisions stowed on the sled. Then he turned the sled around and placed it by the dogs. He unfastened the harnesses with no fuss, and freed the animals which ran off as soon as they had eaten to find the Eskimo dogs. A man appeared. It was Ayallik.

He was cocky. He had a tranquil audacity, and the policeman's visit amused him. In the igloos they used to tell sagas of that kind. It was always the most courageous, and the one who did not fear to venture, who turned out to be the hero. Ayallik felt ambitious to play such a hero. It seemed to him that the role would suit him well. What if he should fulfil his destiny, displace Ramook and take for himself the headship of the tribe? The victory would be easy for whoever could seize his opportunity. Above all, why wait? From the very beginning, he said to himself, he must be the strongest.

"Hey, you!" The policeman was calling him.

Ayallik knew that in every tunnel an Eskimo lay flat on his belly, waiting to hear. He came slowly toward the centre of the open place. The policeman was pulling on his gloves again.

"Who are you?"

"I am Ayallik."

"Where is your chief?"

"I don't know."

"Ah?"

"Probably in his igloo."

"Which one is his?"

Ayallik pointed with outstretched arm. The policeman smiled.

"He does not come himself, he sends you?"

"No."

Ayallik knew that on this cold, dry day, the voices carried. They would all hear the present exchange. The idea amused him. The game became doubly interesting, to fool the policeman and at the same time to fool the people listening. . . .

The policeman nodded. "Tell the others I want to see them all. A crime has been committed here."

His eyes meeting those of the policeman, Ayallik smiled, ever so little, a mere twitch of his lips, which those listening could not see, but which was plain to Henderson, the constable. "Crimes," remarked Ayallik, "are committed in lots of places among the tribes."

"I am interested only in the one that was committed here."

Ayallik bowed slightly.

"I will tell the others that you wish to see them," he said conclusively. "All the others. Ramook, the chief."

"The one who lives with the Montagnais woman?"

"How do you know?"

"We know everything."

Ayallik looked cunning. "And still you have to question people? I will tell Ramook you want to see him."

The insistence was little emphasized, but the policeman

understood. He bowed slightly in his turn. "You will warn Ramook," he said with a flash in his eye.

"And as he is the chief," replied Ayallik, "he will quickly have the others warned."

The conversation had gone on in Eskimo, a language which the constable spoke easily. He made a decisive gesture. "Have them build me an igloo and carry in my provisions. I shall be staying some time."

"How long?"

"As long as I have to."

Ayallik held out both hands and smiled. For people who know everything, he mused, they act peculiarly. To know everything doesn't mean that one has to install oneself in an igloo, that one thinks of staying as long as one has to, as the policeman says. White man's caprice, typical habits which the Eskimo never succeeded in understanding. But what could one do but shrug his shoulders stoically and bear the discomfort?

All this was a considerable disappointment to Ayallik. He had hoped that, if a policeman came among them, he would arrive provided with certain proofs, and that the aid he, Ayallik, would bring to him would be limited to a few well placed insinuations. This would be his road to future power. But if the policeman was going to settle in for an indefinite time, that meant he had only vague suspicions. In this situation denunciation became more difficult. Something in Ayallik, some residue of loyalty, or perhaps of fear, made him hesitate to go any further. He was convinced of Agaguk's guilt, and although he was no longer a member of the tribe, since he had in a way deserted his own people, would not Ayallik infringe the tribal law if he informed on him? Still the constable might, in Agaguk's absence, fix his suspicions on some other member of the tribe concerning the trader Brown's death.

There remained Ramook and Ayallik's desire to succeed him as chief of the tribe. To denounce the son would outrage the father; well, so be it. But how would the tribe accept this outrage? Would Ayallik win something by doing it, or would he simply risk the collective vengeance of the tribe for his treachery, after the policeman left? Ambition and fear were in conflict in the Eskimo's soul. Patience was necessary. An instinctive wisdom counselled waiting. The opportunity might be better tomorrow or the next day.

"Ramook's igloo is there," he told the constable brusquely. "If you have something to inquire of him, go there. He is the chief, I'm not."

Then he turned on his heel and went back to his own igloo, a sudden defiant look in his eyes and an odd smile on his lips.

The Eye

Agaguk could not stop gazing at the child. He spent hours squatting, his back to the fire, watching him. Nothing more, only this contemplation. He did not play with him, he rarely touched him. When the baby cried, Agaguk caressed him, gently, with the tips of his fingers, as if he were afraid of breaking the tiny body. When Iriook gave the baby her breast, Agaguk again contemplated the miracle. This child was his, this future man was in his image. The germinated seed, miracle and mystery!

"I will teach him how to build an igloo," he said to himself. "How to make a snow knife from a seal bone, or a caribou rib. . . ." The baby sucked, a hungry little animal and the milk ran over its cheeks, and Agaguk dreamed. He stood up straight and proud, "My son!" The words fairly rolled around in his mouth, at ease there.

Iriook, propped against the wall, her breast offered to the child, let him stuff himself. She too was dreaming, but differently. She dreamed of gentleness and tenderness. She bathed Tayaout's brown body and held him naked against her skin. She loved to feel the baby's mouth take the milk, feed himself so he would grow healthy and strong. Agaguk often repeated, "He's named Tayaout, a good name. More than anything, it's a brave name."

One day Iriook again pointed to the hole in the ice wall. Agaguk had cut up the better part of two wolves he had killed, but it was not good meat. It was tough and bitter.

"I'll go hunting," he said. But he could not come to a decision. In the meantime, outside, the sun had come back over the snow, and spring was in the air. The tundra would soon be visible. Within the igloo the water ran no more down the walls, and once when Agaguk thrust his arm out of the air hole, at the top of the igloo, he felt that the blocks were half melted.

It was too warm in the igloo now. Henceforth they would all three go naked, the baby because that was the custom when it was so hot indoors, and Iriook because she could not live otherwise in that sweatbox. Agaguk usually wore his skin pantaloons, but his torso was bare.

"We shall run short of meat," said Iriook again a few days later. "Look." There were only two hunks of smoked wolf meat.

Heavy-breasted, the woman was leaning against the ice, and yet she was sweating. The drops trickled down slowly over her smooth dark skin.

"I'm going out," Agaguk said. He took his rifle and went out. He had not been outside for days. Iriook had to bring in even the snow to be melted. Agaguk was astonished to see how the season had advanced. Already down by the river the ice was black, covered with water in some spots. In a few days, a few hours, the current would carry it off and the water would be free. The sun was hot. It burned the skin of his cheeks, it was melting the snow. As he walked Agaguk felt his foot dig into the ground, and each time he lifted it from a deep footprint, he saw the water oozing in. The bottom of his track was black, the water-soaked snow itself was black, or rather grey, like melted metal. Only the surface snow was still white.

On the wind came fresh odours. A caribou fawn bounded along on the other side of the river. Agaguk's shot brought it down. That evening they had a great feast in the igloo. Iriook put the meat on to cook; she kneaded the liver with some flour and fried it in oil, she cut thick slices from the flesh and broiled them in the flame. Agaguk took one of the animal's eyes, went over to the baby and put it in his hands. The child shut his fists on it and lifted it to his mouth to suck.

When they were all full, they went to sleep. Agaguk dreamed that in his village the *Krablunain*, "the Big Eyebrows," as they called the white men, were combing the earth to find Brown's remains. He woke up in a sweat, fainting with horror. He rolled on the skins and rubbed his face with his hands. Awake at last, he was thunderstruck by the dream and could not get back to sleep. He thought he heard a voice calling him. *"Anok,"* he wondered.

There was nothing but the wind, Iriook moaned in her own dream. Agaguk heard nothing more. The night had closed in over him and his family. Outside the loud noises of the cracking ice reverberated over the plain. From the river came the dull pounding of the foaming water. From the south rose a mild wind, stinking of the rotten moss and the decaying underbrush of the white man's country. May came to an end, June began and, with June, the springtime.

CHAPTER 18/ANGAYOK'AK
The Chief

The Montagnais woman always had very sharp senses, of sight, of hearing, of smell. She smelt the coming of the constable. "Ramook!" she said in Eskimo, "*krablunak manitok*! A white man there?"

The man from the R.C.M.P. was already crawling into their entrance tunnel, emerging inside the igloo. "*Kranor itpin*," he said. "How are you?"

"I am Ramook, Chief of the Tribe."

"I am Henderson, of the Police."

Ramook bowed his head and pointed to the bench. "*Namatok*."

Henderson took up his place on the bench, crossed his legs, took out a package of cigarettes and held it out to Ramook. "Want a smoke?"

"No." Ramook remained on guard. His Montagnais wife had watched Ayallik's performance. She had heard some talk going on. What had that ambitious climber given away?

"I shall spend some time among you," said the constable. "I've asked them to build me an igloo."

Ramook scowled. "It's not worth the trouble," he said. "The snow's begun to melt. Stay here with me. They'll build you a hut as soon as the tundra is dark."

Henderson nodded. Two years earlier, he would have refused, because of the smell in the igloo, the foul air, the smoke of cooking. But habit had given him experience. To sleep in a tent in early spring had its risks. Unexpected storms might come, and at that time the wind is especially dangerous. It can arrive from the south with unusual violence, or it may be soft and warm, so that the snow plain may melt away under the sleeper. Who can guess how thick it is or what chasm may lie underneath? The igloo is safe from such dangers. "I'll stay here," he agreed. "If it's necessary, they'll build me a hut, as you say, when the tundra is dark."

He lighted his cigarette. Ramook pretended not to notice him, but his shiny eyes constantly followed every movement the policeman made. "You know why I've come?" asked Henderson point-blank.

"*Nauna.*"

"Sure you don't know?"

"*Naonarlok.*"

"You do know. You and the others too!"

Ramook grinned. His teeth were yellow, and decayed in front. "Me?"

"Yes."

"*Nauna.*"

Henderson had learned patience. In this country of snow and hard living, it was the cardinal virtue. Calmly he undertook the recital he had to go through.

"A liquor trader came here. He was not an honest man. But no one has the right to kill a man, even if he is not honest."

Ramook lifted an eyebrow, bent his head, opened his mouth, the very image of stupefaction.

Henderson went on impatiently, "You know it as well as I do, Ramook."

The Eskimo sighed, and subsided into his former impassiveness.

"This man came here with an Indian, a Montagnais."

Ramook spat on the floor, in the corner the Montagnais woman swore, and Henderson had some difficulty not to smile. This Ramook was tricky. He had been able to marry a Montagnais woman and remain chief of the tribe. That showed an extraordinary ability. The duel was between evenly matched opponents.

"He came here and someone burned him in his hut. The Indian ran away. He reached our post at Great Bay, exhausted."

"Nothing I can do."

"Yes, you can do something. I want you to surrender the guilty man to me."

"*Nauna.*"

"Ramook!"

"*Nauna,* I tell you. I know nothing about it. I have nothing to say."

Henderson stood up. "All right. I'll stay here. When the tundra is dark, I'll search. I have tools. Oh, I know your ways. You have buried the evidence. But I shall dig. I shall dig everywhere, under your own hut, Ramook, everywhere. I shall find it."

The old chief smiled mysteriously. "Nothing I can do," he repeated.

Henderson's patience was wearing out, but he knew it was useless to insist. If Ramook was intelligent, so were the other Eskimos. They would all be faithful to their tribal solidarity. To temporize was the only solution, although the most trying, to stay on, waiting, listening, watching. Who could say that one of them would not sell out? A word dropped in the ear, an act. . . .

Once the snow was melted, Henderson would dig in the surroundings. The logical places to look were not so numerous, and he was almost sure to find somewhere a white man's remains, even if nothing more than a heap of bones or a shred of blackened flesh. He would wait. The white man's law must prevail, and it was his job to see that it did. "Even here," he said to himself.

Here above all, if the Arctic was not to become a vast refuge for outlaws. Henderson decided to go look up Ayallik right away. Of all the Eskimos under Ramook's authority, he felt he was the only one who might speak out.

CHAPTER 19/SIRK'INIK
The Sun

"*Sikrenek nuiok*," cried Agaguk. Indeed, the sun had appeared. But he was thinking of the great sun to come, of the moss turned green, the plants in bloom, the animals whose meat they would smoke for their provisions. The sun of the warm quiet brook, where slept the fish he would catch, the sun of the life without danger, of the naps outdoors before the hut, the patient, nourishing, comforting sun. The clever sun that shines on a caribou antler so worn and polished over the years that the glitter reveals the target to the waiting hunter. The sun of the wild geese, the ducks, the teal, the waterhens, the ptarmigans. The time of the good life! *Sikrenek nuiok*!

Agaguk finished breaking up what was left of the igloo. He threw the hard blocks far out on the moss to melt in the summer weather. And laughing like a child, chuckling with delight, he began at once to build the hut, with Iriook's help. Next time the sun came up he would busy himself with his trapping, but first he would find the places where the animals had begun their new lives. Flat on his belly he would crawl here and there to study the tiny tracks. He would spy on them until he knew by heart the comings and goings of the thirsty beasts. Squatting, his fingers newly skilful at their task, keeping in mind all that he had ever learned, he would push aside the moss, place the trap and bend the spring. Then he would cover the trap, and standing over it would urinate on it so that no scent would reveal it. The smell would not alarm the animal. Whether mink or muskrat or weasel came to spring the trap, it would be for him one prize the more.

"I shall have," he said to himself, "a hundred skins to carry to the post, a hundred of the most beautiful ever seen. With the finest fur. All the winter's provisions." He did not count on the sealskins—those were to be dressed with salt at the sea.

He would go in the autumn, like his cousins of the northern tribes, to ride the first ice floes. He would kill the seal, the bear, he would be the greatest hunter. He would lead Tayaout by the hand over all the tundra and to the great rivers. Look, Tayaout, see the fox, see him run! Look at the bear, the seal. The seal-skin serves us well, child, and the flesh of the seal nourishes us. With the seal's teeth, with its bones, with its tusks we make needles and tools. With its fat we feed the fire, we light the igloo. Father Seal, our Protector!

He was almost ready to throw himself prostrate in adoration. And to think he had to cross the whole land to go seal hunting! Here he would find caribou, sometimes a stray moose, a wolf, some foxes. But the precious seal lived farther away, much farther. "It's not enough," he said suddenly, sweating and panting with the effort. "Listen, Iriook, it isn't enough, we need more."

Ignorant of the thoughts that were troubling her man, Iriook asked, "More of what?"

"The hunt here is the white man's hunting. The Eskimos, the men like me, ought to be in the north. We must go live with the last Eskimos, those at the back of the world, the *Kidlinermeun.*"

"Why? In that country the snow is eternal. They live in igloos the year round."

"I know."

"Then why?"

"*Akragolok aodlanialertugutug.*"

To start tomorrow? Iriook shook her head smiling. She let him talk. Tomorrow . . . his tomorrows no longed disturbed her. She wanted to say, "Exactly when?" Next year? In ten years? Tomorrow . . . . "Here there is sun."

Agaguk looked cross. His fat face shone with sweat. His long arms swung trembling with effort. The hut was built but it seemed to him he would never get through covering it with those big caribou skins.

"There is sunlight here," Iriook repeated. "Soon the moss will be green, almost black. There will be flowers."

She pointed with her finger to a track on a left-over snow-drift. "You see? A mink."

Agaguk was frowning. He was thinking; he had a right to think. Why must Iriook spoil his dream?

Iriook turned toward Tayaout lying on the moss. An insect, a centipede, a dark crawling inhabitant of the earth's crevices, was running over his belly. With his tiny hand he was trying to determine what this new sensation meant. "Look," said Iriook, "see, he's already trying to catch an animal."

Agaguk spat on the moss. "Tayaout will be a great hunter," he said.

He gave up working and stared at the child. It was Iriook who brought him back to reality. "This last hide," she said. "Help me get it on."

Together they threw the big skin with the rough fur on the poles of the pointed hut and spread it out. It looked like an Abenaki tepee, but they did not know that. Now they had only to protect the entrance from the wind, and put stones from the brook around the base to hold the skins down and keep out any small beasts.

CHAPTER 20/APKUTIK
The Voyage

"At the Top of the World," said Agaguk, "in the ice country, it is spring."

But on the tundra, in the latitude where they lived, it was already summer, and Agaguk told himself that up there the sun would be barely warm. This was the time to go. "I'm going seal-hunting," he said next day.

Iriook felt her heart sink. The people who had been north told how the Eskimos got drowned hunting seals. And how they might freeze while waiting for their prey on the edge of a hole in the ice. "You'll come back?"

The question surprised Agaguk. "Have I said I wouldn't come back?"

Iriook sighed. She always asked the same question. "Some of those who go to those countries don't come back. At the village—"

"At the village," Agaguk interrupted, "twenty go every year. How many have not returned?"

He counted on his fingers. "The skin, the fat, the meat, the tusk ivory, the back bones, the teeth—all of that is precious. Three or four seals would be plenty."

"You'll go alone?"

"I've been before."

"Now you have a wife. I can go with you."

He still hesitated. Iriook took advantage of the moment to insist. "I'll carry some of the load," she said. "Coming back, how will you lug the seals without me?"

"They'll be all ready before I start, the skin wrapped around the smoked meat, the fat and the ivory."

"If there were two of us you could kill five seals instead of three."

The offer was worth considering; he had not thought of it before, but since she proposed it. . . .

"And the baby?"

"I'll carry him. He isn't heavy," she said. Agaguk gave in, but he looked sulky. Iriook was smiling. She liked to go on these wandering trips which would take her to the great water, of which she had heard so much but which she had never seen. Happily she got together all the necessities for the journey. First came the biggest caribou skin in which they would roll up to sleep, then another almost as large. The skins would be used also to wrap the warm parkas, the dried meat, the knives and scrapers and the thongs to tie up the bundles for the return journey, and so on.

For his part Agaguk prepared his own pack, which would not be as heavy, so that he could always be on the alert. Who would defend them, if not he with all his agility and his arms ready? He got out his ammunition, cleaned his rifle, and sharpened two fighting knives, one of metal and one of ivory. He put dried meat in his pack, so that they should not lack food, and then the bottles of sewn leather, full of drinking water. By good luck on the trip he would kill some animals, which they would eat raw, rabbits, badgers or even a few birds. And who could say, perhaps a polar bear, a white one such as is found on the shores of the sea?

At sundown that day the two bundles were ready. To carry Tayaout, Iriook had cut and hemmed a leather sling, wide at the middle and narrowed to the width of a strap. She would fasten the baby, seated in her hood, to the middle of this harness which she would carry on her back. The two straps passed under her armpits and were tied securely in front. Beside the child, but lower down and well-tied on her hip, would be her own pack. Thus loaded, she could walk all day without too much discomfort.

"What are we going to do with the dogs?" she asked.

Agaguk shrugged his shoulders, examined the beasts, already fat from their summer feasting on the tundra animals. "They'll find enough to eat," he said. "We'll leave them behind. Don't worry, they'll be here when we come back."

"They'll eat the skins on the hut," Iriook said.

"We'll fold them back and fasten them high up on the

poles. They won't be able to get at them. Nor the wolves either."

And so they arranged matters. There was nothing more to do except to put the lamp, what was left of the dried meat, as well as the other stuff they were not going to take, inside the metal box, which was their most precious possession. They did not fear intrusion. If by chance someone came to the hut to take something, it would be only because his need was desperate. That happened often—no one considered it stealing. No Eskimo would make any fuss over it.

So they left at dawn, Tayaout in his hammock. Agaguk had taken note of the stars, the moss of the tundra, the gusts of wind, then he announced, "We must go this way."

Iriook gave him a queer look. "You won't pass by the village?"

"No."

"You'll go around it?"

"Yes, and by a long way."

"Why?"

He shrugged.

"Why?" insisted Iriook.

"Because I choose to."

They marched all day, not with the uneven step of the white man but with the shorter, very regular pace of the Eskimo, which permits him to go incredible distances with only rare halts for breath. They went according to custom, never placing the foot flat on the ground but only the sole and the toes, using the spring of the muscles to drive the body forward. It is an exhausting and agonizing way to walk for a white man who has not the patience to get used to it, but for the Eskimo it makes the long treks beyond the horizon easy.

So off they went, Agaguk, Iriook and the baby who was laughing as he was tossed about on his mother's back. "Listen to him," Iriook said to her man, "He likes to travel."

And Agaguk smiled, saying nothing, but again entered into a fine long dream in which his son Tayaout became the hero of all the tribes, the man who would be sung about in the igloo evenings. Legendary hunter, powerful as the storm, greater than all the storied heroes, Tayaout, son of Agaguk!

It was a leitmotif hard to stifle; son of Agaguk, grown from his seed, his own creation, flesh of his flesh, issue of a father who would also be hailed—Son of Agaguk!

They made camp at sundown. Perhaps because of his exaltation this first day Agaguk had killed nothing. He had marched with weapon ready. Once they had seen a caribou far off, but that was too much meat to take on the first day. A rabbit too, but Agaguk was lost in his dream and had not been quick enough. The animal was only glimpsed before it disappeared behind a hillock on the tundra. They had stopped a moment, watching for it, but it had not reappeared. It would have been necessary to make a considerable detour to find its burrow. Besides, as it had its summer coat, so like the colour of the tundra, they might not be able to track it. They decided to keep on the march.

When the sun was high, Iriook suddenly felt Tayaout go heavy on her back, no longer braced against her. "He's gone to sleep," Agaguk said.

"Let him," she said. "The journey is harder on him than on us."

When night came they had to rely on the smoked meat again. They ate and went to sleep at once, weary but happy. The baby had hardly wakened up. He had nursed at his mother's breast, less ample that evening because of her fatigue, and then had gone off to sleep sucking on a shred of meat.

Agaguk's sleep was so heavy that two wolves came unscathed to sniff around the packs and made off with a bag of pemmican. He had only stirred automatically, but enough to put the animals to flight. On the wind came a whiff of caribou, and the wolves took off after that new prey. They would not return to the little one-night camp.

At dawn the sharp cry of a wild goose rent the sky, and Agaguk bounded to his feet. He had thought he could sleep with one eye open, and he had heard and seen nothing all night. He noticed the wolf smell, saw the bundles torn open and counted the bags of pemmican. Without a word to Iriook, he made up his mind to be more watchful henceforth. There is danger in life on the tundra—he ought to have been the first to know it. If one of those beasts had carried off Tayaout? He shuddered.

When Iriook had nursed the baby, and lighted a fire to

soften the pemmican, they ate. "Today," Agaguk said, "I'll get some fresh meat."

"A rabbit," said Iriook. "It's a long time since I've tasted rabbit. Later on it will be harder to get one. They'll be rare."

Agaguk did not answer. He already had in mind the route of the day. Now they were in line with the village, off to the left. He meant to describe a big half-circle and come back onto the road that led direct to the star on the horizon, always in sight even when the sun was out. In three days they would reach the region beyond the village.

"How much longer will we still be on our way?" asked Iriook.

He was not going to say how many days it would take. "I don't know. Not long."

"How many suns?"

"I don't know."

She left it to him. He knew the stars, he had by heart the configuration of the tundra. He knew where everything was, and in winter he recognized the snow dunes two days after a blizzard, when they were all new and he had seen them only once.

"Come on, let's go."

They unpacked the bundles. Tayaout took his place happily. That day, in the heat of noon, Agaguk killed his first game, a rabbit as Iriook had wished. The shot stopped him at a rise of ground, just as he was going to make off. Agaguk had only to yell "Ho!" The rabbit, curious at the noise, had hesitated a moment to jump, and the bullet had knocked off his head. Agaguk hung the carcass from a cord of his parka and let the animal's blood leave its dark traces on the moss behind them. Heads bent low, he and Iriook plodded on toward the horizon.

CHAPTER 21/TARIO
The Sea

Now the sky was white and occasionally there came a gust of cold wind.

"The ice," said Agaguk sniffing. "Don't you smell it?"

Iriook nodded gravely. She had never seen the Great Water nor the spring ice. She had heard stories of the seal-hunt, but she had never seen one. The men told lots of stories, and of course easily became the heroes of them, but between the evening recitals and the day's reality, there was enough difference so that she could, in the excitement of this new life in glaring light, anticipate events and feel an unaccustomed pleasure.

"You're happy?"

"Yes, I'm happy."

They had stopped and Tayaout was babbling. "You hear?" said Agaguk. "He too will be happy. He will be a great hunter."

He had no other word of praise to say of his son, only this phrase constantly repeated, synthesis of all his pride. What more was there to hope for, indeed, than that Tayaout should become a great hunter?

"He will be a great hunter, greater than all the others before him."

"You yourself are a great hunter."

"Yes, but he will be greater than I."

While they were talking, standing close to each other, the baby had leaned over and stretched out his arm toward the rabbit's bleeding carcass. Then he had stuck his finger spotted with blood into his mouth and was sucking it with satisfaction.

"You see?" Agaguk said. He was delighted, and he swelled up like a pigeon. The baby liked blood.

"Tonight," Iriook said, "we'll give him some raw flesh."

When they halted, Agaguk skinned the rabbit and Iriook scraped the hide to put it in the pack. Then they devoured the meat dripping with blood. Tayaout had his share, a hunk of flesh to suck on. That night Agaguk had no trouble keeping watch. What had happened put him in a state of exaltation. At first he could not get out of his head the image of Tayaout, his cheeks smeared with animal blood, sucking away on the raw flesh. It was his apprenticeship to manhood.

It was an image that haunted him as a deep and original joy, and which drove away sleep. How many dreams he could found on it! Tayaout well muscled, standing up to a great white bear, rifle at the ready, firing, bringing down the beast, yielding not an inch to fear, defying the animal. Fearless of the growls, of the monstrous mouth!

Tayaout in ambush for the seal, throwing the harpoon, fighting the animal, the triumph of the hunter. Tayaout before twenty wolves, defying them as he defied the bear, firing straight and true, felling the beast, picking them off before they dared attack the man. Triumphant, again and always!

But that was not the only cause for his exaltation. That evening, Iriook, stretching herself out on the caribou skin, had pressed against her husband and made a sudden, impulsive gesture, an intimate caress to which Agaguk was not accustomed. There are initiatives denied the Eskimo woman. The male supremacy and his domination limit the woman to a completely passive role. Even if Iriook, contrary to all tradition, received from the man a pleasure which she did not conceal, she had not really come to yield to the normal physiological impulses that would have been immediately reproved by her husband. She realized very well that Agaguk was far more liberal than others of his age. To press her advantage might compromise what she had gained, which was more than she had hoped for in watching the behaviour of other Eskimo couples. Yet against all reason, she was tempted to obey her impulse, to yield to her first and immediate reaction.

Startled, Agaguk murmured in her ear, "Don't do that. Women don't do that, Iriook."

But soon he resisted no more. Tense enough to break, he savoured this strange experience, while Iriook, her eyes closed, began the experience she had often dreamed of, to be mistress of a pleasure she could give, according to her own passion and her own ability. Afterward came a magnificent madness, a paroxysm of desire which threw them one on the other, equally possessed.

They came to themselves much later, when Iriook cried for mercy. Then he let her go, and she rolled over on her side, almost asleep with exhaustion.

In spite of his weariness, Agaguk could not sleep. To keep him awake there was not only the experience he had just undergone, but there was in another direction the image of Tayaout, intimately linked, it seemed to him, with what had just happened.

Since Iriook had first become pregnant, he had never possessed her without at the same time thinking of the child. First of the unknown, mysterious, anonymous being lying within his wife's body, then of Tayaout, this Tayaout in whom he placed all his hopes and joys. By instinct he linked these two things, refusing to shut off the pleasure of sex and the pleasure he drew from this being he had procreated and who had now come to live so close to him. Without knowing it, Agaguk reached back to man's original philosophy, his first thought.

He stayed awake most of the night. Seated, rifle on knees, he watched the tundra. At one moment the wolves came very near behind him, and he did not see them at once. A fox chanced even nearer. Agaguk heard him and raised his gun. The fox vanished in the night. After that nothing more came, neither man nor beast.

When the moon had fallen to the horizon, Iriook woke and relieved him on watch. Agaguk slept in his turn. And because they had so infringed on their night, they did not start at dawn, but later when the sun was fairly high.

Then came another night, another bivouac with the same pleasures over again. When his turn came Agaguk took a long time to get to sleep, dreaming of this woman who belonged to him, who was not like other women, who was better than the others, and who was so dear to him. Strange thoughts, indeed, for an *Inuk*.

Halfway through the next day they saw the Great Water.

They recognized it by the mists rising toward the sky and by the smell of ice that came on the wind.

They made a halt at the end of the day, just before dark, and Iriook spent an hour standing on the shore looking at the ice close in, the green water farther out, and the floating cakes of ice. Here and there she could see the black spot of an Eskimo crouched by a hole in the ice, or on the edge of a floating block, harpoon poised, watching for a seal.

At daybreak Agaguk drove in the two short sticks he had brought and set up a shelter by stretching the caribou skin from his pack over them. He laid another hide on the ground and arranged on it the ammunition, the rabbit skin and the rifles. He prepared his harpoon, a long piece of ivory tipped with a crook like a fish-hook. The harpoon was tied to a cord, thick as a finger. Another shorter harpoon was at hand too, in case the first one should be lost by carelessness and swallowed up in the Great Water.

"And what am I going to do?" asked Iriook.

"Nothing. You are to wait here."

"Where will you go?" She waved at the floating ice cakes. "Off there?"

She could not forget the tales; it was in this way that men vanished. The big floes were suddenly carried away by the current and they disappeared over the horizon. In these localities few Eskimos owned kayaks. To find them it was necessary to go farther on, where entire villages moved according to the luck of the season, following the seal migrations.

Here only the Eskimos from the tundra came to hunt, those who like Agaguk and Iriook enjoyed two distinct seasons and lived far from the seashore. And so died some men whom the Arctic sea had either starved or engulfed. In this alternative offered by fate, it was enough to encounter a sun hot enough to erode the edges of the floe until the man's weight was too much for it. Drowning or starvation, the result was the same.

"Not there!" exclaimed Iriook. "You'll be swept away."

Agaguk nodded his head. "The hunting is better there."

"But here, on the shore?"

"A fellow can wait for days."

"You've been here before?"

"Yes, before now."

"And you got some seals?"

"Yes."

"You can get some again."

"It will be long, Iriook."

"I'll wait." And she made a gentle movement, repeating, "I'll wait. There's nothing to hinder our staying here."

Agaguk looked worried. "We haven't much time. It will soon be summer here, and the seals will be off to colder water, deeper and far away over the Great Water."

"I would be happier if you did not go out on the floating ice."

"The hunting would be better there."

Agaguk was troubled. It was not customary for an Eskimo woman to argue with a man this way. Even though he was the master, was she not trying to protect him against himself?

"If you don't come back," she broke in brutally, "Who will teach Tayaout to be the greatest hunter?"

Agaguk nodded. All at once the argument struck home to him. Certainly one did not become great only by learning from a teacher. A hunter teaches his son, and the son, if he is of good blood and still more important, if he has double the muscles and the agility and the good eye of his father, will become the proudest of all the hunters on the Top of the World. But if there should be nobody to teach Tayaout?

"I know how to shoot, myself," said Iriook. "But how would I know all the secrets?" She pointed to the sea, and then to the tundra behind them. "Secrets of the ice, secrets of the tundra, all those things that you know, Agaguk. I don't know them."

"That's so."

"Yes."

"If I wasn't there—"

Tayaout was trying to pull himself over the ground in the half-melted snow. He laughed as he crawled along, as if he were discovering a new country that he liked. Agaguk looked at him a long time.

Finally he said, "I won't go on the ice floes."

He searched for a solid stand on the edge of the land ice,

one that was anchored to the soil as well as advancing into the sea. But he also looked behind him, from shore to waves, making sure that the spring thaw had not yet weakened the surface. For little would be needed, a few inches thinner, a weak spot. . . . He had learned on former visits to distinguish between the ice that had been eaten away underneath and the ice that was still thick. In the first kind, dark lines streak the transparent substance. One sees black where everything ought to be pale green or opaque white, while solid ice is of a good colour, with clear tones, without shadows.

He soon found a station which would not be dangerous. If the Eskimos from roundabout saw him there and laughed at his fears, he would pay no attention. He set himself to his task. It looked simple enough.

Seated on the edge of the ice, harpoon ready, he must watch the water, accustom his gaze to sound the depths, to know how to distinquish with no hesitation the slightest movements below the waves. If a seal showed up, he must strike a blow with the harpoon, a blow of incredible swiftness, sure and fatal. Then, the weapon stuck in the animal, he must drown it, fight it to the last movement. Then he must haul the mammal out on the ice.

Immediately he must skin the animal and snatch out the ivory. Then the cutting-up began, to set the fat to one side, to extract the oily reserves, to carve the flesh that made such good eating.

In theory it was easy enough. The difficulty was not only in the movements to be made, or in the launching of the harpoon. Agaguk, like all Eskimos, owned admirably balanced muscles and a magically sure eye. It was the need for patience that was the obstacle, patience which required absolute immobility. Any moving shadow on the water risked frightening the seal. So then a paralyzed fixed waiting could last for hours, even a whole day. Seals did not come for the calling. A man must resign himself to the knowledge that in a day of waiting only one, sometimes two, perhaps none at all, would come.

A young whale a few feet under water could be mistaken for a seal. Knowing that a young whale is only a poor catch and the mere throwing of a harpoon can frighten off the good catches for hours, a man must comprehend the necessity of motionlessness and acquire a sure eye to recognize the best quarry before the cast.

And there too, however easy it looked, that cast was the product of long hours of practice. Agaguk remembered how his father had taken him to the shore of the Great Sea when he was very young. He had been held for entire days to doing nothing but practice casts, one after another, tirelessly, the only way to become skilful at the task. For each cast: a hit!

But when would the seal come? Or the sea-lion? It is true they are not as common as the seals, but sometimes more interesting, for from their skin are made excellent boots, the traditional mukluks. However, Agaguk was not hard to please.

By the end of that first empty day, he would have greeted even a small whale with relief.

CHAPTER 22/UTJUK
The Seal

On the third day of his vigil, Agaguk was tempted to break his promise and to go station himself on the ice floes like the others. It did no good at all to stay where he was, to catch nothing, while that man over there was hoisting his third seal onto the ice. The risk was great and the footing precarious. But where he was the water was already much warmer. It would quickly eat away the ice along the shore. How much time would it still last? Maybe a week?

At that moment, out of the corner of his eye, he saw a movement like a flash in the water. By reaction, in which a nervous reflex rather than any skill played its part, he threw the harpoon. The seal, turning gracefully away a couple of meters from Agaguk, was hit.

From far away he heard Iriook call. She was watching her man the whole time since he left. She had seen him observe the floes since the day before, and she could guess that he envied the catches of the men out there.

And now at the very moment when, knowing Agaguk, she was afraid he would finally go out to the floes, he had harpooned a quarry. She yelled, as much because she was happy as because she wanted to encourage the hunter.

He let the cord pay out, let the seal struggle, but the harpoon had lodged firmly and the water was reddening with the animal's blood. The seal did not struggle long; suddenly Agaguk felt the cord go slack. It was all over, he could hoist the beast onto the ice. He tightened his muscles, arched his back, and with one effort hauled the animal out of the water and to his feet.

It was a magnificent grey seal more than four meters long, a rare prize, for this kind of seal mates in autumn only, and all through the arctic summer takes refuge on the rocky coasts, living in solitude. By what chance had what Agaguk least expected come into these waters?

It was not a crested seal, a common animal whose skin is of less value, that has only short tusks and so almost no ivory. The Eskimos who were at work nearby had taken only ordinary seals. Agaguk had seen that well, even though a few moments before he would have been delighted enough with them himself.

While now, rewarded for his patience, he had won this prize! Iriook had a good right to yell. She ran to him, carrying Tayaout in her arms. "Agaguk, you see! You have a wonderful catch!"

The man smiled, looking at the animal stretched on the ice. It was a fine catch indeed, better than he had ever hoped for. In one throw of the harpoon he had killed an animal twice as long as a crested seal. His patience had paid off double!

"I'm satisfied," he said.

Then he shouted hoarsely and grabbed up the extra harpoon. He had noticed another movement in the water, and without stopping to identify his quarry, he threw the harpoon with a loud cry.

Strike!

Then came the battle. This time it was a hard fight, for the harpoon had gone in near the tail, far from the vital organs, and it was only by its loss of blood and Agaguk's stubbornness that the animal finally yielded. The harpoon had to hold firm until the beast was mastered. His heels well set in the ice, every muscle in his body strained, pain in his back and shoulders, Agaguk held on.

Iriook approached eagerly, and tried to help, but he ordered her off furiously, and she backed away. The contest took half an hour to win. Suddenly, when he did not expect it, the cord went slack. For a second, a terrible grief came over him. Had the seal got away?

But instead it had given up, and resigned itself to its fate. It was not yet dead, for he could see its tail move feebly. This time Agaguk called Iriook to come to his rescue and help him pull the mammal out on the ice. Whether it was heavier than the other or whether his strength had been reduced by the first struggle, they both had to strive hard before at last the new prize rested beside the first one. Agaguk's exclamation was not only joyous, it was incredulous. He pointed to this second animal, as big as the first but unlike it.

"I can't understand it," said Agaguk. "I can't understand it. Where did it come from?"

His astonishment was justified. On the ice rested, now almost dead, one of the rarest seals of these regions. It was a bearded seal, whose exceptionally thick leather is greatly sought after by the Eskimos. They make strong thongs from it and the most durable lacings.

"I've never heard of such a take. People say that others at the Top of the World, or on the Great Island, have caught them, but never here!"

"You see," said Iriook, "you see? It was enough to wait."

That day and the next one Agaguk harpooned four more seals of the ordinary crested species. But with his two prize catches, he had accomplished a feat that would be talked about for a long time.

Other Eskimos—though none from Ramook's and Agaguk's village—came to see the catches, and in the evening they held a gay celebration. Agaguk sacrificed the liver of each animal. First they squeezed out the oil to hand it over to Iriook. Then they devoured the raw bleeding organs. Even Tayaout had his mouth full of it, and seeing him again with his face smeared with blood, Agaguk cried, "He's a man! Look at him!"

They all looked at him, seeing him squarely seated between his mother's thighs, solid as any Eskimo of good race.

Someone began to make up a song. It told of Agaguk the great hunter. And it sang also of Tayaout, who would be the greatest hunter of his time, true son of his father.

The song lasted a long time. Agaguk was drunk with the song—it acted on him like the white man's liquor. He laughed ecstatically all at once, then got up suddenly and began to run in circles shouting, as they all had the habit of doing when they were over-excited. *"Insumane ayorlugo,"* he could no longer control himself.

Iriook clapped her hands, and so did the other women. And while Agaguk ran that way, uncontrollably, the other men yelled and stamped their feet. One of them, brandishing a long knife, screamed, "I'm another man, I'm another man."

The celebration lasted all night. In the morning, they were all bedded down with some woman, not necessarily their wives. Except Agaguk, who rested beside Iriook. After she had appeased him, his body was still shaken by long shudders.

They slept a long time, piled up together like wolves. They woke when the sun was high and their behaviour had returned to normal. Each one took back his legitimate wife and went silently toward the ice, to begin the hunt again. There was nothing more to say, for everything had been said or sung the night before. When they talked again of that night, it would be in their own igloos, during interminable evenings, crooning a song monotonous as the wind of the plains, boasting the exploits of the great hunter Agaguk. But now, back they went to the hunt, for the time to complete the provisions of seal meat was getting short.

Agaguk had estimated the load that all this meat, fat and scraped hides would add up to. He would not hunt any more, for he had enough of a burden.

With Iriook he began the job of cutting up the carcasses which the sun would spoil all too soon. It was a bloody, sticky task, an orgy to which they put their energy without disgust. First they scraped off the fat which they divided into lumps to carry more easily. Then they cut the best parts from the brownish flesh to be smoked. There was no question of being able to carry all that meat. There was too much of it. So they took twice as much time as usual to select the best flavoured as well as the most nourishing. Once smoked, they must plan to carry it on their backs.

"We shall have to travel one extra day, maybe two," said Agaguk, surveying the growing heap.

"What does it matter?" said Iriook. "Once started, nothing need drive us."

It was true. They were in mid-season. There would be no change in the weather for days. As for the delays in hunting, did they not carry full compensation for that?

There remained only the skins to dress. In one way they were the most valuable product of the venture. They had to be cleaned. In a caribou skin shaped into a big basin, Agaguk began to evaporate water dipped from the sea. After three days in the sun, there was left only salt, strongly tinctured with iodine, yellow, sown with bits of seaweed. With this rough product, he treated the backs of the skins, rubbing them into leather. Then he rolled them up and made a package of them. The fifth day the work was done. What was left of the seals was heaped up and strewn for the wolves that would probably come, drawn by the smell. Or it might be the ferrets, tougher than the wolves and just as voracious when they set to.

Assorting carefully the loads for each of them, they tied up the packs. Ivory, flat bones and skins already made a respectable weight. They had wanted to judge the size of the loads before smoking the meat.

It would be too much. And Agaguk could not bear to lessen the supplies of food.

"We won't smoke the meat," he said. "We'll dry it. That will save half the weight, maybe more."

He put the sleeping-skins on the ground in the sun, and with Iriook he cut the meat in thin, narrow strips which they spread on them. For another three days they turned and turned again the strips, watching them lest they go bad. At the end of the third day, the meat had diminished by half in weight and volume. It was well dried and still kept its taste. This time they made it into packages which they put beside the other bundles, to judge better. With the sleeping skins, their few utensils, the rifles, the shells for the guns, the knives, the whole made a considerable load, a weight that would slow up their march a good deal. Besides, there was Tayaout.

"I'm strong," said Iriook, "stronger than you think. We'll go slowly, but we'll get there."

They were up at dawn, their strength at its fullest, their muscles tight. Carefully Agaguk heaped the bundles on Iriook's back. She had already placed the child there. Then, when this was done, he took the bundles that were left and built up his own load. Anyone seeing them would have said they were some new kind of monsters, ambulatory masses, beasts of burden solemnly bearing the world on their shoulders. Only Tayaout was happy now, but he did not know the difficulties of this journey his parents were undertaking.

Painfully, with slow, short steps, they commenced the march.

CHAPTER 23/UNU'AK
The Night

Bent over like porters, they advanced very slowly, stopping often to take a breath. There was not a muscle in their bodies that did not cry for mercy. Evan Agaguk, in his youth and masculine strength, was soon exhausted. Then they halted, and without putting down their loads, they stood a few moments unmoving, rooted in the moss, face to the wind, to slow down their panting breath and their heart beats. They sweated, for the sun was hot and they were thirsty. But the water in their leather bottles was getting low.

"We ought to have gone in a straight line," said Iriook after a few stages, "We might have passed by the village."

Agaguk spoke sharply. "No! We won't go to the village."

He said no more, and his savage obstinacy annoyed Iriook. But she said nothing, and they resumed their march.

Agaguk measured off the distances according to his remembrance of the tundra, according to the stars when evening came. They plodded along; slowly, with difficulty, they drew nearer the river and the hut.

Nights they slept the heavy sleep of exhaustion. If any wolves came around, neither one of them knew it. The only protection they had planned for their packs was to hold them in their arms while they slept. If an animal came to attack them, the movement would have been enough to rouse them. They rested so, with Tayaout and the fruit of their expedition between them. There was no other way, no other watch was possible, for their fatigue was too extreme. They could think of only one thing, once the meal of the halt was over—sleep, to replenish their energies so as to take up again in a few hours the road to the hut.

The day before their arrival, at midday, a caribou jumped up not far from them. First there was the sound, the characteristic clacking of the hoofs, like no other animal's, made by the two halves of the divided hoof hitting each other as the beast ran. Agaguk did not notice it right away. He was walking like an automaton without thinking, his nerves deadened. Suddenly he jumped, as the noise broke into his consciousness. Urgency released in him a small reserve of agility. In a flash he raised his rifle. The beast was there, three hundred paces away, a little afraid, motionless, its nostrils turned toward the smell of danger. But Iriook touched Agaguk's arm. Surprised, Agaguk looked at her.

"Don't fire," she said.

"What's the matter?"

"What would you do with it?"

The caribou was heavy, big and fat, a male in magnificent condition, with unbroken antlers, strongly curved forward. The mane under its neck reached almost to its knees.

"What could you do with it?" repeated Iriook.

The respite had been enough; the animal was fleeing, already out of range.

"I would have killed it with one shot," said Agaguk. "You saw him? A fat beast, ripe for the kill." He was angry. "Why did you hinder me?"

"You would have shot? What would you have done with him?"

Agaguk calmed down. What the woman said was right. He could not carry anything more right away. To leave it on the tundra would mean that the wolves would have devoured the carcass before daybreak. He shrugged his shoulders and unloaded his rifle. They went on their way, but the remembrance of the animal haunted Agaguk. Occasionally he sighed. When would he ever see such a caribou again? As if she were answering his innermost thoughts, Iriook murmured, "You'll find his track again. He'll be browsing around here for some time yet. It's a male, and the female must be somewhere near the river. Perhaps there is a fawn—"

Agaguk looked at his wife in surprise. Where had she learned these things? Nevertheless she was talking sense. If the male was here, such a short while after the calving season, the female could not be far away. And in what more likely place than the river?

"Someone from the village will see him before I do. We are not far from it. By the time I go hunting, it will be too late."

"You'll find him again," said Iriook confidently. "I'm certain of it."

Again there was silence, and the heavy hard march. The sun weighed them down like a leaden cloak. The heat flickered on the low horizon, within echoing distance. A wild goose flew low over them, slanting toward the river down below.

"How much longer?" said Iriook. "Do you know?"

They had branched off the trail that morning, completing the half-circle to avoid the village. Now they were traveling directly south-west. Agaguk stopped, examined the marks on the tundra and the sky, sniffed the wind, consulted some mysterious compass within himself and slowly rubbed his hands.

"We'll get there tomorrow."

"Early tomorrow?"

"No."

When they halted that evening Iriook was staggering with fatigue. Her shoulders freed of their burden, she could hardly walk; her legs were shaky, her ears buzzing.

"I'm tired," she said. Only those words, nothing more, but all the weariness in the world in her voice. Gloomy and depressed, Agaguk dropped on the moss.

"Let's eat," he said. "Let's sleep. Let's sleep right away."

They did not eat the dried meat of which they had such ample provisions, but instead they cut off big hunks of seal fat to eat cold, knowing they would get from fat the energy that other foods would not supply.

For Tayaout, the novelty of being carried on his mother's back had fast worn away. The slower march, and especially the encumbrance of the packs, the greater warmth of the sun made him cross. Often during these last days he cried without knowing why, perhaps because he was tired of being held prisoner. But that evening, after his nursing, he sank into a deep sleep.

That last night the wolves came back. They were less timid, hungrier. First came the old leader of the pack, who was soon rejoined by a female, and then other males, younger ones. In a few minutes the pack surrounded the little camp where Agaguk, Iriook and Tayaout were sleeping.

The silent assemblage approached on velvet paws, with nostrils wide. There was meat in the bundles, fat, all kinds of new and succulent food. The old male came near enough to touch one of the bundles with his muzzle. The other wolves stayed at a distance, watching to see how he made out. He breathed in the odour, drew on all his courage. He tried a timid nibble, to feel out the solidity of one package.

Agaguk in his sleep felt the movement, clasped the bundle more tightly in his arms and made a little sound. The wolf stood still. He stayed motionless a long time, watching the man. Then he tried again, with a hesitant movement, but a little harder bite. This time he stirred the bundle and Agaguk leaped to his feet. Snatching the bundle from the wolf's jaws, he yelled like a devil, running toward the pack. Confounded, the beasts broke up and fled.

Iriook, awakened with a start, frightened to death, screamed and hugged the weeping Tayaout. In an instant all was over; the wolves were dashing over the tundra.

"I'm going to stay awake," Agaguk said. "Go back to sleep, I'll watch."

He remained seated, one arm around his pack, the rifle in the other hand.

"If they come back, I'll kill one or two."

But when Iriook's light snore showed that she was asleep again, sleep overcame him too. He resisted as long as he could, but there came a moment when, without realizing it, he too sank into a heavy slumber. The wolves did not come back.

CHAPTER 24/TIRIGANIAK
The Fox

They reached the hut toward night the next day. Hardly two hours of daylight remained. They had seen the hut from a long way off. Like a point on the horizon at first, their dwelling seemed to grow, to become greater as they came toward it. When they finally got there, they did not utter a word, not even a sigh. Slowly, gravely, they put down their packs, freed themselves from the weight. Then in common agreement, without consulting each other, they walked to the river. There, stripping, both adults and child, they plunged into the warm swift water.

They stayed there a long time, enjoying the coolness, restoring to their muscles their lost elasticity, cleaning the pores of their skin from all the salt and sweat. The sun was fast disappearing below the horizon when they came back to the hut, lighter on their feet, already almost recovered from the journey.

"I'm hungry," said Agaguk.

"I'll light the stove. I'll boil some seal meat in the water." Agaguk nodded.

"It will take longer," Iriook said, "but it will be better."

The man was dreaming of a fresh-killed animal, a rabbit or even a caribou, with its flesh still warm, full of blood, into which he might bite, tearing off pieces to chew on for long moments, relishing the taste. But he would have to get up, to wander through the tundra looking for a track, listening for some yelp, smelling the wind. He did not feel strong enough. "Do as you like," he said to Iriook.

He stretched out on his back, hands under his neck, eyes shut. He was fast asleep when Iriook announced that the meal was ready. He ate greedily, without stopping, emptying the pot, and because he was still hungry he devoured some strips

99

of seal meat, then bit with his fine teeth into a lump of fat he pulled out of one of the bundles. Restored, muscles relaxed by the bath in the river, he did not even stand up, but lay on his side, rolled over to the heap of moss and stretched out on it. In a few seconds, he had gone back to sleep.

Iriook put out the fire, brought the bundles into the hut, let down the skins that they had rolled up to the top and fastened them to the poles. She tied down firmly the panel that served as a door, and then she too lay down. She was tranquil; no beast could get in.

In the morning, when she looked more carefully at the skin of the bearded seal, and realized how valuable it was, she thought of all she could make of it and smiled pleasantly at Agaguk.

"Every year," she said, "We'll go seal hunting."

"It's a long way back," said Agaguk, "and the loads are heavy."

She spread the skin, raised it so he could see it well, put it over her knees and caressed it a long time. "To bring back a skin like that," she said, "just one, the trip is worth the trouble. We'll go every year, if you like."

Agaguk was cleaning his gun. "You going to look for the caribou?" she asked.

"No."

"Why?"

"There are wolves around. The caribou is dead."

"How do you know?"

"I know, that's all."

She did not insist. Agaguk knew what he had to do. By the time winter came he would have killed the necessary quantity of caribou, she was sure. And had they not, to make up a good part of their provisions, all this seal meat and the fat, the burden they had carried for so many days until now?

They heard a short sharp bark out on the tundra. Agaguk leaped out of the hut, yelling "*Tiriganiak!*" In fact, a red fox was running in circles on the tundra. He seemed crazy.

Agaguk stayed near the hut, looking curiously at the beast. Iriook, holding Tayaout close, had come to join him. Suddenly Agaguk burst out laughing.

"You wanted proof of the caribou's death," he said.

"The fox?"

"Yes, look at him."

The fox was still running, and stopped only to roll on the moss. He barked and whined.

"He's mad," exclaimed Iriook.

Agaguk calmly put his rifle to his shoulder, aimed and fired. The beast bounded high and fell back dead.

"What was the matter with him?" asked Iriook.

Agaguk beckoned her to come near. When they came up to the fallen animal, Agaguk bent down, turned its head and showed with his finger the green froth hanging from the half open mouth.

"See that? It's the caribou's gall. Only the fox is stupid enough to break open the gall bladder. Still, he's a smart animal. But he's the only one that does that."

"The gall poisons him?"

"No. But the taste is bitter, and the fox goes crazy. You saw him run?"

"So the caribou is dead?"

"I have the proof of it now."

The sky was radiantly clear, the wind gentle, caressing like the hand of a good spirit.

"You are truly a great hunter," said Iriook. "In all the tribes there is none greater."

It was the finest compliment she could pay, the most sincere avowal of her love. So she gave herself entirely, in those few words which meant something quite different from what they said, but which nevertheless meant the love of a woman, and her pride at being at the side of a man so brave and capable.

"Greater than you, there is none," she repeated softly.

They returned to the hut in silence and there Iriook needed no signal to fall upon the couch. Agaguk, his eyes shining, followed her.

CHAPTER 25/KAPJIK
The Wolverine

The chief's igloo was at the centre of the village. When all the members of the tribe were rebuilding for the summer, Henderson saw that by mutual agreement they had not moved the centre of the agglomeration, had not carried it a hundred feet or so farther on, as was the usual practice. Ordinarily they were concerned with the sewage ditches. The perpetual frozen ground, the permafrost, which is some three meters below the summer moss, and not that deep in those spring days, prevents their digging very deeply. The sewer ditch is a nasty thing. They could not dig? What did that mean? It was foolish to believe that they would imagine digging a wider network of ditches to avoid a shallow ditch. They knew one technique, and they could not conceive of any other. The simplest way was to move the village a little every year. And on this immense tundra, limitless, without zones or markings, perhaps this was really the most intelligent solution.

Henderson had examined the moss. It seemed bizarre to him that the tribe should choose to erect its huts at the same place as the preceding year. The little hillocks, the slumps opposite the cesspools, the waste matter, made it quite clear that they were building at the same site.

"Why?" he asked Ramook.

There had been some councils held, the usual palavers. Henderson had been excluded from them. The two or three times that he had approached them and tried to take part in the discussion, he had succeeded only in breaking up the meeting. He would have given much to hear what was going on, but since the talks were held outdoors and in low voices, he could not take them unaware or spy on them from any hiding place. He spoke to Ramook about the matter.

"You forget who I am," he said. "It's my duty to hear all that you say."

"That's what you think?" jeered Ramook. "Then go sleep in all the huts, go eat in all the huts, go spy in all the huts. We discuss the affairs of the village. It's our right to."

"And if I want to hear what you say?"

"Why?"

"I tell you it's my duty."

"We discuss what concerns ourselves."

Henderson was alone in the village; alone, pitted against the clever and quiet astuteness of a hundred Eskimos. Prudence counselled him not to insist. But suddenly the palavers had their explanation. The reconstruction of the village of huts, after the demolition of the igloos, follows an unchanging ritual in every arctic village. Each of the men instals his hut in the same position relative to the chief's hut which the preceding igloo occupied with regard to the chief's dwelling, even though the village has been moved. In this way the tribal hierarchy is established.

But Henderson noticed that Ghorok, who had appeared to be showing a good deal of indignation during the palavers, did not reconstruct his hut beside Ramooks, but farther away, almost on the outskirts of the village. The fact would have passed unnoticed by a man who was not experienced in Eskimo traditions, but for Henderson, it was very odd. He knew his world too well not to take account of the anomaly. He chose to speak of it to Ramook.

"Ghorok prefers the outskirts," Ramook said without losing his calm demeanour.

"He didn't move of his own free will," declared the constable placidly.

"Who said so?"

"I'm not blind. I saw him making a fuss."

Ramook grimaced. "You think you know more about it than we do?"

"Ghorok didn't like having to move."

"The will of all, that is Ghorok's will. He was not displeased. He obeyed."

"You sent him to live over there?"

"Perhaps."

"Why? Is he in disgrace?"

Ramook hesitated for a breath. "Yes," he said at last.

If he had answered anything else, Henderson might not have classified his words as the first element of proof. But when he saw the tribe meet in council the next evening, to assign the hunting territories, and saw that Ghorok took his place on Ramook's right, Henderson understood that Ramook had lied to him.

Ghorok was then occupying his new location for very different reasons. The constable let several weeks go by, part of June, all of July. He was in no hurry. One evening, after dark, he pretended to go to relieve himself behind the huts and went to find Ayallik. He had decided to sacrifice his nickel-plated pocket flashlight to help the Eskimo find his tongue.

Ayallik, alone in his hut, listened while Henderson spoke to him in a low voice. The man forgot suddenly that he was a member of the tribe. There was the lamp!

There was also the possibility of future gifts. Who could say how far the constable's generosity might go, if the information he gave turned out to be correct?

That was one thing—but there was something more. Over there, there were Agaguk and the girl, the girl that he had taken with him and whom he, Ayallik, had wanted to take into his hut. The pretty girl with the big thighs, the thick body, the smooth skin. Once Ayallik had caught her naked in her igloo. He had held out his hands and touched the hard breasts with the nipples as long as a finger joint. He had to leave, because Iriook had kicked him, but he had never forgotten.

Agaguk, the traitor who had forsaken the village! One of their best hunters, on whom the village depended for its winter's meat, he had abandoned his own people and fled with the girl Ayallik coveted. It would be sweet to know he was taken in the net of the law, carried off, probably hanged, since the white men now hanged Eskimos guilty of murder.

"You got a shovel to dig with?" said Ayallik simply.

"Yes, of course."

"You'll have to use it."

The indirect talk, saying things without saying them, was in true Eskimo fashion. Ayallik spat on the ground. "Give me the flashlight," he said. "If you have more than that to give me, I'll tell you more."

But when Henderson took a four-blade jack-knife out of his pocket, Ayallik shook his head. "No."

"You just told me you'd talk!"

"No."

Henderson showed the knife. It was a first instalment. The light would come later, if the revelations were worth while.

"Take it. You promised me."

"Not today."

"Why?"

"Tomorrow. Come back tomorrow."

"But why tomorrow?"

Ayallik could not have said why. He had a confused feeling that his denunciation ought not to be made all at once, that it was better to dole out his revelations, little by little, as if on tiptoe.

More than anything else, he was afraid of one thing—would not he himself be suspect, for having known about the matter for so long? Suppose the constable took it into his head to arrest him rather than Agaguk? Since the constable's visit, Ayallik had time to weigh the pros and cons of giving information. Although he was still undecided, he rejected the offer.

"Come tomorrow," he said, his eyes veiled. "If I hear anything more, I will tell you."

"But for now, what do you know?"

"You've got a shovel. Then go dig. Go search!"

There was a hidden meaning there which the policeman grasped very well. Silently he left Ayallik to go back to Ramook's hut. The chief seemed to be asleep, and his Indian woman too. Henderson lay down on the dried moss bed that belonged to him and slept also, a deep, satisfied sleep, such as he had not known since his arrival in the village. If he had known that Ramook, distrustful and cunning, had spied on him, followed him to the hut where he had questioned Ayallik, overhearing their conversation, would he have slept so peacefully?

CHAPTER 26/INU'OYOK
He Is a Man

More quickly than the petted white child, the child of the cities who is deprived of the least animal initiative, Tayaout grew. He crept easily. His hands were agile and could seize things, his face was lively, his eyes shone. The sounds he made, the gurgles and grunts, he sometimes added almost articulate exclamations. He would talk early, but it was not in this that he differed from the other little Eskimos. Left to himself, accustomed from his first babyhood to provide for his wants and needs, he had soon learned to roll over, to help himself with his legs to creep here and there. There was a new world on the moss, a country that belonged to him and with which he was in intimate communication. The insects, the rare plants breaking through the fresh carpet of the tundra, the rushing sound of the brook, its shining reflections, all this was on his level. Already he knew how to dodge a blow, to scrabble on all fours while yelling with fright when a mink leaped out of the bushes. A white child would have taken many months to reach this stage of ability. Twice as much time as Tayaout, who, at six months, when the summer sun was warm and the mild wind drove the permafrost deeper under the moss, when the plants rose high and the flowers brightened the tundra, stood alone for the first time.

Agaguk had been transported with veneration before the new-born infant, an almost shapeless lump, without any clear voice or any smile, at the mercy of everything and everybody. He had followed its evolution, he had been carried away with joy when the baby had learned to creep, to run on all fours like a fox cub. But when Tayaout stood up, when Agaguk saw him do so, holding onto one of the poles of the hut and laughing with delight, he became like a madman.

He bounded toward the child, grabbed hold of him, raised

him to his breast and began to run, screaming loudly, in this Eskimo way of expressing outwardly the feelings that are bursting from his throat. He ran about in sheer animal happiness, he cried out without words, like a joyous and grateful animal. He was like a dog whom his master's caress drives wild.

Iriook, standing by the hut, yelled too with the same instinctive impulse. She cried out to see Agaguk's joy, she cried out because she knew the child would soon be walking, because she was alive, because the sun was warm, because her man was crying out. Agaguk took some time to calm down. When he finally came to throw himself down on the moss in front of the hut, he was panting like a tired dog.

"He's a man," he groaned. "Look, Iriook, he's a man."

He set the baby on his feet and held his hands. Tayaout standing, laughed at his new process. Agaguk pulled him forward, one step, two steps. The baby stumbled, caught himself, with a great effort held himself erect.

"He can walk," exclaimed Agaguk. "He can walk!"

Iriook came to squat beside the baby. She gurgled some fond words in her throat. She touched his bare shoulder with her fingers.

The child, in ecstasy, drank in the sunshine laughing aloud, his head thrown back, his throat throbbing. His firm, square body swelled in the effort. His legs, bowed but hard and round, were tense, the muscles showing under the skin. He made some awkward steps, not knowing how to put his feet on the ground, but he stepped forward, his fingers tight around Agaguk.

A bird plunged from the sky, grazed the hut, swerved toward the child and brushed him with its wing. Tayaout made a sound, his hand reaching out for it. His other hand let go Agaguk's and he suddenly found himself without support, tottering in an unstable balance, his face turned toward the bird in flight that he had tried to grasp. For what seemed like a lifetime, the baby stayed thus, proud little man on the endless tundra.

Agaguk and Iriook had been taken by surprise, and now they did not breathe. They seemed to have ceased to live themselves, concentrating all of their own spirit in the body of the child. They became his will, his balance, the duration and the delight of his success.

Then the baby fell. He sat down hard, a dull thump on the ground, but he was still happy, and Agaguk saw two tears roll down Iriook's cheeks.

"He stood up," she said. "All alone. He was standing—he could have walked. Nobody helped him!"

Agaguk found only one word, the only one. "*Inuk!*" Indeed, he was a man.

PART TWO

CHAPTER 1/NIGAK
The Net

Henderson did not go at once to dig on the spot to which his suspicions were leading him. Ayallik's information was clear enough, but the constable did not like the idea of running here and there to verify the insinuation. It was more urgent to lull the suspicions of the men in the village. He wanted more than anything to have Ramook feel secure. To pursue his inquiry he wanted the old man to have complete confidence in his own astuteness. That way he would be most likely to make a false step. Henderson was sure that sooner or later Ramook would do just that.

He waited a week, and since nothing happened, he decided to wait a while longer. All this time, the people felt less distrust. The defences were falling, little by little. Ghorok could smoke his pipe in peace, sitting at the door of his hut. Ramook could walk about, humming some strange tune between his teeth.

It was a vegetative life, a deeply rooted life, a life without motion. Henderson had learned the secret of never resisting any instinct toward laziness, but of yielding to it instead, of emptying his mind of thought, of not trying to reason. The immobility so acquired was worth any cure to him. The vegetable life slowed the racing of his blood, rested his faculties, even though his subconscious did not sleep.

And in truth the subconscious was wide awake in Henderson. Seated, his eyes fixed on nothing much, warming himself in the summer sun on the tundra, he counted no less on that sixth sense which would wake him instantly, with every faculty at its most sensitive, the moment the revealing event occurred.

Then came the alert.

He had stoically avoided Ayallik, who for his part observed the policeman with a wary and sometimes troubled eye. What the man had to offer interested Henderson's policeman's heart. But it seemed to him that he would prefer to discover the secret of Brown's death for himself. He was afraid Ayallik's denunciation might be the result of some stratagem concocted by this ambitious man, and that the proof might be so formal that he would drag back to the post a man who might really be innocent. Henderson did not believe he ought to run such a risk.

He could establish proof, but it would not be possible, since he was a foreigner and held in suspicion by the Eskimos who rebel against the white man's law, to establish any counter-proof, that proof of the proof which avoids condemning an innocent man. He was certain now that Ghorok and Ramook were conniving, certain also that even if Ramook was not Brown's murderer, he knew enough about the affair so that it would be worth while to keep an eye on him. Besides, for several days there had been a lot going on around Ramook's hut.

Kanguak had made the journey to the post, to trade his skins. He had brought back two rifles, one for his own use and the other for trading. He wanted very much two white bearskins which Kolrona, one of the old men of the tribe, had taken the year before. Kolrona had made the journey to the sea that was then caught in the ice. He had crossed the frozen water and gone even to Frobisher Bay, far to the north. It was a two-month trip, and he had made it alone with his dogs. Up there he had killed four polar bears, skinned them and brought back the skins. He had traded two with Brown for liquor, salt and sugar, that new luxury for primitive people, and some bullets for his gun. The two remaining skins were what Kanguak coveted.

"This automatic rifle against your two bearskins?"

Kolrona refused to bargain.

From then on, the discussion widened and grew bitter. Soon a dozen of the men in the village were taking part. They palavered all day, to sleep at last and begin again the next morning. Henderson listened rather absent-mindedly. The worst insults were tossed back and forth between Kolrona and Kanguak, for one was just as stubborn as the other.

In fact Henderson was amused, for from these insults they

passed to the most abject flattery, from the dirtiest slander to the highest praises ever sung. Kanguak wanted the skins. Kolrona wanted the gun, but he wanted to give only one bearskin in exchange. The problem ought to have been simple, for one bearskin was worth at least three guns. But neither Kanguak nor Kolrona would give in.

Henderson understood perfectly well the Eskimo avarice that impelled Kanguak to hold out so long. Polar bearskins are rare merchandise. There are always people at the trading post who offer to bargain outside the law. They will give two jugs full of liquor, even three, for furs of this kind. That was what Kanguak was after, and that was why he was so desperate to have both skins.

As for Kolrona, following rough Eskimo logic, he was simply holding out for a high price, reckoning that his desire for a rifle was foolish and irrational if he had to give up this treasure, these two white bearskins in order to get it. One knew as well as the other the bargaining they had to go through in order to settle things. Hence the palaver!

Many times they came close to blows. Nothing else was to be heard in the whole village except this discussion, going from the central open space back and forth to the huts. Kanguak was not giving in by as much as an inch. Ramook had endured this commotion silently. The first two days he contented himself with smoking his pipe, sitting in front of his hut. He watched the dispute, listening quietly as the antagonists went over the merits of their arguments. Sometimes he nodded, apparently approving what was said. But that was always when Kolrona was talking. Finally he got tired of the whole thing and summoned Kanguak to his hut. Henderson made up his mind not to miss anything that might be said.

"All these discussions bore me," said Ramook. "You'll never win."

"I shall win. Kolrona is an old fool."

"You won't win."

"Why?"

"He's not such a fool as you think. The white man gave three jugs for one bearskin. Why should Kolrona give you two skins for a rifle that is worth one jug at the most?"

"I know, but I shall win all the same."

"You won't."

When Kanguak had left, Henderson approached Ramook. He was no longer sleepy, no longer vegetating; he was completely alert. He had made his first move.

"This white man who gave three jugs for one white bear skin," said the policeman, "was he named Brown?"

Ramook became again impassive. Nothing, no feeling, no emotion, appeared on his puffy face with the veiled eyes. His look was stupid, his lacquered eyes became emptied of any embarrassment.

"I don't know what you mean," he muttered.

Henderson tried every scheme he could think of, and he knew many, to get something out of the man, but all in vain. Ramook realized his mistake and took refuge in silence. Henderson had his labour for his pains. But now he was sure he had not been mistaken. The white man had been there. That was the first fact to establish. Brown had operated in this village. So the Montagnais had not been lying. Someone here had set fire to the firewater peddler.

"You know what I'm going to do tomorrow?" said Henderson.

Ramook looked blankly at him.

"Tomorrow I'm going to dig under Ghorok's new hut, and we shall see what I shall find there."

CHAPTER 2/AGIORTOK
The Bad Spirit

Agaguk picked up the wolf's track early one morning that summer. He had gone out at daybreak because he wanted to catch some fish in the brook. Tayaout was still sleeping beside his mother. Nothing was moving on the tundra. Everywhere there was silence and peace.

In front of the hut entrance, he saw two sharp prints, those of a wolf's forefeet, on the dry moss. Evidently the beast had been down at the brook, where the moss was wet. The prints were dark, still damp. Agaguk squatted down to study them carefully. The wolf must have been remarkably big and long-bodied. The mark was large and the foot healthy, each toe well-defined. The skin of the pads was shown precisely in the fine moss. It was smooth, which indicated that the animal was young. But it appeared to be fat, and how long its steps were!

Nevertheless it was not running at the moment it made these tracks. It seemed rather to be walking slowly, with precaution. The sharpness of the print in the rear and the shallowness opposite the big toe were sure proof.

What had made him come so near the hut? For an old wolf, a solitary, that would be understandable. But this young animal? A young wolf would be hunting with the pack, even here on the tundra. And if Agaguk was not mistaken, if this wolf was as big as he appeared to be by this track, he ought normally to be the leader of a band, acknowledged king of the pack.

Then what was he doing alone, and so near a hut? Wolves do not usually come so near to a permanent dwelling. A bear will come around to smell within two paces of sleeping men. A fox will take such chances if he has some quarry to surprise. But a wolf, never! He will attack a tent, a night's shelter, but he will keep his distance prudently from a settler's hut, all of whose surroundings are soaked in man's odour. And furthermore, he will never come in the summertime, when game is plentiful and he is not hungry.

Agaguk was telling himself these things while he examined the tracks. Then, on all fours like an animal himself, he began to follow the trail. Farther on where the moss was wetter he had hard work not to lose it. But he had a trained eye, and his fingers felt the ground, feeling for the depression caused by the animal's weight. A little farther, and the beast had been running. The tracks were far apart.

The wolf had come in front of the hut, then had described a long circle to return to the brook. He had drunk there, and started off again toward the north. His was the only track.

He was alone. Agaguk would have sworn to it. Alone, young, within reach of sleeping human beings!

The Eskimo was greatly disquieted, for in the bushes near the river, where the wolf had brushed them aside to go down to drink, Agaguk found some white hair caught on the thorns, hair of a pure white, with no touch of grey. It could belong only to that animal, for a wolf will make his own way and will not use the paths made by other animals. A great white wolf!

Agaguk was now sure of his size. Too many tracks showed it clearly for there to be any chance that he might be mistaken. A great white wolf, young and daring enough to come and smell around an inhabited hut! What did this mystery signify?

Agaguk went in to wake Iriook and tell her what he had discovered. She agreed that the event was, if not mysterious, at least uncommon.

"What will you do?" she asked.

"I'll set traps."

Iriook protested. "The wolf is young. He is daring. By the way he acts, by the care he takes to make wide circles before going to drink, he is smart."

Agaguk shook his head, saying again, "I'll set traps. That'll probably do no good at all."

Tayaout was coming out of the hut on all fours. Frowning, Agaguk watched him. He had heard some old songs, the old men of the tribe used to tell some adventures of the ancient times. . . .

"The baby!" said Iriook.

"What about the baby?"

He pretended not to understand. But he did understand, and he looked away. Far away, very far away on the tundra, a caribou was running. Suddenly Agaguk saw it fall. And there, where it had fallen, something white, a nothingness, a glimpse, in the wink of an eye, seemed to move.

Agaguk cried, "Over there, the white wolf! He just killed a caribou!"

It was on the horizon, a long way off. But on the uniform tundra, with no height of land or very slight ones, any movement can be seen. With a trained eye like Agaguk's, one could tell the difference between a motionless low cloud and a man walking, the course of a caribou—and this white point.

"The wolf," muttered Agaguk. "He's staying close-by."

"It's the baby he's after. He wants him. I feel it," said Iriook, touching her breast. "I feel it here. Remember the stories, Agaguk."

The legends said that such solitary wolves spied on children, that they would carry them off.

"No, Iriook, it isn't possible. He hasn't seen him, he doesn't know he's here."

"How can you say that? He could have been watching from far off. Did you watch the tundra yesterday, and the day before?"

"No."

"He smelled him. He came here by chance."

"By chance, so near the hut?"

"You see? That shows it was true, what I said. He smelled him. Far away, but even so, he smelled him."

"No."

"He saw him. He bided his time. He's still biding his time."

The white men say that the rancid odour of the Eskimos keeps the wolves away. But a baby, a baby Eskimo, has no other odour than that of tender flesh. Agaguk was no more reassured than his wife, and if he denied his anxiety so firmly it was only that he wanted to soothe her. He went back into the hut and picked up his rifle. He verified the load of six bullets, then the sight which he set on a branch near the brook. He fired and the branch flew up, cut in two by the bullet. He fooled with the gun, cocking it several times, then, satisfied, leaned it against the hut.

"I'm waiting for that wolf," he said.

"Then you aren't going to set the traps?"

"I've thought better of it. I'd be wasting my time."

All day they took turns. At first it was Iriook who watched the child playing on the moss; when she had something to do inside the hut, Agaguk took over. In his free time, he looked at his mink traps along the brook, within hailing distance of the hut. But he kept an eye on the tundra.

What was this beast? Always the same question, where was the pack? Why the solitude? The leader, wandering alone? He was not wounded, his tracks proved that. The man had as many questions as answers, and the day went by without the wolf's returning.

When night came, Agaguk mounted guard, in a patient, tense, wakeful vigil. He stayed in the hut, but he raised high the skin that ordinarily closed the entrance, to surprise the wolf in time, if he should appear. The night was starry, and the moon described an arc low on the horizon. No wolf howled on the tundra, and that in itself was strange, for the moon usually excites them. Was it the presence of this white wolf that intimidated the packs?

Agaguk watched uneasily. Then the moon set. It was midnight. Now there remained only the faint light of the stars. Slowly the hours went by.

When daylight came Agaguk had not faltered an instant. The dull light turned pink and yellow, and the sun rose in a single leap over the horizon.

The day had come. Agaguk's vigil had been in vain. At least so he thought, going out to stretch his legs in the clear morning. But when Iriook came to join him, he made a tour of the hut with her, and there behind it they saw tracks still fresh. The wolf had even pushed his muzzle a little way under the skins stretched over the poles, right where Tayaout was sleeping.

CHAPTER 3/ANGATK'O
The Witch-doctor

On the tundra, the village huts are queer-looking cones, like ant-hills arranged in a circle. Behind each one is the sewage ditch, a hole where a man goes to relieve himself, balanced in a difficult equilibrium while the dogs, never tied, run between his legs. In the circle within the cluster of huts, the children play at seal-hunting, at throwing down a wounded wolf, at skinning a caribou. Their games parallel their future lives, anticipate their maturity, train them for the life of misery that awaits them. They yell, they quarrel, they chase each other.

The women sit at their doors, chewing leather, sewing parkas with a big ivory needle, breaking up the dried fish, smoking or drying meat to make pemmican. Here and there a pot sits on the fire to try out fat. It will be the winter fuel to burn in the stone lamp, an absolute necessity in the igloo, the frail and essential bridge between life and death. Lighting, cooking, everything depends on this lamp, this fire of clarified fat, reduced to oil which will solidify only when winter comes, and which will be kept stored up high in solid lumps, well protected from marauders. With the pemmican and the caribou skins made into parkas, the three needs are provided for: food, warmth and light.

Kanguak seemed to be resigned, and Kolrona still kept his polar bearskins. Apparently calm was restored in the village. But since Ramook had spread the rumour that the policeman suspected something, that he even possessed a certain clue, everyone held his peace and waited.

Ghorok had been warned. At first he refused to let Henderson in. He stood there, like a rock, an unassailable obstacle like a fortress. He barred the entrance to the hut, his new one, located far from the others, contrary to all tradition. Henderson insisted. Indeed he gave orders.

"Let me in."

Ghorok did not budge. His face was expressionless except for a twitching at the corner of his mouth, so slight that the white man could not be offended. The Eskimo was looking at the men assembled. Coming from the huts, they advanced, making a silent half-circle behind Henderson, cutting him off. Igutak, Siksik, the old Nadloariuk, Hala, Tugugak, Kanguak, Ayallik, Huilak and Hayaluk, almost the whole tribe, the able-bodied men.

Henderson felt what was happening. They had approached soundlessly, but something, perhaps the rancid smell, warned him of the presence of the men behind him. He turned around. The half-circle closed in a little tighter. Over them was the weight of the sun, with no wind, no let-up, and with this was the tundra steaming in a noxious mist. The horizon was vague, shimmering, wavering, the plain was lost in the veil of distant fog, shutting in the circle of the world as the circle of men closed in.

Henderson reckoned the odds. He was alone here, very far from his post. Although he was loaded with authority, he was at their mercy.

"What do you want?"

He puffed out his chest under his tight blue uniform. The Eskimos stood still, but they did not budge from their places.

"It's with Ghorok I'm talking."

"And with us," said Hala.

He alone smiled, but evilly, with a wicked grimace.

He spat on the moss. He held a white man's knife in his hand, a long blade of good blue steel, sharp as a razor. The policeman hesitated. He could probably hold out against them, but would his purpose have been carried out? Finding the bones under Ghorok's hut—supposing he did—would not prove much. Brown's death? Without having the proof, he was certain of it. But the fact of finding Brown's blackened remains under Ghorok's hut did not incriminate the Eskimo. Henderson knew that this hut had been constructed after the crime, and that Ghorok lived there only because Ramook ordered him to.

Nor could he throw the responsibility on Ramook. The

Eskimo had only used his prerogative as chief, and could always plead ignorance.

But Henderson knew perfectly well that the mere discovery of a formal proof of Brown's death did not furnish him with an assassin. The end of the road he must travel, the final stage—to find the guilty man. If he fought with the Eskimos assembled before him, he would anger them. He might also anger Ayallik by doing the same thing. Since it was impossible to play the part of the strongest, he would have to be the most clever.

And then he had to consider if he would win if he fought these men. More than one heap of bones on the tundra and the snow plains of the Arctic are the only remains of imprudent mounties. In some cases the wisest measure for the brave man to adopt is flight. So he relaxed, leaned his shovel against the hut and stuck his thumbs in his belt.

"I shall stay," he said, "a year in your village if I have to. What I want to know, I shall learn."

The tension lowered in the gathering circle. Slowly they smiled a little. The white man's attitude pleased them. So he wanted to see who could outsmart the other. That was a game they knew well. They opened ranks a little. Hala put his knife back in the sheath-cut in his pant-leg. Henderson smiled.

"You thought of killing me?"

"Yes," answered Hala calmly, "I was thinking of it."

"But if you had," explained the policeman, "*tignierpak*, the Big Bird would have come. Men carrying guns would have got out of it. They would have entered your huts. They would have taken the pemmican, the oil, the fat, the fish, and they would have loaded it all in the Big Bird. Then they would have waited for you to speak. If at the end of three days none of you had confessed to the crime, then they would have left, taking with them all your provisions."

"And if we had spoken?" said Hala in a rather worried tone.

"They would have given you back your provisions but they would have taken away the guilty man."

"Where to?"

"To the white man's town. They would have judged him, then they would have put a rope around his neck and hanged him."

Hala giggled.

"I'd have jumped out of the Big Bird."

"It flies too high. You would be killed."

"But they would have sung about me in all the tribes, even those on the other side of the world."

Henderson did not know how to counter this kind of reasoning. He went back to Ramook's hut. The chief had watched the scene from afar. When Henderson came up to him, the Eskimo looked at him mockingly.

"You saw what they did?" said Henderson.

Ramook shook his head. "I am no longer young. I used to see very far, but now it is no more like that."

He stretched out his hand and held it in front of his eyes. "I can hardly see my own hand. I'm an old man."

Henderson had some trouble in keeping back his anger. "You're no older than I am. And if I had your eyesight, I'd be very happy. You're a fox."

Ramook assented with a nod, not without pride. "That's right."

"The people of the tribe are very rash. They threaten a policeman. I shall not forget it. Take care lest the Great White Chief send a troop here to punish you all. I warn you that my patience is nearing an end."

Ramok shrugged his shoulders. "Nobody keeps you from leaving. You're the one who wants to stay."

"Yes," said Henderson in exasperation, "and if I have to stay a year I'll stay."

In a soft voice Ramook murmured, "When the winter comes, we'll build you an igloo, and Hala will let you have his daughter. She says she likes to sleep with white men. She has done it several times at the trading post. She'll like you, and you'll have a fine winter."

In a rage which he could unhappily not fully express, Henderson flushed red and exploded. "I'll get you, Ramook," he said, losing all control. "I'll get you. I don't know yet who killed Brown, but I know it was someone here. And I'll find him, whoever he is. The whole tribe shall pay for the crime."

Ramook remained unmoved. "I don't know the white man's law very well," he said. "That little that I do know is not the way you say it is. If there is a guilty man, he alone will be punished. You can't accuse my tribe of anything."

"I can accuse it of hiding a criminal!"

Ramook had not thought of this alternative. He stammered, "Are you going to punish the mother who wants to protect her child? The father who defends his son?" Then, pulling himself together quickly, "The chief who defends his tribe?"

This tone which Ramook had taken was new. Henderson believed he could distinguish in it a sort of passion, mingled with grief. Inside the hut the Montagnais woman made a muffled exclamation. But the word was said, and Henderson had heard it very well.

He made up his mind to keep working on Ayallik, to drive him to betray his fellow tribesman, to profit from the man's venality. The waiting was exasperating, the tranquil deceitfulness of the Eskimos too efficacious. To get speedy results he might as well count on Ayallik. Who could tell, maybe the man would give away the guilty one?

CHAPTER 4/AMARSIOKGOK
The Wolf Hunt

For Agaguk and Iriook, the peace on the banks of the river had given way to overwhelming anguish, to sick fear, to inner torture. The White Wolf! When Agaguk thought that during that night—when he believed he was doing his whole duty, keeping watch vigilantly—the animal had come close to seizing Tayaout! But why Tayaout? Why the child?

Iriook passed the day with her rifle at hand or slung on her hips while she worked. She did not let the baby play where she could not keep an eye on him and watch the tundra at the same time. The wolf might leap from any quarter. Agaguk, for his part, busied himself with fishing in the brook or tending his traps. He worked furiously. He climbed the river bank, took one beast from a trap, then hurried back to his fish lines and pulled out a fish. His movements were always abrupt and brutal. He was feeling a great rage, the rage that possessed him whenever he came up against an invincible power.

That wolf, an invincible power? One single wolf? Why, one bullet could bring the beast down.

For the first time in his life as a hunter, Agaguk felt himself defeated. Something mysterious was happening on the tundra and the laws of nature were being transgressed. A young wolf is never solitary. The white wolf was. A wolf does not come to smell around settled habitations. This white wolf did.

And besides, Agaguk had used all his senses, his extraordinary hearing, his eyesight like a cat's, his sense of smell which could tell the difference between wolf and fox, mink and muskrat three hundred feet away. Yet in full wakefulness he had mounted guard that night and the wolf had come within an arm's length, and had almost succeeded in carrying off the child. Irretrievably! For against a wolf's flight, what could

Agaguk's human speed accomplish, a biped too slow for the swift animal?

To what bloody fate would the white wolf have taken Tayaout? Tayaout, joy and riches, his only joy, his greatest riches. Tayaout, for whom Agaguk would give the skin off his body, the blood in his veins, his strength and his life. The white wolf was not an animal of the tundra. It was not a beast of nature. It was some evil spirit, an *agiortok*, come to harass Agaguk. For some wrong the Eskimo might have done? But what wrong?

He had committed only one doubtful act, and he still did not really consider it wrong. Brown's death? But the man had tried to rob Agaguk. That was only normal vengeance, a revenge which the Eskimo's conscience fully approved. Why should the evil spirits be so cruel to him for having after all merely rid the world of a dishonest trader? Nobody had come to reproach him for the deed. Then—and how many times would he ask himself the question—why the presence of this evil spirit on the plain?

And why, above all and before all, did he seem to want to attack the child? There was no longer any doubt in Agaguk's mind, the white wolf was skulking around Tayaout. It was the child he meant to harm. And a strange foresight in the Eskimo's heart never stopped predicting that some day the wolf would succeed and Tayaout would die. There it was, the power against which Agaguk feared he might not prevail. The evil spirit, the *agiortok* in the form of a wolf, would be stronger than he.

By nightfall he was foaming with rage. While they were eating he said to Iriook, "Tonight I shall get that wolf."

If he truly believed it, he did not say it again. His wife could see that there was some indecision in his look. He spoke boldly, he put on an air of bravery, but his inner doubt was growing and with that doubt his rage, a useless rage that might even work against him in combat.

The night had come. On the horizon the sun was at rest, a big luminous band which would not disappear in all the summer nights. This midnight sun showed up silhouettes on the plain and left a soft twilight over the tundra. On the other side, toward the east, the stars were brilliant in the black sky. Agaguk was calculating his chances as he sat thinking by the fire.

"How will you get him?" asked Iriook finally.

"He's not like the others. I shall find the way."

He got up. From a heap on the ground he took a caribou skin. Not far from the hut he had a pile of caribou antlers, a sort of cemetery from which he could pick a useful piece of horn when he needed it. He went to it and took out a set of antlers which was almost intact. Iriook was watching him, standing in front of the hut.

"Look after the baby," Agaguk called to her.

She went back in, docilely. He put on the skin, letting it drag on the ground. Then he set the antlers on his head fixing them solidly with a thong. Fitted out like that, he gave a good imitation of a caribou lying down for the night. Under the skin he had the gun on his shoulder, with the barrel hardly showing.

"Iriook!"

Already the shadows were darker close to the ground. From the hut came the smoky glare of the lamp. "Bring the baby with you," Agaguk called. "Don't leave him behind."

The woman took Tayaout on her hip and came over to the dark mass of antlers that hid her husband.

"From here," he said, "I can't see everything. The hut takes up enough room so that the wolf may come without my hearing him. You must keep watch inside too. Put the baby to bed near the entrance. Then open the skins, just a slit. Watch the tundra on that side where I can't see it. You have your gun, if the wolf should appear."

"All night?"

"Yes, and every night if we have to."

It was crazy. They could not keep awake like that, night after night, day after day. But she bent her head without answering and returned to the hut. Some instants later the light went out. Only the silence of the tundra remained, Agaguk's motionless ambush, Iriook's vigil within. And on the bed of moss, the slumber of the child, calm and smiling in his happy ignorance.

CHAPTER 5/PILAYI
The Butchers

The essential thing in this strange country was stratagem, the condition of life, the condition of survival. To the trickery of the beasts, on whom one depends for everything, one opposes human trickery, deliberately brought down to the animal level. For Ramook, as for Agaguk lying in wait for the white wolf over in his home country, there was no way out except trickery. He would use it all day long, month after month, toward the too inquisitive policeman, toward the people of his tribe or the old men.

In the village, everybody was sleeping, save only the policeman Henderson. He had feigned sleep, had even snored a little. It was necessary for his plans that Ramook feel sure of himself. Rolled up on his bed of moss, his face turned toward the entrance of the hut, Henderson was waiting. He had no need to ward off sleep; his senses alert, he was spying. Even a movement of the Montagnais woman tensed his nerves.

The night was well along when Ramook stirred, almost imperceptibly, with scarcely a rustle in the hut. Henderson held his breath.

Outside there was another movement, answering Ramook's, one would have said. The policeman's suspicions were confirmed. During the afternoon, Ramook had conferred with Ghorok, speaking in a low voice. The R.C.M.P. man had not been able to catch what they were saying, but the emphatic way in which Ramook explained something to Ghorok and Ghorok's obvious annoyance indicated a possible plot. His intuition made him decide not to sleep. While he was waiting to see Ayallik again, he would keep watch of Ramook all the more closely, since he was living and sleeping under his roof.

Ramook himself had understood very well that his unfortunate phrase had roused Henderson's suspicions. It was a little thing, but still it was too much.

The Montagnais, for his part, had talked to the police of the visit of this man Agaguk, who apparently lived outside the tribe. He had given them no other information, not knowing himself who Agaguk was or where he lived.

On the other hand, Henderson had not found out much about Agaguk except that he was Ramook's son and that he lived somewhere on the tundra. He intended to go to question him, but it was still necessary to prove that the man was concerned in the affair he was investigating.

The unlucky word Ramook had let slip nevertheless made sense, and Henderson understood then that he was on the right track. That Ramook might be trying to protect his son cleared up some doubtful points in the constable's mind. By doing this Ramook might hope that the tribe would protect him. But knowing the Eskimo, Henderson knew that there was not necessarily any admission of guilt at the base of this feeling of tribal solidarity. The Eskimo is seldom capable of such reasoning. He kills as he loves, as he eats, as he gets rid of a louse in his hair. It was possible that an instinct of self-preservation was guiding Ramook's actions. And more precisely, of protection against the white man's malice.

The Eskimo admits the force of the white man's domination, knows how to recognize it, resigns himself to it, because the white man is the stronger. But his game is to live his ancestral life in constant defiance of the white man, to yield to his instincts, to steal, rob, rape, kill and still remain free within his tribe. This is his everyday pastime, his habit, his way of life. But to outwit the white man, above all a policeman, however agreeable it may be, entails some risk. That night Ramook was going to eliminate one of them, in his own fashion.

First he would attend to Brown's remains, hidden at the site of Ghorok's hut. If they were cleared out, possibly buried elsewhere, far out on the tundra, what formal proof would the policeman have that a whisky trader had passed by there?

Then Ayallik. For Ramook had understood what he was up to when he had surprised him with Henderson. He guessed the man's ambition. His own shrewdness warned him that he had better make sure of Ayallik's silence. Schemes of darkness. All would be accomplished during the policeman's slumber. He must play the dangerous game with skill and dexterity.

His pupils open wide, Henderson tried in vain to make out what was going on in that dark hut. He heard the Montagnais woman breathe, he had noticed a movement of Ramook's, but nothing more. He would have given fortune and future to have the hide, which served as a door to the hut, lifted. So the half-light of the midnight sun, the band of gold on the horizon, might have defined some silhouettes, betrayed some gestures. What should he do? Get up? He was sure that Ramook was not asleep.

He vacillated for several hours, afraid to make any move that might unveil the plot. This was not an unreasonable precaution but rather a matter of prudence. Ramook unmasked too soon would bring the whole village rushing to his rescue. The Eskimo are unpredictable people, capable of uncontrolled rage, particularly in groups. They are like animals which, ordinarily timid and inoffensive, become dangerous if surprised.

In the village, the yelping of a dog that something had disturbed; high above the huts, the occasional cries of owls; and far away, the howling back and forth of a couple of wolves—nothing more. Near the hut an insect, deep in the moss, grated its wings tirelessly.

"Doesn't he ever get tired?" thought Henderson in exasperation.

The noise of the insect filled his ears, grew louder, haunted him. It blanketed everything else; because of it the policeman could not hear anything any more. Was it the monotony of the sound, or the weight of his weariness? Henderson jumped up in a hurry and realized that he had probably been asleep. He had waited too long to get up, to leave the hut. The prudence in which he had been trained had perhaps spoiled his plan. Dawn came, or rather a lesser twilight than the blackness of the night, and when the policeman could distinguish the interior of the hut, he saw that Ramook was sleeping. When the day came, when the sun again rode up the sky, Henderson went out. It was he who found Ayallik's body, stabbed, in the very centre of the place.

And if he had forced his way into Ghorok's hut, he would have seen freshly moved dirt, the patient excavation of a whole night, the disappearance of the last evidence that a white trader had been assassinated in the village.

The question remained the same, the only important one. It took up the whole day in the hut village. Who killed Ayallik? You? Or you? Without let-up, from early morning until night, from one hut to another, every man was questioned, not one was permitted to go hunting. The women and even the children had to face the ordeal too. Seated Indian fashion, his legs folded under him, the moss cushion for his judge's bench, Henderson questioned them all.

It was in vain. What could he do against this impassivity, where sometimes he read, or rather sensed, a contemptuous sarcasm, against these oriental, impenetrable faces, these lacquered eyes, these solid bodies, rocks on which he wounded himself, against the entire tribe, newly welded together, suddenly linked by their ancient loyalties? Henderson felt he had lost his gamble.

In his stupid pride he had been slow to accept Ayallik's accusations, the treachery of one man, perhaps because he didn't like to profit from a betrayal. And now that he had preferred the honour of a patient inquiry to pure treachery, he faced failure. A man, a white man, with means limited by isolation, solitude, the dangerous hostility of the tribe, a man alone could not overcome the obstacle set up by the united silence of the Eskimos.

He questioned them for two days, hoping always for some hesitation in an answer, a word too much, a glance astray. No one claimed possession of the knife that cut Ayallik's throat, no one could identify it. No one had seen Ayallik, no one had heard him. Total ignorance prevailed. But in every look, every barbed word, on every face and in every attitude, there was a hardly veiled feeling of superiority. The united tribe, confronting him! The dull, constant threat, the extreme point of tension. Henderson was playing for his life, and knew it. They might kill him. And even if other policemen came, what could they prove, up against this same tribal silence? Who would be punished?

In a swift decision that to Henderson appeared logical, he

made up his mind to go. He was going without success, but so much the worse. Why should he live in this collection of huts for six months more, to return empty-handed in the end to his police post? Every stratagem of his would be countered by a more able one, that of each individual Eskimo, supported by his entire tribe. Brown's death—after all he was a worthless person anyhow—was no longer of any interest to Henderson. He rose and faced the assembled Eskimos.

"I am leaving. But others will come."

Ramook grinned. "And if you don't leave?"

Now it was time for bluffing, for combat almost body against body, himself against Ramook before the tribe. A single slip, however slight, a moment of weakness, a hasty word, and he would never return alive to his own people.

"If I do not leave, they will come all the same."

Ramook giggled. Henderson gathered his forces together. He thought over what he would say, tried over some phrases in his mind, weighed their meaning and their force.

"Others will come. The big Sky Bird, with ten or a dozen men. And do you know what they will do?"

Ramook had regained his gravity. He looked straight at Henderson.

"The white man's law says this: whoever hides a criminal is as guilty as he. You are then all guilty. They will send a big bird that can hold you all, and you will be carried to the white man's town to prison."

"All of us?"

"Men, women and children."

"The old men too?"

"The old men too."

Ramook thought this over.

"And if you leave?"

Henderson shrugged. He dared not say that even if he left the law would take its course. Merely to shrug the question off committed him to nothing. Ramook appeared satisfied.

"You can go."

"Will someone go along with me? I will pay a guide's wages."

"Don't you know the way?"

"The load is heavy. I have two packs. I came with some dogs, but I can't make them pull over the moss."

Ramook stretched out his hand in an authoritative gesture. "Take only what you need. Leave the rest here."

"Why?"

"Because that's how I want it."

Very suddenly Ramook had become the stronger, and he knew it well.

Henderson had only one idea in his head. He must get away, must flee. He had hesitated to admit the word to his thoughts, but now he could not help it. He was running away, he was saving his skin. He was no more master of events here. Ramook was asserting his power.

"All right. I'll go pack my things."

A few minutes later he set out, alone, on foot, over the tundra. He went toward the south, where the police post was from which he had come. Straight south, with the sun's course as guide. At night there would be the stars. He had food for six days, his rifle and some ammunition. He made his way over the tundra, leaving behind him the village with the tribe assembled to see him go. Ramook was standing before his people, rifle in hand.

When Henderson had gone two hundred yards, Ramook put his gun to his shoulder. The bullet sped, aimed with a sure eye. Henderson fell. Ramook beckoned.

"Come on," he yelled.

The whole tribe ran, a disorderly band shouting hoarsely as they raced toward the fallen man. Henderson was not dead when the leading Eskimos, Ramook among them, caught up to him. He was lying on his back and groaning. Ramook laughed, showing all his yellow teeth. He ran around the prostrate policeman. He drew his knife, cut through Henderson's clothing, and laid bare his body to his sex.

"The man," he said, "the man is the strongest."

He said *Inuk* in speaking of "the man." He was talking only of the Eskimo, not of the white man.

With a turn of his knife he cut off the genitals, and Henderson uttered a horrible scream. With a joyous roar, Ramook threw the organs behind him, to the women who came running up. They tore with their teeth into the still warm and throbbing flesh.

Henderson was still screaming, trying to rise, kicking his legs.

Ghorok had his turn. He leaned over, knife in hand. He pierced the skin of the flank on one side under the ribs and reached the liver, while Henderson awakened the echoes with his terrible cries. With his fingers, Ghorok the sorcerer snatched out the white man's liver and ate it raw, squatting beside his victim.

At daybreak the men of the tribe bore the body much farther way, off any trails which visitors might take. They buried Henderson deep under the moss, so deep that no wolf, and no man, could ever dig him up.

CHAPTER 6/AMARGOK
The White Wolf

The summer would not last more than another few weeks. It had hardly arrived, and already it was giving way to the cold from the north. The short autumn was on its way. Then—the winter!

The midnight sun would give place to the dull, gray, rarely brilliant, always-cold, half darkness. Sometimes it would be as savage as a horde of starving meat-eaters. Already the light of days and nights was not as it had been. The band of gold on the horizon was losing its brightness and was nothing but a dull line, barely luminous. And, in the daytime, wind came cold, freezing puffs, small gusts that troubled the animals and yellowed the moss.

The ground no longer had the elasticity of the warm damp layers, and the chill of the surface would soon join with the ice below and be sealed to the permafrost through the long months to come. At night it was not so pleasant to lie out on the ground, to sleep there, wedded to the earth, sprawled in the moss.

The caribou became scarcer, and the minks' fur began to grow thick, to become more silky. The day before, Agaguk had seen a rabbit. Its sides were white; it was the moulting season and a sure sign of the approaching cold. The time of good living was ending. Coming over the horizon was the time of misery.

And so, in a cold wind, Agaguk wandered about. He had left the hut without following any particular trail, but going almost at random, making a wide circle. He relied on his eyesight, on the instinct he had of any living presence on the tundra. He could stop and without turning around, without making the slightest effort, feel far behind him the presence of the hut and of the two beings who lived in it. Even in darkness, when night, hard on the heels of the day, was falling over the plain, crushing it so as to leave but a tiny ribbon of light, something, some inner alertness, a new rhythm in his blood, a nothingness warned him of its presence.

This would be, on such a night, his best weapon. He would know the nearness of danger at the same moment as the wolf. As soon as the beast sensed him at a distance, he himself would perceive the beast's presence. It was simple; it proceeded from a physical faculty inherited from many generations. But Agaguk would not have been able to explain how the mechanism worked, nor where within him was located the sense that gave the alert. Many times before he had stopped on the tundra, conscious all at once of an animal's presence. He had no need to see it to feel the certitude that it was there, not far away.

And then followed the ambush, the waiting. The animal rose, and Agaguk ate a few days more, or clothed himself, or added to the bundle of raw skins to barter at the trading post.

He kept on walking.

How long, he could not have said. He knew only the direction, and he knew that because of the way he had taken on leaving the hut, he could not go back to Iriook and the child the way he had come, but rather he must bear to the left, toward the big star that was poised in the sky.

But there was no white wolf. In fact, no wolf at all.

If a pack had been howling earlier, and then yelping, it was quiet now. Doubtless the pack had tracked a caribou and brought it down. Now it was appeased, and only later it would begin the hunt again, silently, once the moon went down. But the white wolf? Did he howl with them? Did he hunt with the pack? If he was wandering alone on the tundra, where could he be found? White blot against the darkness? Silhouette perhaps? If he was lurking somewhere waiting, it would be easy. Agaguk would know his presence, would go right to him. He had cocked his gun, the knife with the fine blade hung on his leg. Another knife with a short, very thick blade was at his belt. With one weapon or the other, the white wolf would perish.

An hour went by, another. The moon went down and the tundra grew darker. Standing, motionless, Agaguk scrutinized the vast plain of death. There was not even the sound of an insect.

A tightening in his belly warned him. He felt an animal's presence not far away. He could not have said in what direction or at what distance, but some beast, a fairly big one, not a badger or a mink, was watching him.

Slowly he slid to the ground and squatted, his rifle ready close to his cheek. He must have time. It would be simple to check the direction and the length of the leap toward the animal, but he needed to be close to the ground, to let the wind come to his nostrils, to wait and listen.

A gust went by, rustling the moss, and all was calm again. His eyes at the level of the ground, Agaguk looked slowly around him. In the direction of the hut, at the place where the band of the horizon ended, he saw a shadow against the shadow. There was only a reflection of the light, hardly enough to outline a silhouette. He fixed his eye on the shadow that appeared to stick up over the plateau of moss. He saw the shadow was moving, as if it were crawling. Toward him.

He waited. Some minutes later, he was sure. The odour on the wind was that of a wolf, and the shadow was no longer dark, but gray. And only one animal was capable of creating this picture. The Great White Wolf? No other could make a pale spot on the darkness.

Agaguk, glued to the ground, completely motionless, with his gun ready, waited for the animal to come nearer. Soon the smell was so strong that it made him sick. Now there was not a spot, but the clearly visible form of a wolf crawling on its belly. The wolf also was stalking his prey, seeking to find the silhouette of Agaguk, who was now lying flat on the ground, blotted out in the darkness. Man against beast, two strategies confronting each other. If the wolf came close, Agaguk would fire and the bullet would kill the animal. And if he missed?

Within hailing distance, then the distance of a spear's throw, finally a hundred steps, fifty . . . the wolf was almost within reach of his hand. Only he was coming straight toward Agaguk; he was a narrow target, hard to determine in the night. Agaguk kept his eye on his sights, the beast well in view against the midnight sun on the horizon. Ten steps. It was now or never. Everything depended on one move, on the rapid pressure on the trigger, the aim, the bullet. Less than a second, less still. His fate decided. The death of the wolf? The death of the man?

Agaguk pressed the trigger. The bullet burst from the barrel. But it did not kill the wolf, it only scratched him. He rolled over on the ground and picked himself up ten paces away. At once he was on his feet. Agaguk was standing too, his knife in his fist. The wolf jumped.

A phantom mass, a sort of meteor lanced from the air, landed on Agaguk. Man and beast struggled in the dark. The wolf's jaw was open, slobbering with rage, and with a devilish growling he bit at the man who was fighting furiously between his paws. A horrible wrestling match went on, a deadly gymnastic. At each bite the man's piercing cry rose in the night. The wolf hung on in fury, tearing the man's flesh with his claws, until Agaguk seized the right moment as the animal drew back to plunge again, and pulled back his arm to drive the knife home in the beast's hide. Then he dodged away, but leaped anew on the man, who stiffened against the pain. Great shreds of flesh hung from the animal's teeth. It was a terrible conflict, punctuated by shrieks and growls, where by turns first man and then beast was ahead. Suddenly the knife blade flashed. The fist fell like an arrow, once, then again and again.

Agaguk had the sweet taste of blood in his mouth, which restored his nerve and his grip. Now he was astride the wolf. It was writhing under him and howling. He struck with all his might, his vigor renewed, all pain assuaged. Then he stood up, wiped his forearm over his bloody face and took account of what force he had left. The white wolf, disembowelled, lay at his feet.

Agaguk took off the cord he used as a belt, tied one end around the wolf's hind feet, bent himself to the burden and dragged it over the tundra.

When he reached the hut, Iriook, unable to sleep, was standing there, trembling. Her voice was little more than a whisper, a faint moan.

"Agaguk?"

The man straightened up. "Tayaout?"

"He is safe. The wolf did not come here."

Agaguk pointed to the carcass. "I killed him."

Iriook was crying quietly. "I'm going to light the lamp," she said, "so I can dress your wounds."

From where she was, she saw Agaguk's blood make a black stain which was spreading on the moss. His parka was in ribbons. The wolf had torn great hunks of flesh from the back of his thighs to his shoulders. But there was worse still, and Iriook saw this when the lamplight in the hut fully disclosed her man. Then she began to weep in long sobs, as if she were mourning the dead, and she let herself slip to the ground.

"What's the matter?" asked Agaguk. "What is it?"

She could only raise her head and point with her finger to the man's face. He tried to understand her gesture, and put his hand to his face. In place of a nose there was only an immense hole.

In one mouthful the wolf had torn the nose and part of the cheeks from Agaguk's face. He leaned over as if he were going to touch Iriook gently on the shoulder, but instead of this caress she felt her husband's body fall senseless on the floor beside her. Overcome by weariness and pain, Agaguk fainted and lay unconscious.

Outside the wolf's hind foot was still trembling spasmodically, though the tongue was dangling from the jaws and the eyes were glassy. An owl, crying mournfully, flew overhead. On the horizon a pack commenced to howl. Tayaout woke up whining in the light within the hut.

"The chief is dead," murmured Iriook. Suddenly she felt proud. "The chief of all the wolves," she went on, "of all the wolves on earth and the back of the world, and it is my husband, Tayaout's father, who has killed him."

CHAPTER 7/IKI
The Wound

Squatting on the ground in the hut, Iriook took care of her man.

As the weather grew colder, she had tucked Tayaout away under her parka on her back. Held by a strap that passed under his bottom, he was comfortable there. When he needed air, he hoisted himself up to the collar of the parka and stuck his head out. If he was hungry he had only to slide under Iriook's arm against her side, and seek the generous nipple. If the milk did not satisfy his hunger, he cried, whereupon Iriook put some bits of raw fish in his mouth and he chewed them for a long time, slobbering down his mother's neck.

Stretched out on a caribou skin for three days, Agaguk suffered in silence. Every morning Iriook put a thick coat of bear's grease on his purple wounds, a remedy given her formerly by the old women of the village and kept for this purpose. Every day she went out on the threshold of the hut, where the wolf's carcass still lay, to take a little of the thick saliva from the gaping mouth. With it she traced strange marks on the bear fat. At the same time she muttered words Agaguk did not understand, queer words in an unknown rhythm.

And this made him recall—Agaguk who was of the tundra people—that Iriook was descended from the people on the other side of the world, although she knew nothing of them except what her mother had told her when she was a child. Returning to Agaguk's side, the woman smeared his wounds with this now cabalistic grease. She used an ivory knife, carved from a seal's tusk. With this spatula she pressed the malleable fat deep into the wound, into the recesses of the swollen and ravaged flesh. Agaguk said nothing. He watched her.

He showed nothing in his eyes but impassiveness. His only

admission of pain, a trembling of the muscles, happened once when the ivory knife struck the bone of the cheek that had been laid bare, the debris of the cartilage there in the place where the nose ought to have been.

All the wounds, all the skinned places, were anointed in this way, those of the face, which were the worst, and the others on the shoulders, arms and thighs. When she finished, Iriook and the child slept lying near the sick man. Momentarily relieved, Agaguk also closed his eyes.

He went back over his life, he reviewed it, living over the years. He was going to die, but he wanted to live. He tightened his muscles, he braced himself against his memories to drive away death. He remembered the day when he made his offer to Iriook to take her with him to begin a new life elsewhere, together. He had not been precise; he had spoken of another place without naming it. But he had pointed toward the plain to the south, with a gesture beyond what he could see, farther than the horizon. There, he said, life would begin. He would build a hut, and when winter came, a big and comfortable igloo. Together they would do well there, with meat in store, with skins to clothe themselves, with others to trade for supplies. They would be by themselves, out of reach of the others.

When he talked of getting away, he would often point to the village around them, the people of the tribe. Iriook was happy; she too wanted to leave, to get away from these people. She had never known any real happiness in this tribe.

"I will follow you," she had said.

That was worth any number of promises. He had set to work, getting together his belongings, counting them over. First his arms and ammunition, then the parkas, the skins that he had in reserve, some tools. Whatever was lacking would be Iriook's job to make. He would kill some animals and so procure the bones that were needed. They were the material for the everyday tools and utensils. He would add to them two or three metal knives from the white men, an iron hook, some harpoons he could get at the post in exchange for furs, a bagful of fish-hooks, half of them made of bones he would polish and harden in the fire, the other half of metal gained in trade with the white men.

All this might seem a scanty wealth, but for him it was all that was necessary. And then, in place of the stone lamp for cooking, to heat the cold igloo and light it during the long months, in place of that lamp whose shape had come down to them for thousands of years, did he not have a metal stove, bought from a white man, which he could feed with fat and oil and, if he had a prosperous year, with kerosene? A stove with a wick, black and shining, giving off so much heat that he could burn his hands on it.

Yes, it was more than he needed, more, many times more than any man in the village had. A man's pride, his arrogance on account of the possessions he shows off, his own riches with which to dazzle Iriook.

"Look," he said, showing her the stove and the lamp, "you'll never be cold, and you'll always be able to see clear for your work during the long night."

Six months of twilight, the sun lies below the horizon, waiting. A pale, hardy golden sunrise, a blue and lifeless zenith, and in the north the sombre night sown with stars. And always, over there, the guide star. Always farther on, that star, unreachable, blurred in the distant mists. How hard it was to remember with this piercing pulse, too strong, pounding in his temples. All his wounds were throbbing now, filling his whole body with a persistent sharp pain such as he had never known.

He opened his eyes. Grimacing monsters were marching over the walls of the hut. He heard their savage rhythm in an infernal music. He felt these beasts snuffling about him, weapons penetrating his body, bullets grazing his skin.

It was horribly hot in this new nightmare country. He was no more than a grain of sand which the wind drove over an immense plain. Defenseless, he saw wolves tall as the chief's hut fall upon him. Then a seal as big as a whale struck the wounds in his body with great blows of its flippers, stirring the pain anew, freezing his blood. In his delirium he screamed like an animal.

But the horrible cry that he felt rise from the depths of his being died away into a faint moan on his lips, and Iriook who was asleep woke at hearing Agaguk groan. He seemed to be sleeping very uneasily, but she did not rouse him. She looked at her husband's new face, this monstrous wound.

Never would he be handsome as he was before, with smooth skin, with the face she had loved so much from the first moment when, woman at last, she had felt the desire of man. She was eleven then, a chubby girl, and every night she watched the swelling of her round firm breasts, hard as the stone of the lamp. When her first period came, she had run to the woman in the neighbouring hut, but she had known already what she would hear. It was at that time she had seen again the chief's son, but it seemed to her that she saw him with new eyes.

Agaguk had smiled at her, and she had felt all her flesh move suddenly, an unexpected sensation that gave her pleasure. After three years went by, he had invited her to come with him. When she accepted, she felt a joy she had never known. Like nothing before, a mysterious attraction warmed her body and troubled her heart. She dreamed for hours together, inactive in the winter igloo, and in summer, seated long hours in front of the hut, gazing at the tundra, this immense plateau where she imagined her future life, the new hut, the igloo, her brave and valiant man, and the babies she would have from him. It was a very simple mirage, oftentimes repeated. She thought of nothing but the task to be accomplished, to accomplish it for this man whom she loved and who had chosen her and for the children that she would bear. The passage of the days—she knew no miracle in them if not Agaguk's presence, in itself all miracles and the fulfilment of all her desires.

When he led her to the hut, she could utter no word; she only smiled when he took her by the arm, until there came the sounds of flesh offered as much as taken. There was no dream that had not been made real, no marvels promised that she had not possessed.

Agaguk did not come with empty hands. He had thought of the future, had built a life for himself. He had traded skins for useful objects. He owned a box full of arms and ammunition. If a worse winter came upon them, even so he could hunt, could provide for their needs. He had bullets, rifles, knives, traps. The tundra would have to be utterly deserted, the beasts scattered far before Agaguk's igloo lacked its necessities.

But now she felt all at once totally dispossessed. In place

of Agaguk, who had been at once her dream and her miracle, she saw this new mutilated being, whom she no longer recognized. Squatting beside him, she put out her hand and lightly touched the open wound. Agaguk groaned in his sleep.

"He is still there," she murmured.

Slowly understanding came to her. The mystery would be solved. It was still difficult for her to find Agaguk, for this was no longer he. That face! But what was this? Half a corpse, an apparition. Agaguk groaned again, and something twisted Iriook's entrails. A hand, a force.

"He is still there," she repeated.

She needed a miracle, to recognize the man, to find him again, to hear his voice, what he said, and if he lived, what he might say, to remember his gestures. To recognize Agaguk, in spite of the horror of his mangled face, to find him still as he had been, in spite of the hideous mask. To find him!

She ventured to touch him again, leaned over him and forced herself to kiss him at the very heart of the wound where the flesh had been torn away. Agaguk moaned again and opened his eyes, now sunken in their sockets.

"Iriook?"

Then she knew that she could forget the disfigured features and remember only the man. She cried out hoarsely and threw herself on his breast, straining him in her arms, seeking refuge in her grief.

"Agaguk, Agaguk, it's you!"

CHAPTER 8/IDLU
The Igloo

The snow came, piling rapidly over the earth; the winter
took hold. At first there were only short gusts, snow that ran
lightly over the permafrost that had by now mounted to the
surface. Then one morning of a gray day, the flakes from the
north arrived, whirling thicker and thicker, faster and faster.
By midday, it was a blizzard. The wind whistled over the
plain, and the snow piled up on the sides of the smallest ridges.
After that evening the tundra became anew the arctic plain,
white and motionless.

In the hut, Iriook replaced the grease in the stove with
kerosene so that the fire would be brighter. She stopped up
the cracks, weighted down the edges of the hides with stones
from the brook, and awaited the end of the storm with resignation. Squatting beside the bench where Agaguk lay, she did
not move except to give the breast to the baby tucked away
in her parka and to regulate the stove once in a while. The
dwelling was pleasantly warm. Drowsiness overcame them,
blotting out for them the raging tempest outside, the roaring
wind, the drive of the snow against the supports of the hut.

The next morning there was no more tundra. That day
Iriook built the igloo to replace the hut with her own hands.
At one time she saw Agaguk appear in the opening of the
hut entrance. She went quickly to lead him back inside.

"It is for you that I am building the igloo," she said. "And
for me. It is for the child. Come, we shall not lack for anything. Get well, that is all I ask of you."

Too weak to resist, Agaguk let her lead him in. She gave
him a big hunk of meat. "There," she said, "Eat. Make new
blood in place of what you've lost."

Then she went back to work. By evening the house was
ready. Iriook had built it higher and wider than usual. "A

144

chief's igloo," she said to herself happily. "An igloo of the Good Spirit. For Agaguk."

Inside six people could live and still have room to move about comfortably. The ice bench had been shaped with care and hardened. It was wide and of the right height. She took an hour to polish the walls, to smooth them until they shone like a mirror. She cut the air hole, shaping it into a regular cone as it ought to be. Near the entrance tunnel and over it, she hollowed out a long niche in the wall, two hands' breadth deep and four high; when she was building the igloo, she had placed two long solid bones in the ice. Now they stuck out of the upper corners of the niche. She stretched a wolf skin from them, which she had scraped well on the flesh side and rid of its fur. This way she would have a pantry for fresh meat. The pemmican would be hung from the peak of the igloo, where she had set in the ice several bone hooks, seal ribs patiently shaped.

In the centre of the igloo she made a sort of basin, shallow but even and hard. There she put one of the few pieces of metal that Agaguk possessed, a cast-iron plate that he had procured at the trading post some time before. On this she would place her stove next, that source of warmth, the utensil essential to their lives. The fat for the stove, the oil, the kerosene for emergencies, these would also be suspended at the top of the igloo, in leather or metal containers.

At the very beginning of her work, she heaped up snow in two wooden boxes inside the hut, and pounded it with her hands until it was half melted. Then she carried these two mounds outside, in the fierce cold. By the end of the day the blocks of ice she obtained this way were solid, regular in shape and exactly the size she wanted. She put them on the ice bench, making a sort of arm rest. She would lean against them during the long tasks of winter, the chewing of the skins, the patient sewing, in some cases the removing of hair. At other times, she would be preparing the furs, cleaning and combing out the hair, brushing and dressing it.

She put two caribou skins on the bench, at the end opposite her working place. That would be Agaguk's bed. Then she went to look for her man, and, almost carrying him, slid him into the entrance tunnel. It was quickly done, to the accompaniment of his moans. Tayaout cried under her parka, frightened by these sudden movements which tossed him about and shook him up.

When Agaguk was in the igloo, Iriook stretched him out on the caribou skins. Then she lighted the stove in the centre, and the warmth quickly spread through the dwelling. She had uttered only grunts and murmurs, encouraging her man, comforting him, excusing herself for having to use her strength against him. Now she leaned over him and spoke gently.

"You will stay here alone," she said. "I must tear down the hut."

It took her two hours. When the work was done, the indispensable things were brought into the igloo, the hides that had clothed the hut had come to join the others wrapped around Agaguk, and the ice bench was a warm and pleasant place, comfortable to sit on, with each skin fastened against the wall to serve as a back rest. Already the walls were sweating drops of water and the rancid heat, whose strong odour is the sign of good living, was spreading through the igloo.

Iriook tied the supports of the hut in a bundle and laid them in the snow outside. In the spring, when the snow melted, she would find them there. She hung up the guns in the igloo and put the boxes of shells where the ice bench ended at the entrance tunnel. The niche would serve to keep the fresh meat and the strips of pemmican hung from the top of the igloo. There were surely not enough provisions for the winter; they might lack meat as well as fat, but Iriook said to herself that she could provide if she had to.

Certainly the seal hunt had been successful, but even with all that, the fat and pemmican did not furnish a supply sufficient for a long winter. On the other hand, the warm season had been remarkably short. The trip to the Great Water, the time that Agaguk had lost in hunting the white wolf, and the hours he had wasted formerly in the mere contemplation of his son—delightful and admirable as these were, they were of no use to fill the storeroom—all that time gone by threatened them with famine. All the more, should this winter be as severe as the last one, which kept them from hunting anything, from any hope of getting fresh meat, however poor.

Iriook suddenly decided that the next day she would go

hunting. On the new snow the animals would be running in a crazy way. The migrants would be almost all gone, but a few of them, less endowed with instincts than the others, would be lingering on and would be easy to kill. She would take advantage of their confusion. The day before she had noticed some caribou dashing about in the storm. To kill two or three would make sure of provisions. Caribou tallow is not as good as seal fat, and Iriook dreamed of whales which assure warmth and light for a long winter. But, if they must lack good fat and oil for the final months of the coming season, better tallow than nothing at all.

When she lay down that night, she was weary. But her eyes shone and she felt an inner warmth that she had not known for a long time. In her heart and in her cheeks, there was the flush of joy. For before he went to sleep, Agaguk raised himself on his elbow and looked for a long time over the igloo Iriook had built. Then he let himself drop back and said very gently, "You are a good woman, Iriook."

CHAPTER 9/TUT'U
The Caribou

During the three days following the building of the igloo, the woman did not stay idle. Contrary to all tradition but under the pressure of necessity, because there was no other way to carry out the plan she had made, she entrusted Tayaout to his father and left them alone in the igloo.

Rifle in hand, she went after fresh meat, the last chance for a long time to assure their survival through the winter. Soon there would be only a few scattered beasts on the snow plain, a wandering caribou, half-frozen, a few wolves, perhaps some foxes, a mink looking for a hole in the ice of the brook, or still a badger. But there would be none of the rewarding summer hunts, none of this game within easy reach of a bullet. There would be only the misery, the long spells of cruel winds and the deserted plain.

In the first hour she discovered a caribou track. The cold was a mass resting on the surface of the earth, crushing all life out of living things. A pale light came from the south, but the north was dark. Up there was the six-month night, the terrible endless night of the Arctic, no wind, only the cold, all powerful presence, a cold in bluish colours, paralyzing all energy, inviting to fatal drowsiness.

Her head full of mirages, of marvellous colours and songs of whose beauty she had hitherto been ignorant, Iriook wandered over the plain. She fought against the cold, but a note of alarm in her subconscious warned her that she must soon run, beat her arms, soon flee to the igloo, to the safety of the warm habitation.

And yet, the meat? Was she going to yield before the cold, she who had just beaten back the death that was threatening Agaguk, she who had just built an igloo such as few men could have built? She drove away the mirages. She beat her

148

arms against her sides, now clearly conscious of what she was doing, and meanwhile she looked around her over the plain where surely some animal must be wandering. It was then that she noticed, not far from where she was standing, the caribou tracks.

Crouching down, examining the prints, she tried to remember all that she had heard the men say about the science of tracking, the skilful hunt, the habits of the animals. The tracks zigzagged, the front feet crossing each other. At one place the beast appeared to have fallen on its knees and got up. The image was clear, of an animal half-dead, stupefied by the cold which was overcoming it, ready to yield to superior force.

She was not mistaken. Within rifle range, she saw a heap of snow piled up by the wind. The tracks led to that rise. She knew that behind it she would find the caribou.

Then she ran, her big mukluks bearing her up in the snow. When she rounded the dune, she saw behind it not a single caribou, but an enormous female brought down by the cold and uneasily circling round her a snorting male. She watched the family a moment without moving. Then she shouldered her rifle and brought down the male with a bullet between the eyes. After that she finished off the half-frozen female. Happy as she had never been in her life, she hurried back to the igloo to get the dogs and the leather thongs to pull the carcasses.

She had saved Agaguk. In less than two hours, she had made sure of the winter's meat, by her own strength and her own skill. With what was hanging in the igloo, the two caribou would fully provide for their survival. She made haste.

Wolves might appear, to devour the still warm bodies. She ran now, whipping up the dogs, driving them to the limit of their endurance. The wolves had not come. She tied the carcasses tightly together first and then to the dogs' harnesses. She hitched the malemutes in a fan, to share out the effort, and she fastened herself in front, the long strap under her armpits. And so, pulling and panting, the woman and the dogs hauled the two caribou to the igloo.

Iriook felt as if she would faint from weariness. Nevertheless her task was not completed. The entrance tunnel was too narrow; she could not see how she could slide into it with the beasts, toward the warmth within which she could work at the cutting-up in peace and at leisure. Nor could she wait until the cold froze the bodies to the point where it would be impossible to skin them and cut them up. There was only one thing to do, to call on all her energy. Since she could not count on Agaguk's help, it was up to her to do what had to be done herself.

She entered the igloo. Agaguk was sleeping with the child beside him. The stove was burning well, the heat was good. Iriook rapidly chewed some bits of fat from their reserve and drank a cupful of the water boiling on the low stove. A little recomforted, she found the ivory knives and one of the two metal ones.

Outside, she set to work to skin the two beasts. The skins were precious. There would never be too many of them in store. Especially desirable in her eyes was the female's, with its finer fur. Slowly the cold was freezing the bodies, and Iriook worked twice as hard as before, with nothing in her head but this diligence. She cut and yanked, freeing the skin at a rate she would not have believed herself capable of.

A half hour later the female was completely skinned and the male half done. When Iriook slashed at the neck, the last inch of useful skin, the carcasses were already almost rigid. She had not a moment to lose. With an axe this time, and the larger of the metal knives, she cut the carcasses into four quarters, first in half at the height of the last rib. Then, with great circular sweeps of the blade, she pulled out the entrails which she threw to the dogs. She set aside the liver, the kidneys and the heart, doing the same thing with both animals. Then she cut the back in two by splitting the backbone and the pelvis with blows of the axe. Four quarters in which the blood was congealing were now piled near the skins. Still using the axe, she separated the heads from the trunks and opened the chest from the top. Then she divided the front end of each beast as she had the back, making two separate quarters for each.

Now she could slide the caribou sections into the tunnel. She would finish the job in the igloo. It was time, for already the flesh was almost frozen and the skins were set in a shapeless mass, already frozen together. Iriook patiently pushed each quarter of meat into the igloo and piled them on the ice bench near the tunnel.

Several days' work was ahead of her; she set to it as soon as everything was inside. Outside the dogs were quarreling, tearing into the smoking entrails.

Agaguk had woken up. Unmoving, he looked at the miraculous hunt. Iriook saw her man's eyes widen in admiration.

"Whatever the winter may be like," she said, "we shall survive. We have meat and fat."

Then she went to work. What she had accomplished until then was only the preliminary part, which usually falls to the men. Now came the women's work, the part she knew well and had been used to doing since childhood. She took each quarter and with the steel blade cut the meat into strips and removed the tallow. The big solid bones were set aside to be made later into objects for trade.

She stopped only at meal time, toward evening, when she boiled some of the fresh meat over the flame to give to the child. While she was doing the butchering, she and Agaguk had eaten some of the raw meat, an excellent tonic, which relieved fatigue, replenished Agaguk's blood and was a change for the stomach that was used to smoked meat.

Iriook toiled on. Agaguk was asleep long since, but always the woman's clever fingers cut the strips and piled them on the ice bench. The igloo, big as it was, was cluttered by the remaining quarters, by the bones heaped in two piles, one for the dogs and the other to be kept, as well as by the pieces of meat and the skins which thawed rapidly and filled the room with their odour.

When her fingers were too numb to keep on, and her shoulder muscles ached too much, she stood up, wiped her hands on her parka and went to lie down, taking Tayaout to sleep beside her in the warmth of her body.

CHAPTER 10/UMAYOK
Revival

A month had gone by since the accident, but the ordinary
rhythm of the igloo had really resumed only ten days after the
woman's lucky hunting expedition. Now Agaguk got up,
walked shakily around the fire and went soon to lie down
again, already tired. All the time that she had enveloped him
in patient care, Iriook had little by little got used to Agaguk's
new face. Now that he was getting better, the fear of losing
him no longer troubled her. He would live and he would be
again her master.

But a doubt entered the Eskimo woman's heart. This proud
man had beaten her before, when she wept, and he could not
console her. Would he adjust himself to his fall? What could
she do to give back to the man she loved his will to live as
absolute master of the hut, of the igloo and the tundra? An
instinct awoke in her, told her the gestures to make, the words
to say to convince Agaguk of his continuing power. One
evening she came close to him.

"You are stronger," she said.

A look in her eyes, the smile she gave him, and Agaguk knew
her thoughts. He shook his head sadly.

"I wish . . ." he said.

He made a gesture of impotence. She felt he was miserable.
How ought she to behave after that? Iriook was more familiar
with gestures of submission than with others. But Agaguk held
out his hand and slid it under Iriook's parka up to her belly.
She wanted to cry because without saying anything they
understood each other so well.

"There is nothing there?" he said.

"No. As long as the baby suckles, that's how it will be."

Agaguk sighed and turned his head.

"You could . . ." murmured Iriook timidly.

Tayaout was babbling and the stove was making a humming sound. Outside the night was still and windless. Even the dogs were quiet, doubtless asleep in their holes in the snow.

"You could," repeated Iriook. "Let me help you."

Agaguk did not understand.

Tenderly Iriook took off the caribou skin in which he was wrapped. She saw then how thin he had grown. She too undressed; then she straddled Agaguk, and slowly, almost piously, with sighs and moans that were almost sobs, she drew from him first the beginning of pleasure and then the full accomplishment. But to have been so tender and to have tried so hard, to have worked in these patient and gentle rhythms, had submerged her in a world full of memories, where desires and privations, all too recent, so crowded her mind that she was astonished to reach her climax at the same time he did. She fell trembling against him, to listen a long time to his husky breathing, the sound of almost complete exhaustion. At last he said, panting, "Soon I'll be up and around. I'll go out, I'll go hunting. We must have some furs to trade . . . ."

It was the first time since the accident that he expressed any hope.

Deeply reassured, Iriook wanted to cry again. She could not have said why, but Agaguk's unrecognizable face, with the great hole where the skin was beginning to grow again, was not repulsive to her. Into her resignation, into that fear she had fought so many days without acknowledging, henceforth there crept a tranquil joy, like a need to give which she had until then found no way to satisfy. She looked at the sleeping Agaguk and was able, without shuddering, to imagine the continuation of their days.

Nothing mattered any more, neither the exposed teeth nor the mutilated ear nor the gap where the nose should have been. This horror, which would be a continual presence until death came to deliver her from it, would be bearable because she had at last found the man at the heart of the suffering, still more tender. He remained her most precious possession, more precious even than Tayaout whom he had made. That would be her secret, because for Agaguk the child was more precious than any woman. She must never forget that.

CHAPTER 11/TIGMIERPAK
The Airplane

When the snow disappeared and the tundra once more became green and covered with flowers, when the huts had
replaced the igloos, the Big Bird of the white man landed on
the level ground near the village. Ramook had heard the
throbbing of the two motors. He had alerted the men, and
when the plane landed and rolled up to the cluster of huts, he
was already there, at the head of his tribe, waiting, his face
expressionless as usual.

Four policemen climbed down from the plane, and with
them were two other men whom Ramook could not identify.
They wore white men's clothing, but they had a look about
them that he did not recognize. Were they, to judge by their
bearing, greater chiefs even than the policemen? Six men,
stoically Ramook watched them approach.

Henderson had been buried far off. They would certainly
not think it feasible to search all the tundra. And how else
could they find out what had happened?

The only dangerous traitor, Ayallik, was no longer of this
world. Ramook was safe. He was sure of it.

One of the policemen had two more stripes on his sleeve
than the others. Ramook knew what that meant. He would
speak for the others. He would give the orders.

"Ramook?"

What then, they knew him in distant lands? A big childish
smile appeared on the Eskimo's face. He glanced at his own
people; he saw they were looking at him with great respect—
even Ghorok, the witch-doctor, who asked, "They know
Ramook's name among your people?"

The policeman was in front of them. His men stood back
and at one side, but apart there were the two white men
dressed in shiny parkas.

154

"We know Ramook's name," answered the policeman.

He clicked his heels and looked down at Ramook.

"I am Scott," he said. "We want to talk to you."

"You are the chief?" asked Ramook.

"I am chief of these people here, yes."

He pointed to the white men behind him. Ramook rubbed his chin with his hand. He looked worried. So, the white men were not great chiefs? What were they then?

Finally Ramook said, "Since you are chief, you may come to talk with the chief. But the others will stay there. My people as well as yours."

The policeman Scott was tall, taller even than Henderson. Taller than his companions, young, with dark piercing eyes and a thin mouth. He spoke Eskimo very well and seemed to know the customs and the right way to present himself. Ramook was troubled; he was frightened, but he took good care that no one should perceive his state. He bowed, but not so deeply that anyone could call it servile. With a wave of his hand he invited the policeman. "In my hut," he said.

Scott followed him, and the two men went alone toward the chief's dwelling. Within, the Eskimo took his place on the caribou skin and waited. Scott was seated in front of him, but he remained no less tall, no less dominating. His eyes held Ramook's, who finally turned his head.

"Last year," said the constable, "we sent a policeman here by the name of Henderson. We know that he arrived here because an airplane saw him when it passed over your village. We know that he has not returned to the south. Where is he?"

Ramook narrowed his eyes. "How should I know?"

Scott stiffened. "Know this, Ramook, chief of the tribe. Henderson came to inquire into the death of a white trader. We are almost certain that the white man was killed here, and that in addition you killed Henderson. I give your tribe until tomorrow to surrender the guilty man to us."

Ramook felt rage shake him, the cold rage of an offended chief.

"I am in my own country," he said.

"And so? Who makes the laws?"

"You."

"Then obey my law."

"I obey what I please."

Ramook smiled evilly. "Listen," he added drily, "How many of you are there? Six? And we are fifty."

Scott rose. He smiled in his turn. He looked at Ramook from his height.

"You think you would win? Other airplanes would come, one after another. If a hundred men were needed, a hundred would come, and you would be exterminated. But supposing you are not, supposing you win, where would you go to exchange your furs, or get your ammunition, your new guns, the oil for your lamps? And the cord for your nets? Say now that you no longer know how to weave nets of rawhide, or would you use tarred string?"

Ramook lowered his head and said nothing.

"This evening your women will prepare a meal for us. But we shall sleep in the Big Bird, under cover of our guns. If one of you comes near, he will be shot. Tomorrow morning the guilty man must come to give himself up."

Ramook slowly raised his head. "And if he does not?"

"I have six men, ammunition and plenty of time. Do you know who these two other white men are, those who are not policemen?"

"No."

"They are scientists. Great sorcerers. They have brought magic boxes and spectacles that read the past and make the invisible appear. They will search everywhere in the village. If human blood has been shed anywhere, they will know it right away. They will even be able to tell whose blood it was, in what veins it ran. They will find the remains of a man who was buried, and they will say whether he was white man or an Eskimo. They will search the tundra, with the help of my policemen, and suddenly they will find the invisible emanation of a dead body. They will dig into the moss. They will even be able to say from what gun came the bullet that killed Henderson and to say on what day and hour that bullet was fired. I don't need the criminal's confession. When my two magicians are through, I shall know enough to take the criminal back with us."

He bent over a little, paternally. "You know it, Ramook. The white men are powerful and capable. They have great magic. They talk at a distance, they fly in the air, they fix faces on paper, they know everything and divine everything. What they do not divine their sorcerers divine for them. Do you really think you can win against us?"

That evening, after the white men had eaten and retired into their Big Bird to sleep, Ramook called the Elders to his hut. He told them what Scott had said. When the recital was ended, Ramook murmured in distress, "There is only one thing to do."

No one said a word. The smoky light of the lamp fell on the greasy impassive faces with eyes deep in their sockets under matted brows.

"We have to give up Agaguk," said Ramook.

"Your son?" said Ghorok.

"Yes."

"Give him up to the white men?"

"Yes. It's him or me. I am chief, I have the right to save my own head."

When the others left, Ghorok stayed.

"Leave at once," said Ramook. "Take provisions. Take this gun to Agaguk for me. Say it's a gift. I think he will like this present. When you get back, I will denounce him to the police."

He held out to Ghorok the gun that had been used to bring down Henderson.

"You have to deliver the guilty man tomorrow?"

"I will make them wait for your return. I will make excuses. Go very quietly, make a long detour and come back the same way. I don't want them to know you've gone there."

When Ghorok left, no one, not even the policemen sleeping in the airplane, noticed his disappearance. After travelling all the better part of the night, he reached Agaguk's hut at the end of the following day. He could hardly stand, he had run so hard, with the rifle on his shoulder, the one that Ramook was sending as a gift to Agaguk. He would be thankful to be rid of it.

It was Iriook who greeted him. She was alone, for Agaguk had gone off toward the south, saying he had seen some big birds there. He was going to be away a couple of days. Iriook said nothing of this to Ghorok. She looked coldly at the man, standing in front of the hut and barring the entrance.

"I come to bring a gift," said Ghorok.

Iriook did not speak, nor did she move. Ghorok held out the gun.

"What's that?" asked Iriook. "Who's sending that gun?"

"Ramook."

"What for?"

"He says he's done very little for Agaguk, that he has never come to see how you live. He wants to be pardoned. He will come soon, but in the meantime take this present for Agaguk."

"It's an old gun."

"Yes. Ramook liked it very much. That's why he's giving it to his son."

Iriook was suspicious. She did not like Ghorok, nor Ramook any better. She guessed that there was some plot going on between these two men. She pushed away the rifle.

"Agaguk isn't here."

"He'll be back?"

She hesitated a moment, then she thought it wise to answer, "Perhaps later. I don't know."

Ghorok's eyes lighted up but Iriook grinned. "I, too, know how to kill," she said.

She reached behind her, felt around in the hut, and brought out her own gun.

"I'm armed," she declared, "like a man."

Ghorok shrugged his shoulders. A woman was not worth the risk. A polar bear skin, three freshly killed seals, perhaps, but a woman? He threw Ramook's rifle on the ground. "I've brought the gift. I have nothing more to do here," he said.

"I cannot accept it."

"You'll have to."

He turned his back on the woman and went quickly down to the brook. Iriook saw him wade in and paddle about trying to grab a fish. He emerged triumphant, holding a plump flapping trout which he had succeeded in seizing.

"You see," he yelled, "I don't even have to ask you to feed me."

Seated on the muddy bank, he devoured the raw fish, wiping the blood and entrails from his dripping chin with the back of his hand. When he was full, he got up and went over to where the moss was dry. He stretched out there. "I'll sleep here," he said. "When I'm rested I'll go back to the village."

Iriook watched him for a long time, then she went back in the hut. When she had eaten and the child in turn was satisfied, she went out and saw that Ghorok was still lying in the same place. He was motionless and seemed to be asleep. She let herself down on the heap of moss by the hut, but she remained seated, leaning against one of the poles of the hut. She kept her rifle across her knees. Since Tayaout was now asleep, silence lay over the hut and on the tundra. The moon came up, stood at the zenith and slowly descended. When it set, the stars shone.

Then Iriook got up and went to look around. Ghorok was no longer there. Much later, when she was sure that Ghorok had gone back to the village, she too slept, but still sitting up and with the gun.

She woke at dawn. No trace of Ghorok was to be seen, except that gun which he had left behind and which she regarded uneasily. She did not believe in this story about Ramook. It was not like him to send messengers bearing gifts this way. If Ramook had really delegated Ghorok for this, some other motive was behind it. But what?

All day Iriook reflected on this visit, on this gun so strangely sent to Agaguk. She could hardly wait to see her own husband again, to let him make his own judgment, take whatever decision he pleased. So for long hours she gazed over the tundra, watching for the appearance of that stocky silhouette on the horizon to the south.

CHAPTER 12/AITUSIAK
The Gift Received

Ghorok returned to the village without being seen by the policemen. He glided between the huts at night and slunk home like a thief. Over there, in the airplane, the white men were sleeping. The delay had not been easily obtained. Ramook had to insist and promise. He had pledged himself deeply.

"You want the guilty man," he said to Scott. "All right, you shall have him. But it's no easy job."

"Why? Since you know him. You have only to point your finger."

Ramook grimaced and wrung his hands. He had a role to play, the most dangerous in his life as chief. If nothing convinced Scott, he was lost. He must above all keep the white sorcerers from searching the village surroundings. It was not so much the finding of Henderson's body that presented a great danger, now that Ghorok had carried the rifle to Agaguk, but that the corpse had been mutilated. Scott was sure to know ancient Eskimo customs well enough to picture the scene to himself. He would accuse Ramook, Ghorok and all the village of devouring the man's liver and castrating him. First of all he must delay matters until Ghorok's return. Then Ramook supposed the policeman would focus their attention over there near the river where Agaguk lived.

"Why not surrender the criminal right away?" insisted Scott.

"I can't. Give me another day, two days. I swear to you that he will be denounced to you. I am the chief here, I don't lie."

Scott did not appear impressed. "Two days and then three, and you can prolong the game for a year. Give me one reason."

"You'll see.when I tell you who did it, you'll see."

With that Ramook subsided into silence. He was stubborn, and Scott's threats and curses had no effect. On his return to the airplane, he could only repeat Ramook's words to his men and conclude, "He's promised to give up the man. Unless I use methods which at the moment are revolting to me, I can do nothing."

And they waited. On the morning of the fourth day, Scott went again to Ramook's hut. "Now talk," he said.

Ghorok, having made it back by a forced march, was sleeping in his own hut.

"I'm ready," agreed Ramook. "I had to think hard. And if I tell you, it is only because I wish to respect the law, I want to live at peace with the white men."

"Who killed Brown? Who killed Henderson?"

"I know who killed Brown."

"And Henderson?"

"I don't know."

"You're a liar."

"The man who killed Brown," said Ramook hastily, "is Agaguk."

"Where is his hut?"

"Hold on," said Ramook. "Let me explain. You'll understand. Agaguk doesn't live here."

He pointed to the south. "Down there, a day's journey and a little farther, there is a river. Agaguk lives there, alone with his wife."

"We will go."

"I reflected, I waited, I did not know how to tell you."

"Why?"

"Agaguk is my son."

There was a long silence in the hut. Scott, his eyes wide open, stared at Ramook. He had not really believed that Ramook would denounce a guilty man. In all his experience in the Arctic, this was the first time he had seen an Eskimo betray one of his own people in such a gross manner. What was still more inconceivable, his own son!

"I want peace with the white man," murmured Ramook, with bent head. "The respect for their laws, I had good reasons to ask a delay. . . ."

"I see."

"Henderson left here to go to Agaguk's—"

"You told Henderson that your son killed Brown?"

"Yes. He left to go to arrest him. We have not seen him since."

"Go on."

"After Henderson's departure, Agaguk came here. He left a gun in my hut. When you spoke of your sorcerers, who could tell from what rifle a bullet had been fired, I understood better. Agaguk is young and handsome. He has more knowledge than I. He knows the white man's ways and many of their secrets. He left the rifle here so that someone would find it in my hut and accuse me, myself. He wanted to sacrifice me to save himself. Then I sent Ghorok to carry the gun back to Agaguk's place. He is no longer my son."

"You say that he had also killed Brown?"

"Yes. I can bring you witnesses if you like. The whole tribe will tell you that Agaguk burned Brown in his hut."

In the airplane, Scott reported what he had just heard. "It's too well constructed a story to be easy to believe without some reservations," he concluded. "On the other hand. . . ."

Unless he went to look for Agaguk, how could he be sure that Ramook was telling the truth? With these Eskimos, you never got to the end of the surprises. Since he had taken over command of the police in these territories, Scott had learned that these primitive beings made use of a preposterous morality to justify acts which would have been criminal or at least condemnable among more civilized people. In denouncing his son, perhaps Ramook was not telling the truth, and for reasons which at the moment he was the only one to know. But on the other hand, suppose he was telling the truth? They would go to look for Agaguk.

CHAPTER 13/TUNI'YUT
The Gift Returned

Agaguk came back from the south bringing eight mink, three foxes and a dressed wolfskin, plus two of the big birds that had attracted him into those regions. Farther on he had seen the first swamps covered with bushes and the low rocky hills. If he had walked another two days, he asserted, he would have seen trees.

"Are we then so near the white men's country?" asked Iriook.

"Yes. We could go there some time, to see what it's like."

"To live there?"

"Never."

The woman appeared reassured. "I like this country where we live very well," she said simply. "It's good enough for me."

When she had spoken of Ghorok's visit and showed Agaguk the gift sent by Ramook, he became thoughtful. He was disturbed, and he showed it by the way he examined his rifle. He had never had any confidence in his father; he knew he was avaricious and tricky. He left the village mainly because he could no longer accept that man as chief. Ramook was his father, and he owed him, at least according to tradition, respect and obedience. But he left because he feared he might have to obey dangerous orders—to serve Ramook's personal interests. He had worked this out in his primitive mind. When he departed from the village, he was yielding to an instinct for self-protection rather than acting on considered reflection. When he himself set fire to Brown, he did it because the man had cheated him, because he was moved to see justice done and not for personal ambition.

It had seemed to him that the best thing to do was to go elsewhere and begin a new life, and this had happened long before his encounter with Brown. He wanted to be a long way from Ramook, whose crafty spirit he feared, from Ghorok with his often childish witchcraft, from Ayallik and a lot of others. He wanted to be alone and secure.

And now, today, Ramook sent him this rifle. The reasons which Ghorok had given Iriook were not good enough. Why should Ramook have taken the trouble to send him this gun? Unless the chief of the tribe was up to some dangerous machination.

Agaguk examined the rifle for a long time. Did it conceal some betrayal? This was the first idea that came to him, that Ramook wanted to get rid of him for some obscure reason. He expected that Agaguk would have nothing more immediate to do than to try out the weapon, which would probably explode. Agaguk put his eye to the barrel and scrutinized the bore. Then he tried cocking it; he opened the breech, loosened the loader, pressed the trigger and worked the discharge mechanism, but he found nothing wrong. Nevertheless, did one ever know Ramook's astuteness? The lengths to which he might go?

For a moment Agaguk really thought he would try the weapon, but he changed his mind. If that was what Ramook wanted, why should he fall into the trap?

"What are you going to do?" asked Iriook, who was sitting on the ground in front on the hut.

Agaguk hefted the gun and frowned. Well, what was he going to do? He had thought of tossing it in the river, but that seemed to him too simple.

"I think," he said slowly, "that I am going to give the gun back to Ramook."

But Iriook cried, "No! No, don't go there. That's the trap he has set for you? He wants you to come."

But Agaguk's decision was taken. He had to know. At the very least he wanted to put this object far away from him; he did not know if it was a gift or some evil thing invented by Ramook and Ghorok the sorcerer.

"You'll see Ramook?"

Agaguk hesitated a moment. "No, I don't think I'll see him. I'll hide the weapon in his hut and get away."

"They'll see you."

"I'll arrive there at night. Nobody will know about my visit."

He started a few minutes later, carrying only his own rifle

and the weapon to return to Ramook, some pemmican and a small water-bottle. He would eat frugally and walk fast, without pause.

"Look out for Ghorok," said his wife. "He left a while ago, he'll be ahead of you."

"I'll watch out," said Agaguk. "If I have to, I'll slant away from the route and then if I arrive ahead of him so much the better."

But he knew that Ghorok was a fast walker. Did he not say to himself that sometimes the witch-doctor obtained the aid of the Spirits who wafted him great distances in a jiffy? Agaguk set out then in the direction of the village, suddenly unafraid of Ghorok or the Spirits or anybody there, he was in such haste to rid himself of the mysterious rifle.

Once he arrived, he saw the white man's Big Bird parked on the tundra not far from the huts, and he understood that something serious was happening, but he was able to get into Ramook's dwelling without attracting attention, and to hide the gun there.

When he got home, the journey over, he was sure that this presence of the white men, along with the gift rifle from Ramook, portended nothing good.

CHAPTER 14/POKIAKTALIK
The Policeman

The day after Agaguk's return, the airplane touched down on the tundra near his hut, and the passengers climbed down from it. Scott was first, followed by two other policemen, and by Ramook, Ghorok and Tugugak. Agaguk saw these men come toward him, and stop suddenly as if at a loss. Ramook took another step and seemed to stare at Agaguk He said nothing, but he made a sort of grunting noise in his throat, a questioning sound. Then he turned to Ghorok who also seemed bewildered. The policeman, the one who appeared to Agaguk to be chief, taller, more authoritative than the others, waited patiently, keeping a close watch.

Agaguk did not understand. Without a mirror in the hut, how could he know that his mutilated face not only horrified the visitors but also greatly complicated things for them?

Iriook, standing not far away, stared at the strange procession. It was when she saw Ramook's evident indecision that she suddenly comprehended. These men did not recognize Agaguk.

She had no idea why they were there, but on the other hand she knew that the presence of Ramook and Ghorok among them was a menace. All at once she remembered the journey they had taken to hunt seal. In spite of the fact that they had Tayaout with them, and in spite of Agaguk's intense pride in him, he had not wanted to go by way of the village. More than that, he had made a big circle to avoid it. Iriook had not attached any importance to this behaviour, or been disturbed by it. But the presence here of the policemen, and also of the men of the village, with their chief at their head, was the prelude to some drama. By some instinct, she connected the two events. Besides, she remembered another trip of Agaguk's to his village in the early days of their establishment by the river. Had he not returned with the bundle of furs which he had gone to barter with a white trader? And returned sullen, cross, impatient? Why? What had happened?

The march of events is slow in the Arctic. Sometimes cycles take several seasons to complete. It was not impossible that the policemen's visit was the result of Agaguk's stay in his village, so many months before.

Immediately she pulled herself together, fully decided. This could be nothing but some trick of Ramook's, some wicked plot he had cooked up. Ah! What would she not have given for some confidence from Agaguk, the story of that trip! How much better she could have met the situation today!

The group was still there in front of them, with no one daring to speak. The police chief made a vague gesture, but it was Ramook who bent his head forward and stared at Agaguk.

"Where is Agaguk?" he asked. "Is it you?"

Slowly Agaguk passed his hand over his face. He suddenly realized how unrecognizable he had become. At once he felt reassured. The fear that had overcome him when he saw the police descend from the airplane slackened a little and ceased to bind his chest. He breathed more freely. But before he could answer, Iriook had come forward.

"Agaguk," she said to the men, "What do you want of him?"

Scott was looking at the scene with curiosity. They had not prepared him for the sight of this half-monster. Had not Ramook himself declared spontaneously that Agaguk was young and handsome?

"A white trader by the name of Brown has been killed," Scott said slowly to Iriook. "And so has one of our constables, Henderson. We believe the guilty man is Agaguk. We are looking for him. We heard that he lived here."

Iriook felt a great relief. In a swift turn everything became more easy. Eskimo herself, tricks were not foreign to her mind, even though she often disliked using them. Ramook's irresolute face, Ghorok's and Tugugak's perplexity, inspired her. She came close to Agaguk and took his arm. Her fingers dug into it.

"We knew an Agaguk," she said calmly to Scott.

"We knew one," repeated Agaguk after her.

Even his voice was changed, muffled. His words were hardly articulate through his mutilated flesh.

Scott hesitated. What was going on? Surely nothing that he had foreseen. And Ramook's attitude was no help to him. The old chief stared at the man before him. He seemed to be examining him attentively, looking for something in his face, in his movements.

"Where is the Agaguk you knew?" asked Scott.

Iriook shrugged her shoulders. "I don't know." And, turning toward her husband, she added, "You, do you know?"

It was Agaguk's turn to make a gesture of complete indifference. "No."

The policemen whom Scott had sent with wave of the hand to search the hut were returning, carrying three guns. Scott took them and held one out to Ramook who looked it over carefully. He hesitated a moment as if he were thinking it over. Then he handed it back, shaking his head.

"No, it is not the gun."

Scott handed him the other, and then the third. "And this?"

But Ramook did not even examine them. The last one shown him was almost new, of bigger caliber and modern manufacture.

"No."

The old chief was in a panic. Not one of the rifles was his. He looked about him as if he were searching for something.

"Well!" said Scott.

"My rifle—where is it?"

"It's not one of those?"

Ramook gestured no. "Your men didn't search the hut," he said angrily.

But he felt that it was useless. Ghorok had not deceived him. Iriook had not wanted to keep the gift, or maybe it was Agaguk who had refused it. In one way or another, the result was the same, since Scott was coming to him with different weapons.

"Your men have not searched the hut properly," he repeated. "My gun isn't there!"

"Your gun?"

"I mean the one I sent to Agaguk."

Scott was running out of patience. He asked the policemen, "You looked everywhere?"

The question was futile. The men were experts in their trade.

And the tundra offered very few hiding-places outside the hut. A man was already going through the scanty bushes by the river.

"Nothing here," he called.

There was still identification to determine. Scott went up to Agaguk and looked at him very carefully. "These are quite recent wounds," he said.

The Eskimo did not flinch. Iriook too was very calm. What the policeman said was not dangerous now that she had heard Ramook speak of "his" gun as the one he had sent to Agaguk. She knew his cruelty, however, and the episode of the rifle proved to her that he had fabricated everything, probably in concert with Ghorok. What would he try now?

Scott decided suddenly that he was losing too much time. He might as well throw in his hand. He turned to Agaguk.

"Ramook here says he is Agaguk's father. He has brought us to your hut. He claims that Agaguk killed the two white men. He is corroborated by Ghorok and the other man, Tugugak. I want to know where Agaguk is."

Then turning to Ramook, he demanded, "Can you identify this man? Is he Agaguk?"

The chief of the tribe had withdrawn a little to one side and was talking in a low voice with Ghorok and Tugugak. Did all three of them see a way to send Scott and his men away empty-handed, without harmful consequences for the people of the tribe or for Agaguk?

The man certainly had no intention of sacrificing his own skin for his son, and he would not hesitate to throw on him the responsibility for both crimes. But if everything could be arranged otherwise? The incriminating weapon was no longer there. More, the positive identification of Agaguk had become impossible, at least to the satisfaction of the white man's law. Ramook was practically sure that the Eskimo before him was his son, but what now since no one, not even Ghorok, would have been able to swear to it?

He turned toward Scott, who asked again, "Well, is this man Agaguk?"

"Agaguk no longer exists," said Iriook in a quiet voice. "I don't know what has become of him, but I know that he no longer exists. He has left his village, and that is enough so that he has ceased to exist. Can you understand a thing like that, you people?"

She stared at Scott, calmly but defiantly.

From the moment that Scott had seen the man's mutilated face, his calm assurance, the way the Eskimo stood up to him, he realized that he would have no easy time. And this woman? She too was calm and capable. She defied him, but in a way not altogether displeasing to the policeman.

Scott was surprised, nevertheless, that she could express herself so, talk loud, as the Eskimos say, without being told by her husband to keep silent. Such conduct is not usual among the Eskimos. The woman has no right to palaver, still less to speak instead of her husband. Yet this one did it. Neither her husband nor Ramook protested.

"I want you to know this," Scott said to the woman. "Agaguk went to the village, many months ago. He intended to exchange his furs with a white trader. The man tried to cheat Agaguk. Then he killed him. The Montagnais Indian who was with the trader denounced Agaguk."

"You believe a Montagnais?" said Iriook, spitting on the ground.

"I believe nothing and nobody," retorted Scott. "I am making an inquiry. Listen to the rest. That night Agaguk set fire to Brown, the white trader, and the man is dead. Later a policeman by the name of Henderson went to that same village, and Agaguk killed him too."

Turning brusquely to Ramook, he asked him peremptorily, "Is this man Agaguk?"

Ramook raised his eyes to his son. "Are you Agaguk?" he asked.

Scott threw up his hands. "Then you don't know?" he exclaimed.

"I don't know."

Scott repeated the question to Ghorok, and then to Tugugak. He got the same answer.

"So," concluded the policeman, "you can't identify the man before us?"

"It seems to me," said Ramook hesitantly, "that my son

Agaguk was taller, bigger . . . no, I'm almost sure this man is not my son."

Scott turned to Iriook. "One last time, you," he said. "Are you going to tell me where Agaguk is?"

She tightened her lips and slowly shook her head.

"You admitted just now," went on the policeman, "that you knew Agaguk, but you did not know where he was. Is it possible?"

"Yes."

"If you know him, you would know how to find him?"

"You think so?"

"I'm asking you."

"I don't know. I told you, Agaguk left his village. He ceased to be Agaguk. He is no longer the son of the tribe, no longer Ramook's son. He no longer exists."

Something told Scott, in spite of the doubt they had planted in his mind, that the mutilated man was indeed the one he was looking for. But if the Eskimo's disfigurement was the result of a recent accident, as he had reason to suppose, the identification became difficult. No one in the village had warned him. Of course that was why the woman had spoken with such assurance.

The palaver could have gone on for hours. The tone the woman used and the stubborn look on the faces of Ramook and his companions were clear signs of that. Scott was used to such turns in these discussions; he knew now that all conversation was futile. Each one of the participants had chosen the response that seemed best to him, and would not give in. The trip was a failure.

The gun that Ramook had talked about could not be found, and no one could or would identify the Eskimo with the mutilated face. There was nothing more to be done in this place. Vanquished for the moment, Scott waved his arm. "Come on," he said. "Let's go back."

A few moments later the airplane took off, carrying the policemen and the Eskimos toward the village of huts. Agaguk and Iriook remained alone on the tundra, as was their destiny. They stood side by side, the woman it seemed taller than the man, stronger, filled with a silent triumph.

CHAPTER 15/A'NGNAMARIK
The Woman

Later she finished preparing the meal and called Agaguk, but he did not answer. She found him seated by the river, looking gloomy.

"Aren't you coming to eat?"

He said nothing, still staring at the southern horizon.

"They've gone," she said. "They won't come back."

Silence. She guessed what her husband was thinking.

"I talked," she said gently, "louder than I should have, and too often perhaps. It was necessary."

He was suffering in his pride as a man, she knew that well. But had she not leaped into the breach simply out of the wish to save him? It was his life that she was protecting, and her own at the same time, what she possessed here that was so precious to her.

"Our people say," she went on, "that a woman has no right to think, or to speak. Possibly I am not like the others. I have some things to say, and if I think, it's because I can't prevent myself."

And she added quietly, "I didn't lie."

He turned his head toward her, his eyes impassive.

"I didn't lie," repeated Iriook. "I loved Agaguk well when he lived in the village. He went away and took me with him. Since that time, he has changed. He has made Tayaout. But it is not only that. He has changed. I cannot say how, nor in just what fashion. You see, in former days Agaguk would not have permitted me to speak to him as I speak to you today. I think he would have beaten me. . . ."

She was squatting down near her husband, tracing signs in the dry moss with her finger.

"Those people came here, looking for Agaguk. It was the

172

other Agaguk they wanted, the one who lived in the village. He no longer exists, that other Agaguk. You, you bear his name, but you could bear another and it would be all right, for you are no longer the same."

Agaguk stared at her with an uneasy look in his eyes.

"The man I love," said Iriook suddenly, "is the Agaguk of today, whom one could call something else. They would have taken you away, you know. To the white man's country. They would have put you in prison, and after a while they would have hanged you. I did not want them to take you away, even if you killed two white men."

"I did not kill Henderson, the policeman."

"But you killed the other, the one they call Brown?"

Agaguk lowered his head.

"You killed Brown?" she insisted.

Agaguk took a long moment before admitting it. She waited, patient, uneasy too.

"Yes," he said.

They looked at the water in the river. It was a means of escape, a proceeding that suddenly appeared necessary to them. They needed silence, time to consider and reflect. Agaguk had confessed his crime. He was astonished at it himself. He was astonished too to feel a sort of remorse, an emotion that he had never experienced before. But he found no word to communicate to Iriook what was troubling him. For her part, the woman realized that it was better to wait without saying anything more and to change the subject.

"Where does this river come from," she said at last. "And where does it go?"

He pointed toward the east and traced its course to the western horizon past the place where they sat. "It comes from where the sun rises," he answered, "and goes that way, where it disappears."

"Who told you?"

"I have followed its course far enough to know where it comes from and where it throws itself into another stream."

It was a brook rather than a river, and it was also sometimes a torrent, when stones from its bed obstructed its course. There were stones not only in the bed of the stream, but the bank was made of them, and they were imbedded in the moss for a hundred feet each side, all along the river from source to mouth. The stones were strangely green and streaked. Some old men in Agaguk's tribe and elsewhere boasted that with this stone they could cure many ills. Formerly the sorcerers used to carve it and made strange amulets with evil powers. When the sorcerers grew scarce, from one tribe to another, the young men busied themselves through the idle winter days in cutting curious figures in the stone, or sometimes useful objects engraved and finely worked—harpoon points, dishes, igloo lamps, tools, little carvings, which rapidly became as widely spread as those of ivory or bone or horn, they were in such great variety.

Later on some more inventive Eskimos, with surer talent, sculptured forms which were of no use in the daily life, but which pictured the Eskimo's life, his ways of living, his hunts. Agaguk had seen these figures, made of the same green stone of the brook, patiently carved, polished and repolished. Some white men in the town grabbed these statuettes and paid good money to have them. In the tribes they laughed that people should want to own such useless objects. They said of each of their sculptors that he could do nothing "against his thoughts, *isumane ayorlugo.*"

Seated with Iriook that day, trying to put out of his mind the drama that had just unrolled, Agaguk dreamed that some day he might bring some stones into the igloo and busy himself working on them during the great blizzards. He was delighted with this dream, which filled his mind and distracted him from his remorse and from what had happened a few hours ago. He could escape into this project, think it over and let it ripen. Was he not choosing with his eye exactly the rock he would carry inside, and what he would carve from it?

He would make Tayaout in that stone. He would sculpture his face, his body. He would make him naked, with his hard muscles, his body leaning forward, his hands out to grab something. Already in his head the work was taking shape. Later, when Tayaout should be a man, an image of the child he had been would remain.

So he day-dreamed, losing the consciousness that Iriook was beside him, not even knowing that she also had sought escape, letting her mind wander, staring at the moving pattern of the waves, where the eddies made a sort of eternally changing lace around the stones that emerged as obstacles.

They stayed unmoving and silent for an hour. Tayaout was playing on the tundra, running after insects more agile than he. It was an instant of profound peace in their life together, almost attaining serenity. Agaguk was formulating more and more clearly his dream of some day creating an image of Tayaout, an image that would be imperishable, that would transmit to future generations the emotion that he and Iriook felt in possessing this child. Iriook, in a less precise fashion perhaps, but quite as powerfully in her own heart, could dream of the future. Nothing would be the same any more, she knew. Nothing of their former life remained. In their solitude, separated from the tribal life, they became capable of forgetting the old customs, sometimes of fighting against them. A logical power in Iriook, a reasoning ability that few women of her race possessed, made her from now on hope a great deal for the years to come. She had observed Agaguk, she had seen him free himself little by little from the influence of the tribe. Having fled, he had not been content merely to put himself at a distance, but had gradually thrown off the hold his people had on him. He was alone here, and he was glad of it; Iriook knew that.

She knew besides—and this certainly was the most important thing—if Agaguk had killed a man, he would probably never be capable of doing it again. As an Eskimo, he possessed his own morality, at the opposite extreme from the principles the white men considered normal; killing for him could only be a logical act, a gesture whose consequence must be expected. No one in the igloos, no one in the tribes, would hold it against him. And yet Iriook found hateful this acceptance of murder as a normal gesture. She had never approved of it. In such matters was she different from her contemporaries? Had some human evolution shown up in her? She could not have said, she did not even look for an explanation. Her revulsion was a living thing which she approved, but it did not occur to her to be surprised that she felt this way.

She had divined a hesitation in Agaguk, an embarrassment when it came to admitting his crime. Did he also feel remorse now?

The dream that she was fabricating, seated beside him, gazing at the flow of the river, was the dream of a new life, of their solitary days, their personal undertakings, never shared. It was a great deal, but there might be more. There might be the precise confirmation that Agaguk would never kill again, that he would never be taken away by the white men—his life saved once, and peace for all the years to come!

Her voice startled Agaguk. "I want to know—" she said.

He looked at her serenely, a half-smile on his mouth. He was rousing himself from his beautiful dream; he did not want to break away from it. Already it seemed to him that he held in his patient hands the image of Tayaout that he knew how to create, and which would be like his first work, his conception of the infant in the woman's womb, his work, his own creation.

"I want to know," Iriook repeated. "You killed Brown. If he were still before you today, or if there was another like him who tried to cheat you, what would you do?"

Agaguk shrugged a shoulder. Iriook's question was difficult for him. To live, to hunt, to combat the tundra every day, these were the extent of all his knowledge. But to reason so, not only to foresee events, but to decide a lifetime ahead what one would do, was much to ask of him.

He would have sincerely liked to answer her. He felt the need to reassure her, above all. Certainly, how could he say that he would not kill, when—in reviving the scene with Brown and his rage afterward, his overwhelming thirst for vengeance—he was not even sure he could control his action?

Iriook had put her hand on her husband's arm; she was looking at him impatiently, unhappily.

"Would you do it? That's what I want to know, more than anything. I know that I won't be contented until I hear you say it."

Suddenly Agaguk knew he could answer. There was the peace of the tundra all around them, the cloudless sky, the river flowing at their feet. And there was Tayaout playing near-by, almost naked in the heat of the day, rolling in the moss, uttering once in a while some cry of mysterious joy, the only voice in all that vastness.

Agaguk understood that this was his life, that to turn away

from peace and serenity would constitute a disaster. He could not have put it into words, but he had the consciousness of decisions that must be taken. He felt the peace about him, and he valued it at its full worth. He might lose everything; why take the risk?

"I would not kill again," he said firmly.

Wisely Iriook decided not to ask anything more. She decided also that any tender gesture would be superfluous, and rejoicing embarrassing to Agaguk. She stood up.

"Come," she said. "Come eat. I'm hungry, and you too are hungry."

CHAPTER 16/SA'LAUYOK
Outplayed

On the way back, in the plane that took them to the village, Ramook had thought things over. He had hoped to be able to sit near Ghorok and talk over with him privately what had happened. He wanted above all to learn from the sorcerer why the gun was not found at the place they had agreed upon, and at the right moment. But Scott had installed the chief of the village beside him and the sorcerer Ghorok at the back of the plane with the other policemen.

What bothered Agaguk's father more than anything was the revenge that his son might think up after that visit. Scott, the policeman, had been only too clear. He had declared to Agaguk that the information against him had come from Ramook. Agaguk had not missed the episode of the rifle either. Would this and that not incite him to some vengeance, either against the village or against his father?

If he had to count on some possible vindictive act, was it not best to be done with it, to persuade Scott that the mutilated man was indeed Agaguk? For Ramook did not doubt it. He had never doubted it. If he had hesitated, if he had not dared identify Agaguk, it was because he knew the white man's law. He knew that, in their towns, when Agaguk and his accusers should be brought before the Great Chiefs, they would require a perfect identification, but he knew also that it would be formally impossible in view of the recent mutilation. All this was crowded in Ramook's head. The white men's requirements, but even more Agaguk's anger when he pictured himself being dragged to the towns of the south like a captive beast. He had let go what was worth the most, inasmuch as he had seen there a chance of pulling out of the affair without putting anything at stake, either himself or anyone of the tribe, or even his son.

178

But all that would probably not prevent Agaguk from being angry, and who could tell where such feelings might lead him? An instant ago, his decision had appeared the most logical, but he was now less sure of it. He changed suddenly, resolutely, and while the plane was still aloft he declared all at once to Scott, "Now I'm sure. I remember the parka, the mukluks. The knife in the pant leg is a present that I had made him."

"What are you talking about?"

"Of Agaguk, back there. It was he, now I'm sure of it."

"But back there you weren't."

"No, I know. I think it was the surprise—"

"You had told me that he was handsome."

"The wounds on his face are recent."

"But you don't know if it's he."

"It is."

"But as for me, now," said the policeman, "I can't be sure. The people of your village, your witch-doctor even, cannot swear to it."

Scott did not dare confess to Ramook that he himself was almost certain of having found Agaguk. But he scented some kind of trickery, he perceived Ramook's devious mind, his total absence of morality. Is a man going to inform against his son unless he is the worst kind of criminal possible? Yet it was a deduction he could not avoid.

Scott foresaw also the difficulties of a positive identification. If Agaguk was brought to trial, they would assign him a lawyer to defend him. That lawyer would have a fine time getting the accusation dismissed. So Agaguk's arrest seemed useless and perhaps unjust. Scott had made up his mind quickly, on seeing the mutilated man whom no one dared recognize. Either Ramook or Ghorok or the others had taken part in the crimes. It was even possible that Agaguk had nothing to do with them. The simplest way was to keep on with his inquiry in the village. If it was impossible to reach any satisfactory conclusion, then the only thing to do was to go back to town and file away the whole business.

Scott admitted that Henderson's blood cried out for vengeance, and it was wrong that some Eskimos would remain unpunished for that crime. Wrong, at least, for the future good administration of the territories. But it was still necessary to build a formal proof. This was neither easy nor probable. Besides, Agaguk, or whoever was recognized as the suspect, would be judged according to English law. Perhaps by some stratagem, Scott could accomplish something, but he did not count much on it.

"If you had truly recognized Agaguk when we were there, I might perhaps have been inclined to believe you," he said to Ramook. "But your identification comes too late. And more, I don't wholly believe your story."

Ramook's heart sank. The affair was taking a turn he had not expected. It wasn't as easy to fool them as he thought. He tried despairingly to plan for possible delays, counting especially on Ghorok.

"In the village," he said, "my witch-doctor Ghorok will hold some ceremonies. The Spirits themselves will give you proof that Agaguk is guilty and that he is the wounded man you saw."

Scott's voice remained cold and impersonal. "My own sorcerers are more powerful than your Ghorok. I shall address myself to them to find out the truth."

The airplane described a long circle, losing altitude for the landing. The village was there, apparently calm, a circle of huts about an open space. The dogs were frightened by the plane, by the throbbing of the engines. They were running in all directions on the tundra. Then the pilot cut off the gas and the plane glided rapidly toward the ground.

Ramook was thinking about the white men's sorcerers, more powerful than any he knew, endowed with abilities like no other's. Not that Ramook had any very lively faith in witchcraft, for he had figured out Ghorok's tricks long ago. But he admitted that the white man's artifices by far surpassed the Eskimo's, and that often they seemed supernatural to him. In any case, they were very dangerous.

The village people did not rush forward to meet the airplane. Rather, they stayed near their huts or within them, sullen, quiet, worried. None of them knew, however, that the worst of the trouble was still to come, and that it was now Ramook whose head was at stake. Only Scott could have told them. Ramook and, perhaps, Ghorok?

Scott did not lose a moment. A few hours of daylight remained before nightfall, and he called a palaver.

"I want all the tribe assembled here, before me."

In a few moments the huts were empty and the entire village was grouped in front of the policeman and his men.

"I have not come here for nothing," said Scott. "And I have no intention of passing six months in the village. You have led me up a false trail, this of Agaguk's."

A voice was raised, protesting, but Scott pretended not to hear. He turned to Ramook.

"I have given each one of you ten chances to bring me the real culprit. It was for you to take advantage of that. A crime confessed is often more lightly punished. But you keep me here, you send me off on a wild goose chase, you pile up the expense for the Great White Chiefs to learn who killed Brown and Henderson. I would have preferred a confession, but since you persist in lying to me—"

"Nobody here is lying to you," yelled Ramook.

"And nobody here is telling me the truth," retorted Scott calmly. "That puts me in a disagreeable situation. So much the worse. Since you wish it so, my sorcerers know what they have to do."

He was silent, but no one spoke up. A great silence fell on the Eskimos. Ramook, death in his heart, wondered what Scott was getting at.

"I wish nonetheless to give you one last chance."

He took Ramook by the arm and brought him close. "I want to hear what you can tell me about how Brown and Henderson died," he said. "I want you to say before these people."

Fifty dark faces with impassive eyes, their mongol features accentuated in the sunlight, their brown skins thickly coated with sweat. A horribly ugly old woman, with teeth worn to the gums, spat on the ground towards Ramook. When Ramook shouted some threat at her, she began to moan with fear and fled to her hut.

A young hunter guffawed, but his voice was alone for a moment, hanging above them all. Nobody laughed with him, and he retreated in turn and went to station himself behind the crowd. Only Ramook showed a self-possession that Scott knew was put on, for he still held the Eskimo by the arm and felt him tremble. "Speak," he said. "We are listening."

The chief suddenly cried out, "It's a trap," he said, "don't you see it's a trap?"

But no voice was raised in his behalf. He scowled, and with a rough movement he pulled away from Scott's grasp.

"Speak!"

"It's Agaguk," shouted Ramook. "It's he. He came here and killed Brown. Then he killed Henderson. Anybody in the village will tell you the same thing."

"Who saw him? You? The others?"

Ramook sought some support, looking from one to another. Nothing. Were they going to let him fight all alone?

"I didn't see him, but I know."

"Where is Brown's body?"

"It was burned in the hut, as I told you. As the Indian told you too."

"Nothing left of it?"

"Nothing."

"And Henderson's body?"

"I don't know."

The crowd wavered. A woman on the edge groaned, and Scott whirled around, but he could not make out where the sound came from.

"I don't know," said Ramook. "How can I know? I wasn't there. None of us was there."

"You said he was buried on the tundra."

"I said so without knowing. I think that's how it was. Only Agaguk could tell you."

"Always Agaguk. And yet you haven't even been able to deliver Agaguk to me."

"He's that Eskimo over there, with the face eaten away. I tell you and you don't want to believe me. He has Agaguk's parka, he has his mukluks, I know them . . . he has Agaguk's knife. What more do you want?"

"Some proof, that's all. Henderson's body, more than anything. I know that when I find it, I will know all the rest. And I shall find it."

He saw the effect of that remark. What, he would find the body? Ramook's thoughts were easy to follow. Had not he, the policeman, talked of sorcerers from whom he would demand the culprit's name? These men in different clothing, and the boxes which had come in the Big Bird, the mysterious objects they brought with them—the powerful magic of the white men against which neither Ghorok nor Ramook could do much? And this tribe of cowards, this group of dummies, from which not one voice of support came? Who did not take sides with their chief? Did they forget then that they were bound to that?

"Listen to me," Ramook cried to his people. "I will order Ghorok to send his worst witchcraft on you. Who is your chief?"

People here and there were hesitating, it was plain. There were murmurs, some of the men were talking in low voices. One woman chose to go away, but Scott called her back peremptorily. "You there, get back here."

The woman obeyed, pitifully.

Ramook could no longer contain his rage. He demanded only one thing, that the tribe hold together as a solid block, a block including him. He forced himself to believe, he persuaded himself, that if he had killed Henderson, it was to protect them all, for Henderson had threatened to come back with other policemen. At that moment he was thinking not only of Brown's death but of all the other crimes that had remained unpunished, murders, robberies, simple thefts, of which the whole tribe had been guilty. Henderson had to die! Ramook had killed the constable for the sake of all these people before him. And not a single one now came to his defence, not a single one could find anything to say, a word, a phrase, a false trail on which to send Scott and his men anew. For now he had to answer for more than Henderson's death, for Ayallik's.

The situation was getting worse, and Ramook knew it well. The way in which Scott spoke, the tone of his voice, his look, terrorized the old chief. He was the one the constable was after. He was the one he wanted to hang at the end of a rope. And no Eskimo raised his voice to come to his aid. If Scott wished it, if his sorcerers went to work, what would happen? Desperate, Ramook screamed at the tribe, "But say something. Can't you save me?"

Slowly Scott turned toward him. He was smiling. Ramook's tone had been eloquent, his cry a sort of revelation. The man felt trapped. Scott was rejoicing in his own mind. Once more, by using the most elementary psychology, he was going to succeed, to sow panic in the old chief, to drive him to the wall. Already the man was going to pieces under his eyes.

"I think," said Scott in a joking tone, "that we are wasting our time. I did not want to delay my departure. But since nobody confesses, I shall stay here. My sorcerers will go to work. They will know how to find what is left of Brown's body."

"Nothing is left," said Ramook bitterly. "Agaguk burned it all up. Nothing is left."

"There's always something left of a corpse," said Scott calmly. "Even if it is invisible to you, my sorcerers will perceive it. The constables are going to search all the huts, search the whole village, the moss in this place and the other places where the village was before. They will search everywhere, and what they find they will bring to my sorcerers. After that, it will be easy."

Ramook was trembling, but he fought back his fear. He clenched his hands tight against his body and gritted his teeth. He knew the wisdom of the white men, he knew its efficiency. What was Scott saying there? That he would have his constables search? Here and at the former village locations? Well, Brown's remains would be found, but that did not bother Ramook. In fact, on this his conscience was easy. But Ayallik's body? It had been buried not very far away. As for Henderson's remains, they would give more trouble for they had been carried a long way from the village and buried deep beneath the moss; it had taken two hours of hard labour the day of the crime to dig a ditch which neither men nor wolves could penetrate. As much as he thought about it, Ramook felt reassured about Henderson. Neither Scott nor the sorcerers with him would ever find him. Were they going to search the vastness of the tundra? A winter had gone by. That hardened the moss, and pressed it down. What trace would remain of a ditch dug the year before? Neither Ghorok himself, nor Ramook, could probably find the place. How then would the policemen?

First they went through the huts, as Scott had said, in a patient and methodical search. Every suspicious find was brought to Scott and sometimes to his two sorcerers. The possible importance of the object to the inquiry was estimated. Finally it was set to one side. They did this with the empty jugs that had held liquor and with other objects which seemed to be surplus, knives and tools and mukluks. The Eskimo in general lives frugally, at least as regards material possessions. If one finds more knives in an Eskimo's hut than he needs, or more mukluks or tools, one can reasonably suppose they have been stolen somewhere. But if they used to belong to some victim? That does not amount to a proof; unless each object can be categorically identified as the property of a dead man. That is too rare a case for it really to count in an inquiry. Ramook knew it, even when he had tried to prove Agaguk's identity by those means, but he could not now help being distressed by the methodical investigation that went on from hut to hut.

The guns were all confiscated, each labelled with a ticket on which was written the owner's name. A hundred weapons were carried to the airplane, to the sorcerers who piled them there. Ramook knew that this possible examination of the arms could be the most dangerous. But to lay hands on the weapon that had killed Henderson, they would first have to find the body. Ramook felt tranquil about this; never would they find Henderson's body. As for the gun, it was Agaguk's, and he had it now. To be sure, it had not been found at his place, but Ramook had no reason to doubt Ghorok, and it was very likely that Agaguk suspecting something, had got rid of it. That was what he would have done himself. The policeman then could not find out anything from the weapons they carried into the Big Bird. In the town, Ramook had learned that the white sorcerers could prove from what rifle a bullet had been fired, with the aid of their mysterious apparatus. From this to identifying the guilty was only one step. There must also be a corpse, and only by this possibility could Scott come out ahead. On this account Ramook had nothing to worry about. Ah! He was smarter than the policemen, he knew it well, and he had no more need to tremble.

A wide smile appeared on his face, and he stuck his hands in his pockets, casting a defiant look at Scott.

But at that very instant, Ramook saw a policeman come out of his hut, and what he bore in his hands, Ramook could identify all too well. It was precisely the rifle that had shot Henderson. It was precisely the weapon that he had sent Ghorok to carry to Agaguk. Panic seized him. He dashed toward the policeman, running and yelling. "What's that gun? It isn't mine."

He might better have kept quiet. His hysteria could have only one result, to draw Scott's attention, as it did not fail to do.

"Give me that gun," said Scott to his subordinate. "Where did you find it?"

"In the chief's hut, hidden in the moss."

"Hidden?"

"Yes, there were two others there, but this one was hidden, and not the others."

Scott who had begun to despair, now had an air of great relief. The search of the other huts had not given much. Scott did not know too well what to expect, but he had a vague hope of finding some clue, of turning up some precious indication. And now here at the last moment, when his men were going through Ramook's hut, the last one remaining to be inspected, this gun appeared, a find that seemed to upset Ramook completely. At that moment Scott decided to gamble everything on one throw.

"I think," he said, "that we are not going back empty-handed."

He turned on his heel and went over to the airplane. Ramook saw that he made the white sorcerers come out. He held a long discussion with them, out of earshot of the tribe. They all punctuated the talk with wide affirmative gestures, seeming not only confident but amused.

Ramook watched the scene without stirring. He felt a knot form in him, twisting his heart and his stomach. These white men were .the devil. Where did that gun come from? How could it be there? Was it not some trick of Scott's? With no possible error, Ramook recognized the weapon. It was the one that had killed Henderson, the one that he had tried to palm off on Agaguk. He looked around for Ghorok, but before he could find him, Scott returned and spoke to the tribe.

"My sorcerers are going to work," he said in a firm voice. "They are going to get into the airplane and fly over all the tundra, up to two hours march from here and farther if they have to. Then they will begin again tomorrow and every day after. They are going to make their magic boxes talk. If there is a body buried out there, the boxes will tell."

Ramook tried to snigger, but it was a sad sound, hardly a grating chuckle.

"Don't laugh," Scott said to him. "You know the power of our magic. You have been to the town. You have seen the wagons that move by themselves, without dogs to pull them, the hundreds of big birds that fly in the air, and so many other things. We are very powerful magicians. It is easy for us to know if a man has been buried in the tundra."

Ghorok sniggered too, but with no more enthusiasm than Ramook had shown.

"You, Ghorok," cried Ramook, "Confound the white men. Prove to them that you are still a great magician."

The appeal was useless; how could Ghorok confound the white men when he was at the very moment dying of fright?

To Scott, Ramook shouted, defying him, "You come here and you lie. You pretend to fly through the air and to know through your sorcerers that there is a body in the moss. And you think we're going to believe that?"

The sudden firm voice of Ramook brought an access of confidence to the tribe; they laughed. One nudged another with his elbow, they found this warning of the white man very funny. But Scott lifted his hand and imposed silence.

"I cannot reveal to you all the secrets, but I can tell you this. You have seen a corpse before now. You have seen its eyes? The eyes do not die at the same time as the body. They die long afterward. So a body looks at you for months and years afterward. The magic boxes know how to perceive these looks, even if the moss covers them. The Big Bird will fly very low over the tundra, and all at once when one of the boxes perceives Henderson's look, we shall know where his body is."

Encouraged by the laughs of the tribes, still ringing in his ears, Ramook boasted, "You will never find Henderson's body that way. Your boxes will be no good. Henderson was buried with his face to the earth."

Behind Ramook, Ghorok uttered a cry of rage—no words, only a sort of roar. Now all was lost, and the tribe understood it. The smile on Scott's face grew wider, the gesture that sent his men converging on Ramook was eloquent. They had the guilty man, and they would not easily let him go.

A woman, Tugugak's wife, now called out. She was younger than the others, and like Iriook, more advanced, more tender also, and the life of her people sometimes disgusted her. Also, she hated Ramook.

"It's he," she exclaimed. "He killed Henderson. He killed Ayallik too. We're afraid of him."

Scott jumped. Ayallik? Were they going to cram another corpse into his hands? It was surprising that anyone, especially a woman, should so raise a voice among the tribe. But Scott had counted on it. He knew that if he could impair at all Ramook's hold on the tribe, his enemies would not be slow to overcome him. All that he had to do first was make him a suspect, and the rest would follow of itself. It had not failed; the woman's voice was soon seconded, this time by Oonak, one of the old men. He advanced toward Scott.

"We want to live at peace with the white men," he said. "We want to respect their laws. Ramook and the witch-doctor would not let us. I don't know who killed Brown. Some say it was Agaguk. It's possible. But Ramook might have killed Brown and accused Agaguk. He killed Henderson, that's sure. We all saw him. And I saw him kill Ayallik with my own eyes."

"And you didn't try to prevent Henderson's death?"

Oonak shrugged his shoulders. "Ramook was the chief and Ghorok the sorcerer. What could we do?"

Now the tribe was drawing away from Ramook. Only Ghorok stayed by his side.

"And will there be someone among you who will come with us to the town, to witness at Ramook's trial?"

"And Ghorok's," corrected Oonak, "he is Ramook's accomplice. They did it all together."

"And Ghorok," conceded Scott. "To try them and have them punished. Who will come?"

Ten hands went up.

"There's room for only five more in the airplane," said Scott. "You, what's your name?"

"Oonak."

"Then pick four men and come along. You will be in the town only a few days."

"We shall be back before the cold weather?"

"Yes."

Oonak selected four Eskimos whom he led to Scott.

"Good," said the policeman. "Now, let's go."

Visibly relieved, the policemen got ready to depart.

"You see," Scott said to Ramook, loud enough for the tribe to hear. "The magic of my sorcerers is great. They were able to discover the guilty man, even without going anywhere, without using their magic boxes. Would your sorcerers claim the power to do as much?"

But Ramook heard nothing more. He had been outplayed. Scott's stratagem had been greater than his. In the face of the tribe, he had been humiliated, accused; and even his own people rejected him. The game was lost, and he was there, fainting, insensible to everything. What could he say now, and why speak? They would judge him and he would be hanged. His life was over. He offered no resistance, when one of the policemen led him toward the airplane. Nor did Ghorok.

In the history of the tribe, as it would be entrusted to the songs at night, Ramook had ceased to exist, and so had the sorcerer.

The airplane took off as night fell and disappeared in the sky, taking Ramook away forever.

Life began anew. Agaguk could not have said whether Ramook was still at the village or whether the police had taken him away somewhere. The summer was already ending; he had to hunt, to cut up the meat, to smoke it. His work awaited him, constant, every day's burden.

And then there was Tayaout.

But even more for some time past, there was Iriook. It seemed to Agaguk that the relationship between them was no longer the same. Something new had come into their everyday life. Was it a respect for the woman that he had never believed he possessed before? Since the visit of the policemen, he had not possessed her. It was not because of hate or indifference. Rather, it seemed to him difficult to be himself with her. Timidity hindered his gestures, and he felt confused. And, nevertheless, nature rebelled within him. He felt his flesh burn, he would have liked to bite, to scream sometimes. And when this malaise took him at Iriook's side, when he reached out his hand toward her, this same shyness overcame him anew. He saw again the image of Iriook, stronger than any man, standing up to the policemen, speaking up as no woman ought to speak up, but knowing how to find the right words, at the very second when they were necessary. In short, she had saved Agaguk's life, and he could not forget it.

In the end, it was Iriook who made the advances. But not as Agaguk would have expected. With new words and astonishing demands.

"Some day," she said, "I shall have another child."

She had spoken with no previous warning, while for an hour they had been slowly chewing on their evening meal.

"You will sleep with me and you will give me another child."

190

Agaguk did not answer. But he had raised his eyes to hers and stopped chewing.

"It will be a girl," she said. "I know it."

Agaguk remembered what she had said before. He foresaw she was going to talk about it again. Without saying a word, he got up, went out and started down to the river. But Iriook was ahead of him. She barred his way, trembling.

"If it is a girl," she said in one breath, "I shall keep it."

Agaguk was troubled. Why did she talk about such things? Is it permissible for a woman to discuss such matters? Is it not the prerogative and the duty of every Eskimo to decide the fate of the newly born, without the intervention of the wife?

"Say that I shall keep her," moaned Iriook.

Agaguk could not answer. Too many contradictory thoughts weighed on him. It went through his mind that he owed his life to Iriook, and in more than one way. Who had cared for him when he was wounded by the wolf? Who had cured him, if not she? And she had hunted the animals, and butchered them. Thus she had provided for the winter's needs, provided for all of them in the igloo. She had guided his tottering steps, she had done everything, given everything that he might live. And when the policemen had come? Without her, they would have taken him to prison in the town and would probably have hanged him.

But the girl? This girl baby, which some day they might have and which Iriook wanted to keep?

They did not live in a village. They could not count on others to feed them if they lacked pemmican or fish. They were alone here, dependent on their own resources. They were hermits, with all the dangers of the tundra around them. A son goes hunting when he is young, he brings his own subsistence to the home.

A girl?

Indeed if there had been four men to clothe, a girl would have been necessary to help her mother. But they were only two, and there was exactly work for one woman.

Another mouth to feed? What of their survival? Nevertheless, if he was there at all, to whom did he owe it, if not to Iriook?

The woman's cry was passionate, almost strident. Her eyes were desperate.

"I want to keep the girl," she cried.

Agaguk tried a last evasion. "Do you know what will come? If it is a boy, you will have cried for nothing."

But Iriook shook her head and wept. "It will be a girl, I know it. I know it!"

Agaguk stood first on one foot and then on the other. He was raging inside. Ramook had been nearly right. Why let a woman speak so loud?

"Shut up," he yelled.

But Iriook implored him. "I want to keep the girl. I've earned her."

The word was as brutal as a slap. So, from now on she was going to take this tone? What she had done was only done so she might keep the girl she wanted to have? And he would have to be eternally grateful? He went up to her. Suddenly his rage was stronger than any reason. "You talk too loud," he cried.

His fist shot out and landed on Iriook's jaw. Then Agaguk was on her, kicking her and jabbing her with his clenched fist. The blood ran down her face, and still she cried, "I want to keep the girl. I want to keep the girl!"

When Agaguk was too tired to strike any more, he fell on Iriook and possessed her. She took time to welcome him. But soon the longing was stronger than her resentment and she began to moan, but differently from before. Agaguk recognized her pleasure as he plunged into her with powerful strokes. And when they were still, he heard Iriook's voice, raucous, insistent, deepened by pleasure, murmuring in his ear. "Say that I shall keep the girl."

CHAPTER 18/ATSUPLUAYOK
The Wheel

When Oonak returned from the town where Ramook and
Ghorok had been hanged, he took on a new importance in the
village. Perhaps he had been more authoritative than the
others; he had known how to speak at the right moment. How
could these things be explained? They formed a circle around
him, by instinct, without any concerted movement.

"Oonak," said one old man, "Now that Ramook is no more."

He said no more. Other voices blotted out his; there was
the phenomenon of discussions that reached no definite end,
of ideas left half-expressed, until all at once the voices died
away, silence prevailed little by little, and the words of the
old man were gradually realized.

"Oonak," said a young man hesitatingly.

He looked at the others and the others shook their heads,
poked Oonak in the belly with their fingers, laughed, nudged
each other in the ribs with their elbows.

Oonak? One of the young men summed up the general
opinion more soberly than the others, "You could be our chief."

How did they reach that conclusion? By the excellence of
the man, but in the arts that belonged to the tribe. The
standards were sometimes surprising. Oonak was a good
hunter. He was skilful in preparing skins. He had no wife and
said he did not want one. He built the most solid and the
roundest igloo, he hunted seal like a man of the sea country.
He knew how to speak, and he was not afraid of anyone now.
With him no one had any need to fear a betrayal. And since
he was beloved by all?

So is history written.

Dealing with a tribe or an empire, is man ever free from
new beginnings? A Caesar—and for a tribe of the ice country,
Oonak.

"You could be our chief."

He wavers back and forth, reflecting. What would it be like? Oonak thinks that it would be pleasant to come out of his igloo in the morning and give orders. Who would settle things, decide, promulgate decrees? But what made one side of the coin so attractive did not make the other one pleasant enough for the clever Oonak to lose his head over it. What punishment is inflicted on chiefs who err in their judgments, for a day's failures?

The stories peddled from village to village and tribe to tribe made that clear enough. This one's ear had been cut off, that one had been emasculated, another had been exiled, become homeless among his own people and in the biggest country in the world. They spat in the face of another one, and took away his wives. These stories were repeated with immense enjoyment of the proceedings, with pleasure in the adventures. Torture is not outmoded among the Eskimos. They take great delight in it, on occasion.

The case of Ramook alone, for example?

Many of the chiefs whose legends are told on the winter evenings, heroes of the absurd, wear as the jewels in their crowns the cries of suffering and the most frightful mutilations.

With average luck, certainly Oonak could hope to survive. Others were dead with their hands behind their necks and without a sigh, enfeebled by age and voluntarily retired into their last igloo. It was only a pity that it could not be so for all. This was what Oonak was meditating on.

But there was more. Against the joy of being chief must be balanced the burden of the task, burden less cruel than the possible tortures, true, but work for every day. A tribe would depend on him. He would be master, but still this authority had to be exercised with no let-up.

Oonak dearly loved his liberty. He was a bachelor, with no wife, no children, nobody, no obligations. It was thus that he had cast his lot. He made up his mind then to stay this way.

As chief, would he be free? Could he sleep when he liked, hunt when he pleased, travel if he felt like it? What would they say of a chief's undertaking an expedition to the Top of the World? Or to the Great Water? At his own convenience, for as long as he wanted to be away? There would be grumbling in the tribe, they would pass from the enthusiasm of his early days to progressive discontent. No, Oonak did not want to be chief.

He freed himself from the hands pressing upon him, from the congratulations each one was already showering on him.

"No," he said, "no, I do not want to be chief. There are others for that."

But who? The Old One insisted. "Name one," he said. "Point him out with your finger. What other?"

Oonak was uncomfortable. He would have liked to run away, to be very far from there. His discomfort was above all made of impatience. He had refused, he had meant to make it final, the end of these discussions which he did not want to hear.

The Old One opened his toothless mouth and spat out his words: "I tell you, you are the chief. There aren't any others."

But there are some acts which a chief must not commit, some attitudes he may not assume, some urgent solutions that are forbidden to him. Tradition requires that the chief should reign alone, that any democratic concession should be considered a sign of weakness. The only thing for Oonak to do was to take a step forward which would allow him two backward. "I lay down a condition," he said.

He looked at the sun of midday, at the bare plain, and came back to examine his hands. It was necessary that each one hear what he had to say. Point by point, without possible confusion.

"My condition," he said after a while, "is that I should not be alone. I will be chief; there will be a council of Old Ones, a council of men, and the council of women."

"Of women?" It was almost a cry of horror.

"Of women?"

Oonak, more audacious, more advanced, had lived in the white men's country. He had even been to the big cities of which the stories tell. He had ridden in the metal Birds, and down there, they said, he had entered vehicles each one more fantastic than the other, moving by themselves, going here and there. The recent voyage, which he had made in company with Ramook, Ghorok and the policemen, had not been an adventure in itself. All he had learned on these trips his people distrusted. Nothing virulent, nor even very precise, but an uneasiness, a vague resentment, which was manifested most of all on his return some years before. The fact that the predictions at the time, the warning that some of the old men had given, the fears of some in the village that they might have to submit to Oonak's new ideas, had never been realized, and that no one finally had any reason to reproach Oonak, had reassured many. However something of this still lingered in their minds. It was inevitable.

The residue of distrust in the tribe left sufficient enthusiasm so that they desired to make Oonak a chief, but it put them on their guard as soon as he tried to express an idea which was too evidently related to his experience among the white men.

"A council of women?"

It was too much. One spat, another laughed, but in an anxious tone. They cursed, too, among the more virile, those who had women in their igloos.

An elder of the tribe said, "It's a white man's fashion."

He had such a tone of contempt in his voice that Oonak burst out laughing.

"That's right," he said. "A white man's fashion. I learned it down there. Let everybody have his say in the tribe, the women as well as the men."

The theory was unacceptable. Were they now to give a voice to the women? They shook their heads. An elder came up to Oonak, stared him in the face and went away at once, with long strides, and a disgusted air. Oonak did not restrain his delight. He could stay free, no one now would want him as chief. The tribe scattered, each one going off to his own affairs which suddenly became pressing. Oonak returned to the obscurity that suited him, became again a member of the tribe, alone and happy, because it was indeed so that he intended to remain. He was free above all to leave at will, to live his own life, with no burden on his shoulders, without obligations to which he must submit.

Oonak returned to obscurity, and in the chronicles of the tribe he ceased to exist, he became again a single member of an anonymous collectivity.

They still had to find a chief.

They pitched on Tugugak, who refused but for other reasons than Oonak's, secret reasons which he dared not confess. For some time he had been dreaming of starting off for the Top of the World. There was good seal hunting there, and an entirely different life, the permanence of the one igloo in the eternal winter. But he intended to go alone, to abandon his wife and children. Men were always hanging about his hut; his wife would be quickly adopted by one of them. But this was hardly a project to be talked about ahead of time. Nothing must hold him back, and discretion was the price of his liberty.

As chief of the tribe, he would have been tied down by responsibility. The honour would have pleased him, but the fact that it would block his plans made it unacceptable. He gave a cold refusal, without discussion.

They insisted. A dozen men were massed in front of his hut, holding a discussion. Time was pressing. A tribe without a chief is a tribe in decadence. They must have somebody. No one offered himself. Oonak put forward forms that were not to be thought of in 'this primitive government; Tugugak refused even to discuss the matter. They took an hour to accept this second refusal. Then they went to an Old One's hut, a long low hut where they sat in a circle and weighed the pros and cons of the situation. It was becoming serious.

"No one consents?" asked the Old One.

They had all the reasons. They would have liked, one and the other, to propose a candidate, or even to offer themselves, but then what would become of this project, that dream, such an escape now planned for, this voyage, that hunting trip?

A chief is bound to the tribe. He goes where the tribe goes, he does not depart alone. It is a very heavy bond, almost an imprisonment. In the eyes of those they had considered, one must be a fool or crippled or excessively sedentary to accept such a job.

Or like Ramook in his day, ambitious and dishonest and eager to seize the opportunity of this honour for tyranny and personal riches. Had not Ramook quit hunting the day someone proposed him as chief? He required a tribute from all of them which kept his provision reserve well furnished. He did not pardon any who were stingy, or even the unlucky ones who could not supply the required part from their hunting trips. Ramook, taken prisoner by the constables, had departed a rich man, according to the standards of the tribe. They had quickly sent the Montagnais woman back to her own country and pillaged the storeroom of the hut. To the astonishment of each one, the bundles of skins alone were worth their weight in gold.

Present among them, Ramook had been respected, or at least obeyed, which often amounts to the same thing. They had been very careful not to break down the authority that had been confided to him, so strong is the tradition that rules the election of Eskimo chiefs. Now that he was gone, no one would have consented to elect a replacement so greedy and dishonest. This did not alter their way of looking at things; Eskimos have little respect for laws and morality; the well-being of the community proceeds according to very different laws. In virtue of these laws they were going to choose a chief. Above all, they were concerned not to repeat the adventure of Ramook.

To decapitate a tribe by removing its chief unsettles its ways of living, bores all the men by imposing long palavers on them, provoking uneasiness among them, troubles which they would like to be spared. Thus they had not gone hunting for several days. This might damage their life for months to come, since the stores they were using up were not being replaced as they ought to have been. But Oonak did not want the post and Tugugak refused. To whom should they turn?

In the stinking hut, terribly hot and smoky, the men seemed discouraged. For a moment no one spoke. What was there to say? Who was there to name? Did no one want this post?

"I know," said the Old One, "I know who!"

Ten heads turned toward him in a hurry, looking for relief to their pain, in curiosity as to what they would hear.

"He is," said the man sententiously, "a son of the tribe. He would be a good chief."

"Who?" one of the men finally ventured.

The Old One shook his head. "It's a question," he said, "if he will take it. I was thinking of Agaguk."

"Son of Ramook," said one of the men, his voice hardly a murmur.

"Son of Ramook," agreed the Old One, "that means nothing, really. He is not like him, and you know it."

He had one final argument, the most important. "Perhaps he killed Brown," he said. "He was not captured. That rid us of Ramook."

Avenging assassin, Agaguk had not been captured! It was an exploit to tell of on winter nights. He had the qualities of a chief, cleverness, intelligence, authority, ability, youth, strength. They approved now; in the hearts of the assemblage there began to rise some enthusiasm.

"Who will go to his home?" asked the Old One. "Me, I cannot."

Three men stood up, Alignak, Hayaluk and Nattit. "We will go," said Nattit. "We will leave tomorrow."

There was nothing to do now but wait.

CHAPTER 19/SIVUDLIPA
The Hero

Nattit led the way, Alignak and Hayuluk followed. The summer was ending, and yet the heat lay heavy on the tundra. There was no shelter, no relief from the hot damp mass of air that rested on the infinite plain. To travel there at all was exhausting, to walk as the Eskimo walk, with firm rapid steps, could fell a man in a few hours, even an Eskimo with his extraordinary endurance. In the memory of man, they had not known such hot and heavy weather. Their faces were dripping with sweat when they reached Agaguk's hut. Their parkas, unfastened at the neck, showed their naked chests, trickling with sweat too.

Agaguk did not bother with much ceremony in receiving them. He felt a vague embarrassment at this contact with his own people. By preference, solitude suited him best. Outside the most urgent needs, it was as well to stay away from a place of which he had no pleasant memories and for which he felt no homesickness.

But since three of the tribe had come, Agaguk was not going to drive them away. He would listen to them. That was more than he would have considered doing, if he had been warned of this visit. Then, taken unawares, practically cornered, he made up his mind to be neither hostile nor cordial.

No invitation was given, no offer of anything, no welcome. They did not enter the hut, the pemmican remained hung high, and Agaguk found sufficient a brief nod to them. They were all full of their mission, anxious to make it known, and they did not seem to notice Agaguk's coldness. Nor his disfigurement, of which they had been warned.

"We come in the name of the tribe," said Nattit.

Agaguk bent his head a little. Alignak dropped on the ground, his legs crossed.

"The way is long," he said.

He snatched the parka off his shoulders, and exposed his body to the breeze that ran over the surface of the moss. Hayaluk did the same. Nattit remained standing, as did Agaguk.

"Ramook was taken to the town," went on Nattit. "Oonak came back and told us that the white men had hanged him, and Ghorok too."

"Oonak said so?" insisted Agaguk.

"Yes."

In these matters, it is better to have the news from an Eskimo rather than a white man. He will tell the truth without altering it, finding nothing more to say when it comes to the white man's oppression, which appears in itself sordid enough. A white man will moralize. He will alarm people, he will call up the evil spirits. He will sometimes tell what is not true. Kakkrik, an Eskimo from a tribe on Baffin Land, had been taken to the town for having killed his two brothers. A white man peddled the story in his village, saying that Kakkrik had been put to death by the white men. Ten years later, Kakkrik came back—unfortunately, since in his absence his wife had taken three husbands. The first was dead, and she was living with the other two. She had ten children, of whom six were living. Plus Kakkrik's six, this created difficulty. Kakkrik killed one of the two husbands and three of the children. He stopped his massacre only when someone told him that the white man had lied; the woman, believing herself free, had naturally taken other men. They impressed on Kakkrik that she had to take three men to replace him, proof to all of his great virility. This flattered Kakkrik, and after that he lived with the remaining husband and his wife. This husband had to hunt for two and submit to Kakkrik; he could receive a visit from his wife only once a week, well supervised by Kakkrik to make sure that the man did not show himself too enthusiastic. As the story is told on the winter evenings, all this could have been avoided, and Kakkrik would have had only one replacement to kill on his return, if the white man had not lied.

The news about Ramook had come from an Eskimo. It was a guarantee of its truth; past experience proved it.

"They put him to death?" asked Agaguk, but without curiosity.

"Yes."

He searched his mind, and found no emotion. Ramook was dead, it was all over, Agaguk himself felt nothing. He even experienced a certain relief, and did not hide it from himself.

"That's how I guessed it would be," he said.

Alignak balanced his head from right to left, whining softly, "Aye-aye."

Agaguk glanced at him curiously.

"The tribe is desolate," said Alignak. "Our chief is dead."

The voice was hypocritical; Agaguk did not believe a word of such sentiments. Desolate, the tribe, that Ramook was dead? Worried perhaps, possibly distracted, but desolate? Words say what they wish to say; they are used as needed, nothing more. But then they can be employed to falsify ideas. Like Alignak's words. What was he getting at?

"The tribe," Hayaluk said, "needs a chief."

Silent, Agaguk waited. Nattit touched his arm.

"The tribe has palavered," he said, "for long hours, long days."

"It was not easy," whined Alignak.

In the hut Iriook was listening, with beating heart. She knew well they were discussing grave matters, but what could she do since, in these things and for this time, Agaguk must feel himself master? It was quite enough for her to impose her will on the man in other things, without intervening today in this debate. Tayaout was playing with an ivory knife, squatting at his mother's feet. Outside, the men had fallen silent again. They had expected to find Agaguk more friendly. They had hoped to have to say little to make him understand the purpose of their visit. And as all three feared a refusal, they did not dare venture further, except for the sake of their pride.

"We have come," Nattit began afresh.

He sought words to finish the phrase. Hayaluk stood up and came to Agaguk. More determined than the others, he was going to come to the point.

"We thought you would be a good chief, if you want to return to the village."

The word was spoken.

Agaguk, who was by now prepared for this, showed no emotion. He looked at them each in turn. Nattit, fat, stupid, tricky, Alignak, the whiner, who could never find weather to his taste, hunting to his satisfaction, life according to his desires. He was small, thin in contrast to the others, a poor hunter, of little use to the women whom he fondled without giving satisfaction, unskilful in everything. And Hayaluk, crafty, muscular, talkative, noisy, a braggart.

Why did they come here to look for a chief? What was going on in the tribe? And what profound reason made them pick Agaguk?

The Eskimo reflected, considering his decision. A man does not become chief so young in the tribes. The honour was attractive. But it meant a return to life in the village. Agaguk did not want to lose what he had, most of all the peace, the isolation, the liberty to decide his own least movements.

There was also Iriook. She was plump and attractive. Once Agaguk had gone a rifle-shot from the village, they would surround the hut, men like Hayaluk, like Nattit, like plenty of others, harassing his wife. There are the tribal laws of good sharing. A man is sometimes obliged to offer his wife in consolation to some solitary neighbour, to a recent widower or to someone who is unfortunate by no fault of his own.

Agaguk, strangely enough, felt no taste for granting her favours to the needs of the tribe. He had never imagined giving up Iriook, were it only for an hour. Without being able to express by what process he had come to feel this instinctive jealousy, he felt the evil, and he wished to have nothing to do with it. Iriook was his own. It was she above all whom he wanted to protect from the village, from the tribe, from the demands that living together provoke.

And what would he do in a group, when he abhorred gregarious life? He was happy here. On the other hand, the honour attracted him. He could become one of the young chiefs among the Eskimo. It was no small honour. Sung of at the night feasts as a great hunter, as the chief younger than the youngest chief of the distant tribes . . . .

"We can help you," said Nattit. "We can take down the hut, carry your goods to the village. With four of us, and Iriook besides, no need to wait for winter and the help of the dogs."

Agaguk shook his head. "No," he said.

Three astonished faces stared at him. "No?"

Nattit made a face. Alignak possessed a new pretext for whining. Hayaluk stepped forward, almost threateningly.

"We offer you the chiefship, and you refuse? You have some conditions to lay down?"

"No."

"Then why do you refuse?"

Agaguk made no reply.

"We will hunt for you," said Nattit. "All your provisions will be assured."

Agaguk pointed his finger at Hayaluk.

"Why isn't he the chief?"

"I don't want it," said Hayaluk.

"I don't either," said Agaguk.

He had made his choice. His voice revealed only a cold determination. Discussion became impossible.

"Listen," said Nattit. "If you will accept, we will—"

But Agaguk interrupted with one word. "No."

Nattit made a gesture with his hand.

"No," Agaguk repeated coldly.

Later they started back to the village. They were going to march all night, since the weather was cooler and the road easier.

Left alone with Iriook, the Eskimo felt satisfied and happy. If he had let himself be drawn by the alluring offer he would have regretted it later. He knew that now. The peace of the tundra surrounded him, the quiet sky, the beauty of the evening. All this familiar dusk, whose remotest nook he knew well, of which he possessed the entire mastery. He was a sort of king, greater than any chief, ruling a country rather than men, this rich plain rather than twenty huts and their inhabitants. He shared with no one this country he inhabited, with no one save his wife, whom he had chosen and to whom he was bound. King of a kingdom, absolute monarch, he had to render account to no one. The three emissaries had departed, and he had watched them pass out of sight on the tundra. Then he sat down on the ground, as he often did before going into the hut to sleep. He contemplated the sky and the stars. He knew he was completely at peace, free and content to be alive. He felt a step, a presence; Iriook came to sit beside him.

"I heard," she said after a little.

"Yes."

She touched his arm. "I was afraid you would accept."

He shook his head. "I did not accept."

"You did right."

Later she revealed her thoughts.

"With time, you might perhaps have talked. At an evening feast, you could have boasted of having killed Brown."

"They know that I killed him."

"But as you have never said so, they would denounce you in vain. They have no proofs. A jealous man might go to the constables to say that you boasted of the crime, and nothing more would be necessary."

Agaguk admired this reasoning. He had not thought of this possibility. Nothing like it had crossed his mind.

"Why," he said, "have they come to ask me? There are others, Komayiak for instance. He leaves nothing to be desired, he is the age for a chief, he is a great hunter, he is powerful."

"Has he killed anyone?"

The question astonished Agaguk.

He had never been skilful in this tribal life, he had never known how to become interested in the subtleties of the collective life, the currents of opinion, the levels of power. He had not understood why they came to offer him the post of chief. He had not even tried to understand. He avowed his complete ignorance. And, behold, Iriook brought forward an idea.

"Did he ever kill a man, this Komayiak?"

Agaguk remembered that this had a certain importance. Ramook, his father, had not accepted the honour in his time as a prize for virtue.

"You killed Brown, and the police can't prove a thing. They think down in the village that this is a great thing. They reason like that. As you too reasoned, not so long ago."

"And is it for having killed that they would make me chief?"

"Perhaps." And she added, "Not just for having killed but for having killed and not having been punished by the white men."

Agaguk shook his head. "You don't know what you're talking about. You weren't there when they held their palaver."

"But I know it is for this reason they decided to come. Komayiak has never killed anyone, except his daughters at birth and his mother's mother when she was too old to chew the skins. More than anything, he has not killed a white man."

"No, that is so."

"You are their hero."

He weighed the word. It was a fine word. It was a delight, something very pleasing. Heroes do not come by the dozen, nor every day. To be sung about and have stories told about one pleases a man.

Iriook spat on the moss.

"A hero who has killed, is he a hero?"

Agaguk did not know. He hesitated.

"Tell me," Iriook insisted.

Silence fell between them. The peace of the tundra invaded their hearts. Agaguk thought of what had happened, of what a move to the village would mean. Iriook was right. What better than this chosen life? What did the rest matter? He stood up. "Come," he said. "Tomorrow I must go hunting."

CHAPTER 20/ATSAK
The Bear

Tayaout was five years old when a bear from the forests to the south, a black bear, came up on the tundra where Agaguk lived. The animal had been wounded. Dazed, it had fled without knowing where it was going. This had brought it to higher land than it was used to, and now it was lost. The wound was not bleeding any more but the bear felt weak, so it cowered under the bushes near the river and waited.

Agaguk was hunting farther away at the time, Tayaout at his side. He did not see the bear nor notice the odour, for the beast was hidden on the other side of the river. In the evening the animal took care not to move for fear of attracting the wolves. He did not feel the strength to confront them. He took four days to recover his strength; at the end of this time he came out and went to hunt. He found little game on the tundra, even less than in his native forests. Still, he killed a weasel with one blow of his paw. Higher up the river, he saw some fish swimming between two currents. He entered the stream and caught ten or so, which he ate. On the opposite bank he found some berries, which he devoured. Then he crossed over and found his hiding-place again. He was full, and better still, no one had noticed his presence. One instant, Iriook thought she saw something moving, far up the river. But she had work to do in the hut, and she did not linger to watch outside.

By a sort of miracle, the bear could rest another three days in his thicket without being discovered. It was not Agaguk who noticed him, but Tayaout. There were some stones at a narrow place in the stream, and one could ford it easily. Agaguk had not gone hunting that day, and the child was playing alone in front of the hut. He took a notion to cross the river and go along the other bank. In the bushes he saw a dark mass that roused his curiosity without his being able to identify it. He went up to it, stretched out his hand and touched the bear's back. Tayaout, barefoot, coming against the wind, had not aroused the bear's attention for it was sleeping. The animal shuddered a little at his touch. His instinct was not completely alert. Then Tayaout pulled harder at the fur, a child's rough and careless gesture. The bear jumped, rolled over, struck in the air with a paw, found himself on all fours, rose to Tayaout's height at once, set his back to the thicket and roared. It was a sequence of movements so rapid that they seemed merged into one.

Tayaout yelled, a long desperate cry that mingled with the animal's growling. Nevertheless the bear did not feel any rage, but instead an uncontrollable fear, a confusion of all his senses and his instincts. He did not recognize this enemy. Tayaout did not smell like a man. The child did not move but he yelled and the bear growled, both of them the prey of mortal fear. In the hut, Iriook heard Tayaout's cry and the bear's growling. She yelled too. Agaguk was setting traps downstream; he heard the bear's growling and Iriook's call, but not Tayaout's.

The lot was cast, in time counted by the tiny fraction of a second, the flick of an eyelid, the instant of half a breath, a shudder. To release the bear from the spell, to make him leap on Tayaout there was needed only the least impulsion on a muscle, an infinitesimal click, the message along a nerve. Agaguk was already running, ready to kill. Iriook was coming out of the hut, rifle in hand. She raised it to her shoulder, sight on the bear.

But before she could press the trigger, before Agaguk in his mad race could arrive, the scene changed as if someone had suddenly brought to life some motionless figures.

Tayaout, who was crying, suddenly roared, if you can call by such a word the sound that came from his tiny throat. He rolled over on the ground and picked himself up with a stone in his hand. The bear rushed on him. He threw the stone, hit the animal on the muzzle, the bear staggered, stopped and ran in the opposite direction, fleeing its assailant.

Iriook fired at the same instant. She had followed the bear in her sights, even as it fled. The bullet broke the animal's skull and it fell.

The bear was dead. Iriook, shaking, ran over the stones of

the ford and grabbed Tayaout in his arms. Agaguk arrived on the scene, crying, almost weeping, dancing about, clapping his hands.

"Did you see?" he cried. "Did you see Tayaout? He made the bear run away. He hit him with a stone!"

He tossed the baby in his arms, throwing him in the air and catching him, and Tayaout laughed and cried in delight. Iriook was smiling through a face flooded with tears, admiring this brave baby, already almost a man, up to his waist, who threw stones at a bear as if it were a frightened mink.

"Tayaout," cried Agaguk. "Tayaout!" He found nothing else to say, nothing else to cry out.

CHAPTER 21/SARAGLOVAK
The Liar

Iriook waited several days to express what she had in mind, what she had not said before, what bothered her. One morning when Agaguk had not gone hunting, she made him sit down with her before the hut. Tayaout was playing near the river. He was naked and he went into the water at times, amusing himself by grabbing the crawfish and throwing them to the fish.

"Agaguk," said his wife.

"What is it?"

"Something important to say to you."

"I'm listening."

"The trader Brown, you killed him?"

"You know that. You asked me before and I told you."

"Yes, I know."

"And then?"

"Ramook has been hanged, let us say, for having killed Henderson, for having killed Ayallik. But you?"

"Me?"

"Are you like those men of the village? Or did you flee here to live differently?"

Agaguk did not answer. He looked hard at his wife. Now that he had this mutilated face, she could not tell what he was thinking except by observing his eyes. And at this moment his gaze was steady but told nothing. She could not guess what he was thinking.

"If you are not like them," she went on, "to have killed a man ought to trouble you."

"Why? He wanted to rob me of my furs."

"You might have been satisfied to take them back, without killing him."

"What do you want?"

"Nothing. To know—"

"To know what?"

"Are you sorry you killed him?"

Agaguk waited a long time without answering, then he made up his mind.

"Why do you keep talking about all these things? Are you a woman like the others?"

"Yes."

"One would not say so."

"I am, nevertheless."

"In our tribes, in our villages, the women don't talk so loud, and they don't trouble themselves with what their menfolk do."

He was trying to defend himself, going for once beyond his new ways of looking at such things.

"Well then, I am not like the others."

"I can see that very well."

"I am Iriook, that ought to be sufficient for you. And what are we here, alone in our own country?"

The man bent his shoulders.

"We are as we are."

"That is different from the others."

"Perhaps—"

"You regret having killed the white man?"

"I don't know."

"You were younger, you had not lived here very long, you did not know me much."

"I know."

"And you did not have Tayaout."

The man clenched his fist.

"Tayaout," went on Iriook, "he is what counts. If someone set fire to him some night?"

"Brown was not Tayaout. Brown was a white man who wanted to rob me."

"But maybe he had some people who were waiting for him in his country. If you went away, if someone killed you, I would wait for you. And never seeing you return, I would cry."

Again Agaguk fell silent. Then after a little, "And if I regretted having killed Brown?"

"For a life taken, a life must be paid."

"I don't understand," said Agaguk.

"I am not talking about today. But if there came a time when you had to choose? To give a life for the one you took?"

"I don't know what I would do."

"You would give it, that life?"

Hesitation. "Yes, perhaps."

Tayaout at the river, called out. "Aya!"

He was standing in the water, holding a big fish flapping about over his head. Agaguk rose to his feet.

"Look," he said, "I must go to the river."

It was clear that he was making his escape, but he had said enough to satisfy Iriook. Touched, she looked at both of them, her men, her children, this Tayaout already so sure of himself, and the other, this Agaguk who was going to regret a crime, a sentiment which no Eskimo would ever avow, a woman's sentiment.

And coming from this strong male, this master before whom she went on her knees. Strong, the male Agaguk? But wherein lay his strength? In his muscles? In the scope of each gesture? In the effort of raising a caribou carcass from the ground? In the embrace? Or then as life willed it, in the calm defeat of his enemies, in his sure march, beating down obstacles with a rush—slow, inexorable strength.

Agaguk could not analyze his force. He awoke in the morning, exiled from a land of unconsciousness whose geography he had not comprehended. He entered into another country, this one familiar to him, the habitual abode of his daytime hours, and so reassuring. For each enemy a weapon. For each menace a defence. Upright, fully conscious, capable of performing the day's ventures, Agaguk felt no fear. He knew the method to victory over every dangerous beast. Against the cold, against the great winds of the tundra, against the lightning in the summer sky, he knew the surest shelter. He knew how to dig in, if it was necessary, to run at the right time, to stand and fight if that was the thing to do. But the night? But sleep? If there was any breach in his wall, any weakness in his strength, it was during his dreams at night. He did not say this. He would not have known how to say it.

If he was troubled on waking, how could he explain to Iriook that during his sleep enormous wild beasts, nameless, against whom he had no defence, fell upon him and devoured him? The wound on his face, painful every night, was reopened every night by the beasts of his dream. Every night he rolled on the ground, helpless, crying for aid, imploring, groaning.

He did not suspect that when he writhed in nightmare, when the sweat poured off him, that a worried Iriook, raised on one elbow and wide awake, was watching him. Sometimes she shook him to drive away the bad dream. But she had learned when very young that it was best not to fight dreams, that they are the inhabitants of the lands of sleep, that they dwell there, free and powerful, and that to drive them away one night brings them back, a thousand times more menacing, the following night. So she could do nothing. This went on for months.

Every day she had her work to do. Her eternal task would end only with death. And for Tayaout, the rapid growth, the increasing consciousness of the world around him, the equilibrium more complete every month, the muscles more and more docile.

And the marvel of the tundra. Soon, the misery of the snow plain.

For the winter was returning. They had hardly come out of the one before, when already the wind whistled every night, cold and insistent. In the morning the moss was frozen stiff, and there was no respite except in the middle of the day, when the warmth of the sun quelled the north wind and it was almost mild.

There was no green left. The tundra became dark again. In the places where the water oozing from the moss spread in puddles, ice formed each morning and every day took a little longer to yield to the sun.

The summer birds were flying to the south. Some geese that Agaguk had spotted, some of which he brought down, took the road to a sunnier country. Soon the tundra would be firm and hard, the permafrost would mount to the surface, and the first flakes of snow, fine as salt, would be flying over the moss.

Suddenly it would be winter.

And how would they fare, in this dangerous time? The hunting had been good, and provisions would not be lacking. The furs already formed an imposing bundle to exchange at the trading post when spring came. The skins for their own use—those of caribou, wolf and a few fox skins, and the sealskins that remained—also formed a precious reserve.

The box held ammunition for the whole season and some over. They would lack neither sugar nor salt, and there was a large bag of tea, a luxury Agaguk was proud of. The fat, the tallow and even the oil, product of patient distillation, assured the indispensable reserves of fuel. The winter could come, they would lack nothing.

If the Eskimo's soul was troubled, it was not the possible misery, now postponed to another winter, that caused it. There was something else that he could not explain. The episode concerning Ramook, perhaps, the visits of the police, the accident? He could not have said.

Still more than all these things—the uncertainty of life which he had early learned to meet, the tricks of the combat with the police, the disturbances in the village which made up part of his life and which this life could bring—more than all this, an uneasiness would not let Agaguk rest.

Each day he discovered Iriook a little more, in a slow revelation which, it seemed, was never going to come to an end. And what he discovered left him thoughtful.

In the first days together he had loved well the beautiful smooth face of his wife, her sturdy body with the solid muscles, which he embraced with pleasure. He had desired Iriook in her body. Then, as the months went by, he had come to appreciate her ability to accomplish her tasks, her strength, her resistance.

Then the child had come. A son, and the profound gratitude of Agaguk. He had discovered, through this birth, the husband's attachment that he had for Iriok. He had discovered that anything that hurt his wife hurt him too, and he was overcome with the need to strangle, to strike and even to kill. The emotion he felt drove him mad, but what sense was there in this animal desire to kill when Iriook suffered?

After the accident, the woman was revealed anew. Formerly she had been the precious female, dependent on him, but to whom he was attached as he was to his rifle, his traps, his bullets, to the metal stove or the lamp hanging in the igloo. When the accident happened, when Iriook took patient care of him, when she hunted for him, when he saw her distressed, devoted, attentive to his least complaint, she became to him something more than a female. He felt an inexplicable embarrassment.

It was not in his race and tradition to let a woman transcend the female role that thousands of years had imposed on her. Nevertheless, before the policemen, Iriook had displayed a calm, unmoved, baffling guile. She had saved him, that was certain. And Agaguk had found the proper words, accusing Iriook of knowing how to speak too loud, louder than women of the tribe ought to speak. If she was more than a female, was she then a woman? But what did that mean?

And what exactly was she saying now? To pay tribute for Brown's death? Today would he burn Brown with the same cold-blooded indifference? Would he think twice before doing it?

Iriook had said, "You were younger. . . ." But it was a short time in terms of years, of months. What did she mean? To grow old, that is time passing. He did not comprehend any other kind of aging than that.

Now if a girl was born of her pregnancy, she would insist on keeping it.

After all the rest, this was the sort of blow that made him afraid; Iriook's hold on him, her power, this was what troubled him. Iriook's power.

The word stung him. He could not bear the thought. A female more powerful than a male? He should have been able to flog this woman with rawhide lashes. To master her. Even, in loving her well, he must remain master in his hut, master in his igloo.

He wandered over the tundra, his eyes alert, seeking game to bring down, and in his head there was a whirlwind that made him ill, that oppressed him. What had Iriook become? Stronger than he?

Must he preserve a life to ransom Brown's death? This was a new morality which he did not know. He must let the girl-child live? Well, the provisions would not fail this winter, but what of the next? The boy was growing rapidly; in a little while he would bring in his share of the provisions, but a girl? Let there be just one bad winter, then the extra mouth to feed would be an enormous burden. He must resolve to oppose this. If he permitted it, Iriook would walk all over him. He would allow himself to be patient, he would be distressed over it, he would help her with her work, if she needed help, and he would let her talk. But he would kill the girl at birth!

He would have to do it secretly, of course, warning Iriook once the deed had been accomplished.

He returned that evening fully decided, his eyes hard, and in his heart the answer to all his misgivings. Iriook could be a woman like all the other women of the tribes; she could bend to tradition, to a need and, indeed, to a necessity. The girl would not survive, it was not necessary that she should survive, were it only to teach the woman the place she ought occupy in her husband's life. Female, female with a great heart, good and hard-working, clever and able to hunt as well as a man, but no more than a female. The master, that was he.

When he entered the hut, evening had come, and the stove was crackling, warm as ever. Nude, Iriook awaited her man, seated, her thighs spread, her breasts high. She was smiling. The hairy sex was dark and mysteriously inviting. Everything in Agaguk crumbled, all his resolutions, the influx of power. He advanced silently toward her. The child, indifferent, was playing on the moss bench with some rawhide thongs.

There was a pleasant dusk in the hut. A good odour of sweat, of hot grease and gamy meat pervaded the hut and intoxicated Agaguk. He growled hoarsely and fell upon her, with nervous, searching, almost brutal hands. Agaguk, the powerful. . . .

CHAPTER 22/NIVIAKSIAK
The Girl

At the village, life had long since gone back to its usual rhythm; they did not even talk any more about Ramook and his crimes. Ghorok's wife had taken another man into her igloo, a bachelor who had no one to chew the skins and keep the flame alive in the lamp.

Oonak traveled to the Great Water to kill seals. He was accompanied by two young fellows of the tribe with whom he shared a dwelling. One of these was beaten to death when he was asleep, and his seals were stolen. It was Kuriaak, the mother of the victim, and another woman who talked too loud, who denounced the guilty man. But nothing was done to Oonak, for he agreed to give back two seals and pay a hundred rifle bullets.

A woman lost all her blood one night. She stood with her legs apart on the ice bench and the blood made a spreading pool on the ground. They sent for the new witch-doctor, and he put warm pads filled with sacred charms on her vulva. That accomplished nothing, and the woman died early in the morning, as if she were going to sleep. They thought she was saved, for her blood did not run any more, but she was dead.

One of the old men, Hala, went outside the village, built himself his last igloo and shut himself up there without fire and without food. He died a few days later. He had not hunted for two years. He had come to the end of his road.

A child died of a pain in the belly which the witch-doctor did not cure.

Onaituk's wife left her husband to go to live with another man, who already had a wife but who wanted two, intending to double his pleasure. Onaituk's wife accommodated herself well to this state of affairs and quickly made a baby for her new male.

So unrolled this chronicle of a peaceful life, the days when something happened were only a tiny fraction of global time. One could count by the dozen the days when nothing happened. Hunt, rest, sleep, meals, the women's work, the daily coitus, the boredom of time that goes by with no shocks.

This rhythm of life, a sort of cycle daily renewed, was not so very different from that lived by Agaguk and Iriook. That nothing tragic occurred to the young couple did not weaken the dull anguish prevailing in the igloo. It rankled under this apparent peace, through the long days and the luck of the occasional hunts and in spite of the routine occupations, there was a mounting tension which possessed Agaguk.

The second child was soon to be born.

Nothing else was really important. Iriook walked heavily, and her breath was short. From one day to another now, she would take to her bed, and the baby would come out of her belly. What would it be?

"A girl," she said once, as if she were continuing her thoughts out loud. "It will be a girl."

Agaguk, stretched on the ice bench with his hands under his neck, neither moved nor spoke. But he felt his heart beat faster.

"It will be easy, this time," said Iriook after a while. "It is always so with the second."

She counted on her fingers.

"A woman in the village had fourteen. As I show you on my fingers. She had trouble only with the first one."

This time Iriook had not waited, motionless and stoical, for the baby to grow within her. No day passed in which she had not done her work, using her muscles. She accomplished all the tasks of the Eskimo woman without complaining.

The baby would come easily, for if she touched her belly, the muscles were firm and hard, and she had solid legs. And what would be born of this belly? The male that Agaguk wanted? Or the girl that she desired?

"It will be a girl," she repeated.

Agaguk fretted inwardly. He had days of strength, days of weakness. For an hour he would be certain that he would kill the child if it were a girl. And the next, he would be indulgent to Iriook's wish, swearing to himself that he would let the girl live, just as he had promised.

He was in torment, a new state for him, who had never known moral suffering. There was enough trouble these days, the fear of famine, the fear of perishing, the dangers— a thousand and one constant menaces lying in wait for him on the snow plain—his whole life indeed, as well as the difficulty of surviving from day to day. There were enough things to disturb him without his having to experiment with others. But the others came without his looking for them.

He did not know it could be possible to suffer for a single woe, for a single dilemma. He was well caught, he found it hard to reflect on this problem. He succeeded in comprehending it only with difficulty.

One instinct stuck firmly in his mind, which his trouble dictated, directed, modified. Iriook must not cry. And even when he felt all-powerful and master of all, something muffled within him, a voice which he perceived without quite understanding it, kept telling him that if he strangled the girl at birth, Iriook would cry.

And that, he did not want.

Each day Iriook grew bigger. Now she was enormous, her belly a balloon, her breasts like leather bottles, her brown face stained with whitish patches. The winter was well along when a sign came to her. Almost nothing, a sharp pain that ran through her from left to right and then vanished. A blizzard was scouring the plain, immense, destructive, heaping up the snow. There was nothing living, only the roar of the wind, the monstrous drive of the snow.

For some days Agaguk's face had foreshadowed the bad time coming. The blood-red scar had become livid. Sometimes it pained him dully. With the lamp-light exaggerating the cavity and the shadows, he was more horrible than ever to look at. As long as they spent half their time in the hut and the rest indoors, Iriook did not have to fight against the hideousness of her man. In the igloo his ravaged face became a frightening presence.

A blizzard came which lasted three days, four, and was

entering on its fifth day, when Iriook began to feel a queer panic within her. Was it her condition, the nervous exaltation of her pregnancy? She was not sure.

Agaguk was before her like a nightmare; this face where she could no longer read any expression, which was no longer human, struck her as monstrous. Yet this was the face with which she must henceforth live her life. What kind of fate was this to endure? And for how many years? Was it measured in months, in seasons or in revolt?

"The baby will be beautiful," she cried. "It will be a girl more beautiful than the Great Snow, more beautiful than the flowers of the tundra."

Her pain had just left her, and she had for refuge and assurance only this cry, sign of the pain in her entrails, the compound pain of her imminent delivery. The other ill was so subtle that the woman could no more, any more than Agaguk, grasp its sense, that of the fear of living. Above all, of living before this man.

Each one, the Eskimo and his wife, was held far from the other by this heavy and secret thought, too tensely to be able to express it to each other so that together they could overcome it.

"Will it be a girl?" Agaguk wondered.

"It will be a girl, and she will no more be able to live with that face than I can," Iriook said to herself.

She transposed the horror. It would not be she, Iriook, who could not live thus, but the girl who would be born, gentle and pretty, who would recoil in terror before Agaguk her father.

But Tayaout did not recoil. . . .

The days became hours, and each hour the length of a day. The minutes were counted by heart beats, a heavy, piercing rhythm, driving the blood in the temples. In Iriook, the rhythm went according to nature, multiplying in her. In Agaguk, it was the sum of accumulated silence which he did not know how to break, an anguish, a fear, and with the passage of the hours a growing resolution that he must in spite of everything obey tradition.

If the sun had come out on the tundra, and if his gun could have brought down some game, he might perhaps have conquered that instinct. It might have been enough if there were signs of good luck outdoors to reassure him of a future in which a girl could survive. Sign from heaven, a glimpse of sun, three animals in his gun sight . . . but the blizzard?

That also was a sign from heaven. If the wind lasted until the moment of birth, would that not be the voice of the Bad Spirits? *Agiortok!* They have spoken. The girl shall die!

Dull thud of his heart, a heavy blow, the girl shall die! Beginning again, an obsession, the girl shall die! Every heart-beat an affirmation.

Outside the wind screamed.

Agaguk went over and over the things he knew in his head, the experience of ages. A bad summer, the cyclic scarcity of animals—told in the songs, this was—the presence on the plain of the Evil Spirit, and nothing to eat when mid-winter came. That could mean famine in the igloo. In such times, a girl, an old man, a sickly child are burdens to be destroyed. Beating of the heart, the girl shall die, thrown out to the dogs and the wolves at birth.

And Iriook?

Iriook? She would cry—nevertheless she must not cry. He would not be able to bear it. Outside the wind grew fiercer. It was a hell. But the old men said that blizzards have been known to last weeks without ever slackening. And these blizzards, the old men affirm also, always come when provisions in the igloos are getting low.

A white man said one day, "You Eskimos eat too much, especially in the idle season. You are gluttons. It takes the meat of ten caribou to feed four Eskimos during one winter."

The white men always know how to say big words and give advice. The Eskimos know how to live. To each his own wisdom. And if there is one bit of wisdom that Eskimos possess, is it not, reasoned Agaguk, to avoid useless mouths?

That was how he must talk to Iriook, after the death of the girl. He would have to convince his wife that it was not only a custom to carry on, but the necessity of survival. The baby would die because even if nothing was lacking just now, it was necessary to think of the next winter. And of the other winters, until the girl could chew the skins, sew and in that way earn her dole.

Agaguk made his resolutions.

The time came and took them both by surprise. The old women were right. For the second child, and since the woman had kept on working up to the final day, the birth was hardly painful.

The moment arrived without preliminary labour. One moment, Iriook felt a terrible pain shoot through her body. She fell on her back. Already the child was going to be born.

CHAPTER 23/N'AKOKSANIK
Happiness

At Iriook's cry, a savage, tortured wail, Agaguk leaped up. Remembering Tayaout's birth, he swiftly pulled off the woman's clothing. She was extended naked on the caribou skin, her face twisted, her swollen belly a monstrous mass upon her.

Awakened by her cry, Tayaout was weeping in fright.

Agaguk, squatting at the woman's feet, observed impassively the gaping opening where already could be seen the head of the infant about to be born.

"It will not be long," he said in a calm voice.

They were his only words.

Another pain tore Iriook, and already the infant was emerging. The head slid out of the belly, easily, as if some hand within were pressing a sack to squeeze out the contents. Iriook did not cry out again. Only one moan rose from her, a hundred times less horrible than on that first night when Tayaout was born.

His hands extended, Agaguk waited to grasp the child, then suddenly in a final effort the new being slid and fell into them. With a sure motion he cut the cord with an ivory knife. Higher up, very far it seemed from Agaguk, Iriook was moaning—so far that the man heard nothing of it. A great buzzing was in his ears; he stayed squatting, holding the child. He had eyes only for its sex.

A girl!

It was now or never. He must take advantage of Iriook's semi-consciousness, of the baby's momentary quiet.

Agaguk crawled like an animal, holding the slimy little body with one hand. Silently he made his way toward the tunnel. He knew what to do. Once outside, he would strangle the girl with a decisive motion, breaking its neck at the same time.

Then he would throw the body in the snow. The wolves and the dogs would quickly feed on it, and in the morning nothing would be left.

He crawled, the rubbing movement of his body the only sound, so slight that it took a very keen ear to detect it. Tayaout had gone back to sleep.

Agaguk was just reaching the tunnel when suddenly Iriook's voice, calm and implacable, was raised.

"Agaguk!"

He froze. The child against him still did not move. He turned his head. The woman was sitting up. Rifle in hand, she was aiming at him.

"Now make her breathe," she said.

He hesitated a moment. Then he stood up, silent but tense as a harpoon cord. With a nervous finger he emptied the baby's mouth of the mucous accumulated there. He hung her by the feet from his calloused hand, and with the other hand he struck her back. The baby did as Tayaout had done; she curled up suddenly. A long wail burst out echoing against the icy walls of the igloo.

"Give her to me," said Iriook.

She held out her arms and Agaguk came to place the baby there.

Iriook examined the plump body for a long time. She felt the dimpled limbs, touched the black down on the head. Slowly, with an almost coaxing gesture, a gesture of almost sensual caress, her hand slid over the baby's belly and touched lightly the swollen vulva. Iriook contemplated carefully the baby's sex, then her body and finally her head. Then she smiled. It would be a beautiful girl. Content, she laid the child on the caribou skin beside the rifle.

Agaguk had not stirred. If he felt any rage, he did not show it. Iriook, her look impassive, half sitting, leaning against the wall, pointed to the child with her finger, and to the rifle also.

"That's not the way to do things," she said.

Agaguk still did not stir.

"Listen to me," said Iriook. "You must be the one to decide. I do not wish to force you."

Agaguk dug in his heels. So it had come to this? To win by logic? The habits transmitted to him, the fears of many thousands of years, are not easily expressed. He sought for words. Iriook was ahead of him.

"You were going to kill my baby?"

He did not answer at once.

"Speak," insisted Iriook.

"Yes."

"Without telling me?"

He shrugged his shoulders.

"Without telling me?" repeated Iriook.

"Yes."

She had circles around her eyes. Her belly, still very big, seemed to be hurting her. Sometimes spasms of pain shook her.

"I cannot keep her," Agaguk said.

It was his first argument, the only one he had to offer. It must not be. It was against all logic. Later, perhaps, when Tayaout would be grown . . . .

"Some day Tayaout will be hunting," he said. "At that time, we will keep a girl, maybe two. . . ."

Iriook shook her head.

"No," she said. "I don't understand you."

"It's all that I have to say," said Agaguk dully.

Iriook made a weary motion. She pointed to the ice bench. "Sit down," she said, "listen to what I'm going to tell you. Listen well."

It was clear that she was still in pain. Waves of suffering passed over her face. Her eyes were clouded, her mouth twitched, foam appeared at the corner of her lips. And yet a new strength emanated from the woman, which held Agaguk, which riveted him there. He obeyed, he sat down before her.

"It is our life that is at stake," she said with difficulty. She spoke in a heavy voice, which pain suddenly altered. "Do you understand, Agaguk?"

She insisted. He said nothing.

"If the child perishes, what will remain? If you take away my baby, what will I do?"

He defied her with a look. "You are not an Eskimo woman," he said, falling back on his last defences. "You talk too loud. I could make you be silent."

"I will go away. I will take Tayaout with me! I will take

some skins, my rifle, some ammunition. One morning you will wake up and I will not be there."

"Where will you be?"

"I don't know. I will be gone away."

"I will follow you. I will kill you and take Tayaout back."

"No, you will not know in what direction we have gone."

"I will find him again. You cannot take Tayaout away from me!"

"And you want to take away my baby?"

Suddenly she fell back. Her belly contracted, and she groaned like a frightened beast.

Agaguk looked at her, disturbed. He knew that if she began to cry, he could not refuse life to the baby girl. But Iriook sat up again, her eyes dry, and her look met Agaguk's without flinching.

"It's over," she said. "Only a pain."

She resisted the pain, a combat betrayed by her movements, the panic in her expression, and even more by the drops of sweat on her forehead.

"What will you do, Agaguk?" she asked after a time.

The Eskimo rose, slowly, his arms dangling, his eyes staring. He dared not make any motion, he did not feel ready to. He stood there, sullenly, his neck deep in his parka.

"Speak," said Iriook, "Say it. What will you do?"

The baby wailed; Agaguk turned his gaze toward her.

"She ought to be washed," said Iriook.

He jumped, he seemed to come out of a dream. What was happening? Who was going to be boss in this igloo? A woman? The woman who had just given birth?

He cried suddenly, "I am the master! The child must die. And you will not go away. And if you ever try to take Tayaout away from me, I will kill you like a dog."

The old atavism was taking over. He forced himself to believe that the woman before him could weep, could implore, and that he did not have to obey her. He did not even have to bother about her. He leaped suddenly, releasing muscles that carried him toward the baby wailing on the caribou skin. Before Iriook could move, he had seized the child and was running to the tunnel. But Iriook's voice stopped him again. This time it was a wild scream, an original cry such as Agaguk had never heard. The woman was on her feet; she had no gun, she held out her bare hands. And her body with the still swollen belly was grotesque to see.

"No, Agaguk, don't kill her. Listen to me," she begged.

"A life for Brown's!" she cried again. "Agaguk, listen. See what you can do. The baby's life against Brown's. And you shall have peace as long as you live. I promise you!"

She wept in great sobs that broke up her words and shook her body.

"Agaguk, have pity. Leave me my baby. Don't kill her."

The man did not move. Once more he was paralyzed by the woman and her tears which he hated so much, against which he became so powerless.

"Leave me my baby."

Nailed to the ground, Agaguk was incapable of budging. Something kept him there, a power so complete that he did not wish to oppose it. Iriook held against herself the arms she had held out, begging him to lay the baby in them. Hate took the place of entreaty and pain on her face, a hate such as Agaguk had never imagined, in her expression, in the twist of her lips, in her whole face, burning and indescribable. A new need rose in the man's heart, to destroy this hate, for all at once it appeared to him that the future would be lived in silence, one day after the other. Never again would he know the former caresses, only this hate with which he would have to learn to live. He knew he was incapable of that. But why would she not understand?

"You must understand," he said. But in pronouncing the words he realized their uselessness. If he killed the baby, he would be killing Iriook with the same blow. At least he would be killing all that in the woman had been his joy, his pleasure. As the image of the years to come suddenly appeared intolerable, so his memory of former times revived. Iriook's smile, her tender gesture, her sensual wail in the night, what she had been to him, each step that she had taken beside him, the feeling of peace and security that he had with her beside him, their entire life together came back to him, pushing aside the ugly image of the future. None of this harmonized with Iriook's present implacable, unfeeling look.

"Go kill the baby," she said in a cold voice. "Go ahead. Do what you like. You are right, you are the master."

She turned away, fell on the ice bench and cried, "But go on. Since you want to, go on. I'm not hindering you. I will go away. I have no need of you, nor of Tayaout, nor of the baby."

It was true that she could go away, at night, silently. And even if he caught up with her the next morning, would he not have to kill her? But then? Dead or living, would she be as he saw her now? After a long while, Agaguk came slowly toward the woman. Hesitatingly, he held out the child to her.

"Take her," he said.

They stayed thus for a long time, one before the other, incapable of speaking or moving. Iriook hugged the baby against her, hid her between her breasts. And slowly, as gradually as as it had come, the hate vanished from her face. She raised a glance of mute tenderness to Agaguk. She understood, Eskimo and woman, through what conflict the man had passed, what victory she had won. The man appeared so great to her that she moaned softly. Nothing in his mutilated face frightened her any more, nothing repelled her. And what could she give Agaguk in return?

She could not have expressed what she knew of new-found happiness, of sudden and tremendous joy. In the dark moments of her pregnancy, when in the narrow confines of the igloo she could hardly bear to live before her husband's ravaged face, she would not have believed it possible that this hideousness could one day appear beautiful to her. And yet the miracle had come about. Agaguk before her, almost beautiful? In any case, so gentle, so good, so generous. She put out a hesitating hand, and drew it lightly over the mutilated face.

"Thank you," she said. "Thank you."

She was trembling on her feet. Her belly, still heavy, was an ugly mass, bulging over her sex.

"Lie down again," said Agaguk. "There, lie down."

He helped her to stretch out, the baby beside her. Within him rose a warmth, a pleasure he had never before experienced. He was happy. He did not want to fight any more. The baby would live because Iriook wished it so. He touched his wife, his hands caressing. And he touched the baby.

"She will be beautiful," he said, "as beautiful as Tayaout."
Who shall inherit the earth?

"She will be beautiful," he repeated. "Beautiful and strong."
Suddenly Iriook screamed. "You're in pain?" asked Agaguk.
She nodded her head, desperately.

"In your belly?"

"Yes."

"But what's the matter?" he exclaimed.

He saw Iriook's body contract under the pain, and twist about.

"Iriook, tell me why. What's happening?"

Instead of answering, she cried out again, screamed like an animal, a vibrating, terrible sound, which died away slowly in a long, soft moan.

"Agaguk," she groaned in the pause, "Look!"

She opened her thighs wide. Stupefied, Agaguk saw that another head was emerging from the vagina, that another baby was ready to be born after the girl. As before, he held out his hands.

This time, it was a boy.